FINI FLIGHT

A SPECTRE THRILLER

C.W. LEMOINE

This book is a work of fiction. Names, characters, places, and incidents are either products of the author's imagination or used fictitiously. Any resemblance to actual events or locales or persons living or dead is entirely coincidental. The views in this book do not represent those of the United States Air Force Reserve or United States Navy Reserve. All units, descriptions, and details related to the military are used solely to enhance the realism and credibility of the story.

Cover artwork by ebooklaunch.com
Edited by Beverly Foster.

Copyright © 2019 C.W. LEMOINE
All rights reserved.
Trade paperback version.
ISBN-13: 9781097655854

"The guy you don't see will kill you."

— *Robin Olds*

THE *SPECTRE* SERIES:

SPECTRE RISING (BOOK 1)

AVOID. NEGOTIATE. KILL. (BOOK 2)

ARCHANGEL FALLEN (BOOK 3)

EXECUTIVE REACTION (BOOK 4)

BRICK BY BRICK (BOOK 5)

STAND AGAINST EVIL *(BOOK 6)*

THE HELIOS CONSPIRACY *(BOOK 7)*

FINI FLIGHT *(BOOK 8)*

SPECTRE: ORIGINS (PREQUEL SHORT STORIES)

Visit www.cwlemoine.com and subscribe to C.W. Lemoine's Newsletter for exclusive offers, updates, and event announcements.

PROLOGUE

Jon Chang-Ha massaged his temples as he sat at his desk. He closed his eyes, thinking of his wife and daughter. They had been taken nearly a decade earlier and forced to work in a North Korean small arms factory. A family picture he had hidden in his wallet was all that remained of his beautiful family.

Jon didn't know for sure, but he had already come to terms with the fact that they were both likely dead. Conditions in the factories were barely survivable. Workers were exposed to asbestos, mold, loud noises, and diseases from the other workers on a daily basis. They were given little water and even less food. It was a death sentence.

But Jon had no choice but to steel himself and do his best work for his country. As the number two scientist for North Korea's Intercontinental Ballistic Missile and Nuclear Delivery program, Jon spent most of his time under the watchful eye of

Dear Leader himself. Any slip-up would guarantee his death by artillery at point-blank range.

The lights of his modest shack flickered off and on as the last train to Pyongyang rumbled by. It was the same train he had taken many times before to report the status of their research to Dear Leader. The *click clack* of the cars traversing the rails made him cringe. He had grown to hate everything about his life.

As the lone bulb in his one-bedroom apartment flickered back on, Jon took a deep breath and exhaled slowly. He retrieved the thumb drive he had taped to the inner wall of the top drawer of his desk and shoved it into his pocket. It was his only hope at vengeance for the life with his family that had been stolen from him in the name of country.

Grabbing his work briefcase, Jon turned the light off and exited the tiny apartment. He was still wearing the dark gray military uniform he had worn all day. As a senior scientist within the military's most important program, it was his best chance of avoiding confrontation with any North Korean soldiers he might come across.

As he exited the apartment building and walked out onto the street of Changjon, he noticed an eerie quiet. It was well after dark and less than an hour until the mandatory curfew. He had never been out so late and immediately ducked into an alleyway when he saw a pair of soldiers walking on the other side of the street.

Despite his position within the military, he was still terrified of the consequences of being seen after dark. Discretion was not a word in the vocabulary of the average North Korean soldier. He had seen far too many innocent people arrested for far less.

As he hid from the soldiers, Jon looked at his watch. He had less than thirty minutes to make it to the rendezvous point before the curfew went into effect. He steeled himself and emerged onto the street, ignoring the soldiers as he continued toward his objective.

They glanced his way and saw his rank, stopping to render a sharp salute as he walked by. Jon quickly returned the salute and continued forward, hoping they wouldn't cross the street to question his intentions at this hour.

Reaching the end of the block, he glanced back and saw that the two men had continued down the street. He breathed a short sigh of relief and turned right to head toward the docks.

The street was dimly lit, but Jon made it to the end with little trouble. He found the apartment building where he had been instructed to go. He looked around to ensure no one had followed him and then used his key to open one of the outdoor mailboxes. Inside, he found another key. He took it and deposited the thumb drive before placing the new key in his pocket and continuing toward the docks.

As he reached the gate to the harbor, he pulled the key from the mailbox out of his pocket and placed his briefcase on the ground. He fumbled around with the lock until suddenly he heard footsteps behind him. He spun around and saw a soldier with a flashlight. His heart raced as he dropped the key and froze against the chain-link fence.

"Halt!" the soldier ordered as he shined his light on the sixty-year-old general. "State your intentions!"

As the solider approached, he immediately saw the two stars on Jon's collar and snapped to attention. "General, I am sorry!" the solider said.

Jon once again tried to calm himself. Although he was a general in rank, he had been a scientist his entire career and had little interaction with the military rank and file. He wasn't sure what the proper protocol was to make this young soldier go away.

"It is quite alright," Jon said softly. "Please return to your station."

"General, I must ask for your identification first. I am terribly sorry," the soldier replied.

"Is that really necessary?"

"I'm afraid it is, sir."

Jon pulled out his laminated identification card from his coat pocket and handed it to him. As the soldier shined the light on Jon's hand, he saw that it was shaking nervously.

"Are you alright, sir?"

"I am fine," Jon said as the soldier took the ID.

"May I ask what your purpose is here tonight?"

Jon considered the question for a moment and then sternly said, "No, you may not."

"Sir?" the soldier asked, taken aback by Jon's sudden change in demeanor.

"Is there a problem? Shall I speak to your commander?" Jon asked angrily.

"No, general. No problem at all," the soldier said before quickly handing the ID back to Jon. "I am sorry for disturbing you."

Jon nodded and the soldier turned to walk away. As he turned back toward the gate, Jon realized that he had dropped the key into the gravel. He started to panic as he dropped to his knees and struggled to find the key in the darkness.

As Jon fished around for the key, the soldier turned around and saw him on his knees. He walked back and shined his light on the ground. "Can I help you find something, general?"

With the assistance of the light, Jon immediately located the key and stood.

"Found it," he said as he held the key up.

"Will there be anything else, sir?" the soldier asked.

"No, that's-"

Jon froze as he saw three more lights approaching. One of the men called out to the soldier standing in front of Jon.

"Sir!" the soldier replied as he waved his light.

"Carry on, soldier," Jon said, trying to shoo the young man away.

The three soldiers continued toward Jon and the confused soldier. Jon struggled to get the key in the lock as he tried to hurry and get away before the others arrived to ask more questions. The padlock clicked open and he removed it from the chain.

"Corporal Pak, what is the meaning of this?" one of the approaching soldiers asked. "Who is this man?"

The approaching soldier shined his light on Jon and immediately saluted as he recognized Jon's rank.

"General, I had no idea you would be here," the soldier said. "Forgive us for intruding. We were not notified of your visit."

Jon slowly removed the chain and nodded. He saw the rank on the soldier's uniform and realized that he was an officer, probably the corporal's commander. "It's quite alright. Please, carry on, Captain."

"Sir, may I ask what you are doing here at this hour?" the Captain asked.

"No, you may not," Jon said, hoping the same tactic would work on the officer.

"Respectfully, general, I'm afraid must insist. This is a fishing harbor and is off limits at this hour."

"Captain, I appreciate your diligence, but your corporal has already verified my identity. My purpose here is none of your concern."

The Captain stood there under the glow of the flashlights as he considered his next move. As he and Jon stared each other down, a look of recognition suddenly flashed across the Captain's face.

"You are a member of Dear Leader's National Science team!" the Captain shouted. "I have seen you before."

"Yes, keep your voice down," Jon said. "I am here on a special mission sanctioned by Dear Leader himself. You mustn't delay me any further. He will be very angry if you continue."

The Captain seemed to consider the threat for a moment and then suddenly became very serious. He raised his rifle and pointed it at Jon. "I am sorry, sir, but I am afraid you must come with me."

With a flick of his tongue, Jon removed the cyanide capsule from his teeth and bit down. The poison caused him to collapse as he started convulsing. He said a prayer to be reunited with his wife and daughter in the afterlife as his consciousness faded.

CHAPTER ONE

Freddie "Kruger" Mack maneuvered his GMC Yukon Denali down the winding dirt road lined by trees on both sides. His GPS had long since given up trying to find the address, dropping him off at the end of the main highway where it turned into loose gravel.

He followed the gravel road until it stopped at a metal gate with a call box. He lowered his window and pressed the button marked simply "2" and waited for a response. After a few seconds, the call box buzzed and a red light on the attached camera illuminated.

"It's me," Kruger stated as he looked directly into the camera.

Without a word, the gate opened. Kruger drove over the cattle guard and continued down the driveway past a log cabin. A dirt road beyond the cabin appeared to be freshly graded.

After a few hundred feet, the dirt road turned into a concrete driveway that led to a much more modern home.

Kruger parked his SUV behind a three-quarter-ton diesel pick-up truck and killed the engine. He took a deep breath as he stared at the newly built home, wondering if he was sentencing its owner to death after being out of the game for so long. He had been struggling with what he would say since leaving Virginia. He hated to show up under these circumstances, but they were truly out of options.

He shook off his doubts and exited his truck as the front door of the house opened. A blonde woman emerged, holding the hand of a toddler with light brown hair and bright blue eyes.

"Kruger! You're early! It's good to see you again," she said as she picked up the boy. "How have you been?"

Kruger frowned and then asked, "Is Spectre here?"

"He went with Bear to pick up some steaks. He said he'd be back before you arrived, but you're a little early. Is everything okay?"

Kruger forced a half grin as he walked toward her. "Sorry, just a long day. Thanks for having me. It's good to see you too, Michelle."

The wife of Cal "Spectre" Martin, Michelle Decker Martin was a former FBI agent and prosecutor. Together, she and Spectre had helped take down a corrupt and despotic U.S. Vice President, and more recently had helped stop a group of billionaires from destroying Western civilization. They had worked with Kruger and his team, but had since retired to the quiet life in rural Louisiana.

"Will Jenny or that other pilot be joining us?" Decker asked, referring to Darlene "Jenny" Craig, a former pilot with the top-secret organization known as Project Archangel, but who now worked for Kruger.

"Just me," Kruger said gruffly.

"Well, come on in," Michelle said, motioning for him to come inside. She gave him a hug as he reached the doorway and then ushered him in. Their German Shepherd named Zeus briefly sniffed Kruger and then followed them into the living room.

"Nice house," Kruger said.

"Thanks, although not as nice as yours," Michelle said with a grin.

"I'm only in it for work," Kruger replied.

"What group are you working with these days?"

"Maybe it's best to wait until Spectre gets here and then I'll explain everything," Kruger said.

"Is that why you're here today?" Michelle asked as she put Cal Jr. down and handed him one of his toys.

"Unfortunately, yes," Kruger said.

"Does Cal know?"

"What did he tell you?" Kruger asked.

"That you called from out of nowhere and said you needed to talk to him," Michelle said.

"That's about all he knows," Kruger said. "I wanted to speak to him in person."

Michelle turned and squared off with Kruger. "What's with all the secrecy?"

"You know the drill, Michelle," Kruger said. "Everything I do is classified at some level."

"Yes, I know the drill, and that's what I'm afraid of," Michelle replied. "It's been – what – a year since Helios?"

"Sixteen months."

"So, almost a year and a half. Which, by the way, caused my husband to lose his job, nearly die, and almost attempt a Presidential assassination...but who's counting?"

"I'm sorry," Kruger said. "If there were any other way, I wouldn't be here right now."

"You saved our lives, and for that we are truly grateful. But please…please don't drag him back into that life."

"I'll explain everything as soon as he gets here," Kruger said softly.

"You sound just like Lyons," Michelle replied.

"I guess it comes with the territory," Kruger said.

Michelle sighed softly. "Make yourself at home. I need to go see about the baked potatoes," she said as she turned and walked into the kitchen.

Kruger sat down on the couch in the living area. He noticed a lone book on the coffee table and picked it up.

"*Instant Justice* by Cliff Hanger," he said to himself as he studied the cover.

Kruger was flipping through the pages when the door opened. Spectre and his long-time mentor "Bear" Jennings entered carrying groceries. Kruger put the book back on the coffee table and stood to meet them.

"Kruger! Good to see you, buddy," Spectre said with a smile. "I see you found my book."

"*Cliff Hanger*?" Kruger asked as he picked the book back up.

"Much catchier than Cal Martin, don't you think?" Spectre asked with a grin as he continued into the kitchen to deliver the groceries.

"A former fighter pilot must take down a top-secret organization hell-bent on world domination with the help of a few unlikely friends," Kruger said, reading the back cover. "Is this about you?"

Spectre placed the bags on one of the kitchen countertops and headed back into the living room to greet Kruger. "No. Why does everyone always think that?"

"I don't know, bub," Kruger said as he shook Spectre's hand. "Maybe because that's exactly what happened?"

Spectre shook his head and laughed dismissively. "It's 100% fiction. Trust me."

"I'll take your word for it," Kruger said as he turned to shake Bear's hand. "Good to see you, Mr. Jennings."

Bear frowned as he shook the red-bearded operator's hand. "I have a feeling I can't say the same about seeing you. Cal told me you called from out of nowhere and needed to see him."

"I promise, I will explain everything," Kruger said.

"How about now?" Michelle asked, returning from the kitchen.

"Fair enough," Kruger said.

Spectre picked up Cal Jr. as they took their seats around the coffee table in the living room.

"Two weeks ago, a high level North Korean scientist named Jon Chang-Ha killed himself after being discovered during an escape attempt. He was the number two man in their nuclear program, specializing specifically in their EMP technology," Kruger began.

"Killed himself or was killed?" Michelle asked.

"Based on what we know, he killed himself," Kruger replied.

"Was he defecting?" Bear asked.

"It's highly classified and I can go to jail for telling you this outside of a vault, but yes, he was working with a team out of Langley," Kruger said.

"What does that have to do with us?" Michelle asked impatiently.

"Despite his death, we were still able to pull intel off a thumb drive he left in a dead drop for us. Without going into too many details, we learned that an attack on mainland U.S. is imminent."

"It's been imminent for months now, hasn't it?" Bear asked. "Or is that just smoke and mirrors from the CIA?"

"This is a no-shitter, bub. The thumb drive verified that they have the technology in place to pull it off right now."

"What kind of attack are we talking about?" Spectre asked.

"Multiple ICBMs fitted with EMPs that could take out everything west of the Mississippi River," Kruger replied.

"So, you go in and take them out. You have guys – like yourself – trained to do just that. Besides, that country would cease to exist within minutes of launching anything at the U.S.," Bear argued.

"Well, we have a plan, which is why I'm here," Kruger said before turning to Spectre. "I need your help one last time, bub."

"Dude, come on," Spectre replied. "I have *one* kidney, remember? I'm no operator. Never have been. I write books and take care of my family, which is all I want to do now. I'm finally happy."

Michelle grabbed Spectre's hand and squeezed it as she glared at Kruger.

"I get that, bub. I really do. But I wouldn't have come here today if there were any other way. You have a firsthand experience that no one else in the world has. And to be honest, you're the only person I know I can trust for something this critical," Kruger argued.

"I'm sorry, but my answer is no," Spectre replied. "I've given enough for my country. It's time for someone else to pick up the torch. My son is my future."

"Even if it jeopardizes your son's future?" Kruger asked. "We're not talking a minor inconvenience if they do this. It's the end of modern civilization in the United States as we know it, and probably the end of this country."

"We've been long overdue for a good flush of that toilet bowl in Washington anyway," Bear interjected. "We'll be fine out here. We can fend for ourselves."

"There's a war brewing. The only question is whether we fight it here or there. But rest assured, you will fight it, one way or another. Even if that means fighting until your last bullet here," Kruger answered.

"So be it," Bear said as he folded his arms and sat back in the recliner. "Molon Labe."

"You really think the threat is that real?" Spectre asked.

"Again, I wouldn't be here if I didn't," Kruger said. "Look, I'm not asking you to be a door kicker. I just need your expertise and your critical thinking skills. I need the mind that came up with that tactical plan you executed in Cuba."

"Cuba?" Spectre yelped. "What does this have to do with Cuba?"

"With limited numbers and relatively little firepower, you infiltrated a foreign country and recovered a prisoner and a fighter jet," Kruger said. "I need that kind of thinking."

"I don't know…" Spectre said.

"$10 million dollars," Kruger said. "Wired directly to your account. Tax free."

"From who?" Michelle asked.

"Doesn't matter. You'll get ten million and the peace of mind knowing that Cal Jr. will grow up with a chance at a decent future."

"What good is the money if Cal Jr. grows up without a father?" Spectre asked. "Trust me, I did that. It sucks – even with a good father figure in your life. It's just not the same."

"Like I said, I'm not asking you to be a door kicker. I just need your outside-the-box thinking," Kruger replied.

"So, he only does the planning?" Michelle asked.

"And the training and minimal support," Kruger replied. "That's it. I wish I could explain more, but it's really sensitive and highly classified. I've already said way more than I should."

"Ten million dollars to train someone else?" Spectre asked incredulously.

Kruger nodded. "It's that serious, bub."

Michelle and Spectre exchanged a look. Michelle nodded slowly as Spectre kissed Cal Jr.'s forehead.

"When do you need an answer?"

Kruger looked at his watch. "Twenty minutes ago."

"Typical government bullshit, always waiting until the last minute," Bear said.

"Bear, what do you think?" Spectre asked. "Seriously."

Bear eyed Kruger. "You two have been through the shit together. If it were any other worthless government shill, I'd say hell no. Even knowing the stakes, I don't think you should do it. But, I know you, Cal. If you don't go, you're going to let it eat at you. And ten million *is* ten million."

"It's not about the money," Spectre replied.

"I know that, but it doesn't hurt."

"I'll let you three talk it out," Kruger said as he stood. "But this is time critical. I'll need your decision by morning."

"Wait, aren't you going to stay for steaks?" Michelle asked.

"I'll pass," Kruger said. "I really need to get going. Call me when you make your decision, Spectre.

CHAPTER TWO

Spectre could feel his chest tighten as he passed the Blue Angel F/A-18 on display outside the front gate of the Naval Air Station Joint Reserve Base New Orleans. He made a right turn at the red light and joined a short line of cars waiting for the sentry to check their credentials.

He wasn't quite sure why he felt so apprehensive. It wasn't that he thought the sentry would arrest him or that he might be denied entrance as a civilian. Kruger had made sure that his credentials as a Department of Defense (DOD) Contractor were valid, and his record had been wiped completely clean by Kruger's hacker named Julio Meeks.

There was no record of him being an unwitting participant in a plot to assassinate the President of the United States and tear apart the fabric of Western society. There was no trace of his time spent in prison after being framed for the murder of a sitting U.S. Senator. To everyone outside of his inner circle, Cal

"Spectre" Martin was nothing more than a combat veteran who had left the military to pursue a civilian career.

But Spectre knew better, and the more he thought about it, the more he realized that going back to his most recent squadron was the cause of his distress. It had been here that he had finally hung up his G-suit for good. It had been with this A-10 squadron that he had finally had enough of dealing with bureaucrats posing as leaders and their extreme risk aversion. He had sworn he would never deal with the military again.

And yet here he was, waiting in line as the sentry gave directions to the driver in the car in front of him. He had managed to let Kruger talk him into one more mission. That's the way it always seemed to go.

After Kruger had left, he had discussed Kruger's proposal in great detail with Michelle and Bear. It had been a tough decision, but by the end of the night, Spectre had decided it was in the best interest of his family and his country to accept. Besides, he reasoned, it was a fairly low-risk advisory role. It wasn't like he was parachuting into Pyongyang or anything.

With the decision made, he had called Kruger and told him that he was willing to help. Kruger thanked him and then gave him his first assignment – go to the Sensitive Compartmented Information Facility (SCIF) at NAS JRB New Orleans for a Top Secret briefing. He had left a contractor ID and visit certification letter in Spectre's mailbox on his way out. That would be all he needed to get in. They would discuss the plan via secure video teleconferencing once inside the SCIF.

He studied the ID as he waited in the line to enter the base. It was an older picture, but Spectre doubted the guard would care. As the car in front of him cleared, Spectre lowered his window and pulled up to the sentry.

"Good morning, sir. Any firearms or contraband to declare today?" the guard asked as Spectre handed over his ID.

"None to declare," Spectre said. It wasn't exactly the truth – he had a concealed Glock 19 holstered near his appendix and a short-barrel M4 rifle locked in a case under the back seat. But it wasn't a lie either, since he was only answering the question of whether he intended to declare either of those weapons to the guard standing in front of him. And that was an honest *no*.

The guard scanned the ID with his handheld scanner, then returned the ID and motioned for Spectre to continue. Spectre thanked the guard, then raised his window as he maneuvered through the barricades and onto the main road.

He turned left and headed for the address and building number Kruger had given him. He parked in a visitor's space, and then walked into the building's lobby and signed in with the sailor manning the security desk. After Spectre's credentials and visit certification were verified, an intel analyst emerged from behind a steel door and escorted him in.

The analyst walked Spectre to the inner vault and then handed him a red folder. As Spectre opened it, the analyst set up the video teleconferencing software and then excused himself, closing the door as he walked out.

The MI-6 liaison for the covert unacknowledged group known as Project Archangel appeared on screen. Agent Sierra Carter gave Spectre a short briefing on the situation in North Korea, reiterating much of what Kruger had already told him.

"Your folder contains a list of aircraft possible for this mission," Sierra explained.

Spectre flipped through the aircraft profiles in the folder. They were standard data sheets on various countries' fighter, attack, and even cargo aircraft.

"Kruger believes you are the most qualified to plan this mission; however, he is working another angle that he is holding close to the vest. I recommend you find two pilots that have experience in a variety of aircraft," Sierra said.

"I think I have a candidate or two in mind," Spectre said. "I'll be in touch."

* * *

Spectre left the SCIF and headed out of the building to retrieve his truck. As he drove out and reached the main road, he turned left toward the flight line instead of right to exit the base. He hoped his first candidate was working today.

Spectre followed the base's main road until it came to a T intersection and then turned right to parallel the flight line. As he neared the squadron operations building where he used to work, he looked to his left and saw a pair of A-10s taxi under the sun shelters and shut down. It was hard not to miss flying the "Hawg." Despite being relatively slow and underpowered compared to his first jet, the F-16, it was still his favorite aircraft.

The parking lot of the operations building was mostly full, but Spectre was able to find a spot near the back of the lot. He took a deep breath and exhaled slowly as he killed his truck's diesel engine.

He walked to the front door of the building and picked up the phone to call the Ops Desk to have someone let him in. Although he was pretty sure they had been lazy and hadn't changed the door's cipher combination, he didn't want to cause any issues by walking in unannounced. He was a civilian now, after all, and had no business being in the squadron without an escort.

When a female airman answered, Spectre identified himself and his reason for the visit. A minute later, the door opened and Major Tim "Kaiser" Von Rader greeted him.

"Spectre!" Kaiser said as he extended his hand. "What brings you here?"

Spectre shook Kaiser's hand. When Spectre was the Director of Operations, Kaiser had been the squadron's token single dude, constantly getting into trouble with online dating. One such encounter led to Kaiser's abduction and eventual rescue by the secret paramilitary organization run by Kruger called Odin.

"Is Woody around?" Spectre asked, referring to Major Trent "Woody" Hardick. Woody was a former Navy F/A-18 pilot who had transitioned to the Air Force Reserve to fly A-10s. Although still new to the A-10, Woody was an experienced combat aviator, and a good friend in the squadron to Spectre. The perpetual businessman, Woody flew with the squadron ten days per month while spending the rest of the time pursuing real estate ventures.

"Yeah, man, he's just about to brief for a flight. Is he expecting you?" Kaiser asked.

"I don't think so," Spectre replied. "Can I talk to him real quick?"

"Sure," Kaiser said as he turned to escort Spectre through the building.

"Still doing the online dating thing?" Spectre asked as they walked toward the ops desk.

Kaiser laughed. "Nah, I gave that up after *the incident*. I met a girl at a car show a few months ago. I think I'm hopefully done with the single life."

"Nice, man, congrats."

"How are Michelle and Cal Jr.?"

"Doing great," Spectre said. "Michelle opened her own private practice and Cal Jr. is growing like a weed."

"You still with the airline?"

"Nah, I moved on from that," Spectre answered. "Long story."

As they reached the ops desk, Woody and a few other pilots that Spectre didn't recognize were huddled around a computer looking at the weather radar.

"Woody, you have a visitor," Kaiser said as the group turned to see Spectre.

"Spectre!" Woody yelled. "Holy shit, man!"

Woody and Spectre exchanged a half-handshake, half-hug. "It's been forever, broski. How the hell have you been?"

"Doing great," Spectre replied. "Listen, I know you're about to brief. Can we talk for a second somewhere private?"

"Sure, man," Woody said with a quizzical look. "Everything okay?"

"Everything's fine," Spectre said.

Overhearing their conversation, Kaiser said, "You guys can use my office if you need to."

Spectre turned around as Woody pointed to the Director of Operations office. "You're the DO now?"

"Somebody had to do it after you left," Kaiser said.

"Congrats, buddy. You've earned it."

Spectre and Woody walked into the office and closed the door behind them. Spectre took a seat at his old desk while Woody sat in the chair across from him.

"Let me guess, you're recruiting me for a secret mission," Woody said with a grin.

"Actually, yes," Spectre said.

Woody laughed. When Spectre didn't respond, Woody suddenly turned serious. "Wait, what? You're serious?"

"Very serious."

"I thought you were writing books now," Woody said with a confused look. "Is this about the sequel? Are you finally ready to be a bestseller after writing the Woody Chronicles?"

"Depending on how this goes, we may have plenty of source material."

"Okay, seriously, what's going on?"

"You did some contract work in Southeast Asia flying the F/A-18, didn't you?"

Woody nodded slowly.

"And some of the countries you flew with had a mix of American and Russian equipment, right?"

"Yeah, but I never flew anything other than the Hornet."

"But you're familiar with the other aircraft?" Spectre asked.

"Dude, what's this about?" Woody asked impatiently.

"I can't talk about specifics here. We'd need a TS/SCI vault and a higher level of classification, but I came here because I need your help. I've been tasked to put together a team for a highly sensitive mission that I believe your background makes you uniquely qualified for."

Woody sat back and considered it for a moment. "Go on."

"You'll be put on military orders and sent TDY to Nellis for training."

"Working for…"

"Me."

"Is this some UAV gig?"

"No, it's definitely manned. Which is why I'm putting together a team of people I can trust."

"Flying what exactly?"

"That's not something I can talk about here," Spectre said, eyeing the door. "I'm also not quite sure yet, if we're being completely honest."

"What about my background? What kind of gig is this?"

"I wish I could tell you more, but I promise you that it'll be perfectly clear once you're read in."

"So, I'm just supposed to leave my family on trust?"

"Yes. But you'll be paid generously for it."

"Sorry, brah, but this is just my part time job now. I'm doing real estate development now. I don't do this for the money. But just out of curiosity, how much are we talking?"

"Eight figures."

Woody's eyes widened. "That's a lot of diapers. But still, I don't know, man. I learned in the Navy not to sign up for anything unless I knew every detail, disclaimer, and every word of the fine print. You're my friend and I trust you, but this sounds sketchy, brah."

"How about this – come to Nellis with me. Listen to the full-up briefing of what we're trying to do. If you're on board, great. You'll be generously compensated above and beyond just going on orders. If not, no worries. We'll make you sign a non-disclosure and send you back home. No harm, no foul."

Woody sighed. "Fine, but if the Woody Chronicles becomes a bestseller because of this, I want royalties."

"Deal," Spectre said with a grin.

CHAPTER THREE

Spectre had plenty of time to think about his next sales pitch on the drive from New Orleans to Fort Walton Beach in the panhandle of Florida. His next candidate was someone he'd gone to pilot training with, but they had regrettably done a poor job of keeping in touch afterwards. Aside from the personnel file and flying schedule hacker Julio "Coolio" Meeks had managed to obtain for him, Spectre wasn't even sure the man would be there.

Major Jonathan "Sparky" Lynch had graduated both Undergraduate Pilot Training and the F-16 Basic Course with Spectre. They had been good friends both on and off duty during training but had lost touch after Spectre left the Air Force shortly after being grounded in Iraq in 2009.

But despite their hiatus, Spectre knew that Sparky was perhaps the most qualified person for the mission at hand. After graduating F-16 school with Spectre, Sparky had gone on to graduate the F-16 Weapons Instructor Course at Nellis before going to Test Pilot School at Edwards. He had flown nearly every fighter in the U.S. inventory and a few foreign fighters like the MiG-29 and Su-27 as well. His experience and training made him a perfect fit for their mission.

And most importantly, Spectre trusted him. They had been neighbors in the dorms during pilot training and had spent time together off duty riding their motorcycles and shooting guns at the local ranges. Sparky was a good pilot, but an even better friend.

Spectre reached Eglin Air Force Base late in the evening. He checked into the Air Force Inn and found his room. All of the facilities had been renovated since Spectre had last been to the base three years ago, an experience he would have preferred to forget.

But like in New Orleans, Spectre had a history at this base. He had last been there investigating the shoot-down by radical Islamic terrorists of an F-35 during its test phase. That pilot had been the son of a United States Senator, a man with whom Spectre had been working to investigate the U.S. Vice President after Air Force One was hijacked over Midway Island.

Spectre was staying in the very building in which Senator Wilson had been assassinated by a bomb planted by one of Vice President Johnson's mercenaries. Spectre had been framed for it and had spent time in prison after confessing to the crime in order to save his wife. The scars and lost kidney were constant reminders for Spectre of the consequences of such evil.

Spectre tossed and turned that night, thinking back to the day the bomb went off, and running through what he might say to Sparky. He wasn't sure how much Sparky knew about Spectre's past, but it was doubtful that Sparky didn't at least know about his incarceration.

After a fitful night of off and on sleep, Spectre took a shower, ate a protein bar, and headed to the squadron to intercept Sparky before his flight. He arrived just as pilots were starting to show up for work and went through the same routine of calling the ops desk as he had done in New Orleans.

This time a young male airman showed up at the door and escorted him into the building after checking Spectre's identification. He brought Spectre to an office with multiple cubicles where Sparky appeared to be checking his e-mail with his back to the door.

"Major Lynch," the airman said. "You have a visitor."

Sparky spun around in his chair and immediately stood as he recognized Spectre.

"Spectre! Holy shit, what are you doing here?" Sparky asked, reaching out to shake Spectre's hand.

The airman excused himself as the two shook hands.

"Is there somewhere we can talk in private?" Spectre asked.

Sparky looked around. "This is the flight commander's office. It's as private as any place without going into the vault."

Spectre nodded and closed the door behind him. He pulled a chair from a nearby cubicle and wheeled it next to where Sparky had been sitting.

"How the hell are you?" Sparky asked. "I heard about what happened here. How'd that work out?"

"Big misunderstanding. It was all cleared up," Spectre said. "Have you been okay?"

Sparky smiled. "Yeah, man. Just started flying the F-35 for the test squadron here. It has had its share of bugs to work out but it's a pretty awesome aircraft when all systems are online."

"Listen, we definitely need to catch up later, but I'm kind of pressed for time and we need to get down to business. I'm here because I need your help."

Sparky leaned forward in his chair. "Of course, brother. Anything at all. Is everything okay?"

"Yes, everything's fine with me," Spectre said, realizing that it might have come off the wrong way. "I'm here about a project I'm working on that I think you'd be perfect for."

"What kind of project?"

"It's classified, so I can't really go into details here. But I can tell you that you'd be flying. And I know you love it here, but you'd be temporarily reassigned to Nellis until it's over."

"Okay..."

"You'd be assigned to work for me. I know it's kind of a leap of faith, but I'll be able to explain more-"

"I'm in," Sparky said, cutting Spectre off.

"You are?"

"Are you kidding? A flying job working for you? Of course I'm in! Where do I sign?"

"Sparky, this is serious," Spectre warned. "It's a no-shit mission."

Sparky waved his hand dismissively. "Dude, I know the drill. You'll explain when we're in a vault. But on principle, if you're in, I'm in. Case closed. Do I need to book my flight in DTS?"

Spectre was taken aback by his old friend's immediate answer.

"You don't need to talk to your wife?"

"Divorce finalized three months ago. Fuck her!"

"I'm sorry to hear that," Spectre said. He had either missed it in the personnel record Coolio had sent him, or it was too new to have made it into Sparky's file.

"Are you sure you're okay?" Spectre asked.

"Absolutely!" Sparky said enthusiastically. "I can't wait to find out what it is. Unless..."

"Unless what?" Spectre asked.

Sparky suddenly turned serious. "You're not going to make me be your backseater, are you?"

"No," Spectre said, laughing.

"Good," Sparky replied with a grin. "I get sick when I have to fly in the back."

"Alright, then," Spectre said. "Don't worry about travel arrangements. If you're in, I'll contact you with a time to meet the aircraft. A jet will pick you up from here and fly you to Nellis where we'll brief you on the operation."

"Shit hot!" Sparky replied.

CHAPTER FOUR

The all-white Gulfstream 650 taxied to a stop in front of the Base Operations building at Eglin Air Force Base. The pilots didn't shut down its engines as the lineman chocked the wheels and the airstairs lowered.

Sparky jogged out from Baseops, carrying his duffle in his left hand and a backpack over his right shoulder. He was greeted by an attractive younger woman wearing a dark gray pantsuit and sunglasses.

"Major Lynch?" the woman asked as she approached him. Sparky hesitated as he barely made out a British accent over the engine noise.

"I'm Sierra Carter," the woman added as Sparky stopped. "I'm here to take you to Spectre."

Sparky relaxed slightly as he heard Spectre's callsign. He shook the woman's hand.

"Do you need my identification?" Sparky asked.

"That won't be necessary, we've already positively identified you," she said.

"How?"

Sierra pointed back to the Baseops building. "Facial recognition based on those cameras."

"Do *you* have an ID?" Sparky asked as he turned back to her.

"No," she responded curtly. "Now, come along, we have a long flight ahead of us."

Without waiting for him to respond she turned and motioned for him to follow her back to the waiting luxury business jet. Sparky stood there watching her for a moment and then jogged to catch up, his duffle skipping along the ground as he tried to hurry.

As she reached the stairs, Sierra once again turned and stopped Sparky.

"Your mobile please," she said, holding out her hand.

"What?" Sparky yelled, struggling to hear her over the engines. Sweat was starting to bead on his forehead from the hot Florida sun and the effort of dragging his bags a few hundred feet.

"Give me your mobile phone!" Sierra repeated.

Sparky fished it out of his flight suit pocket and reluctantly handed it to her. She removed the micro sim card and the battery and continued into the airplane. Sparky followed her up the stairs, watching as she deposited the phone into a metal container and the other items into a separate one.

"Hey!" Sparky protested. "What's all that about?"

"You're off the grid now, my friend," a voice to his right said.

Sparky turned and saw Woody, an old friend he had met when Woody first flew Hornets and Sparky was an F-16 instructor. They had fought each other many times in the airspace over Fallon Naval Air Station and had become good friends.

Woody was sitting in a large leather chair with a napkin tucked in his t-shirt as he worked on a T-bone. Unlike Sparky, it was hard to tell he was a fighter pilot or even in the military. His dark, spiked up hair was much longer than Sparky's high and tight, and he was wearing a Metallica t-shirt and blue jeans.

"Woody?" Sparky asked, dumbfounded as he blocked the door. One of the pilots squeezed by him and closed the door before retreating into the cockpit as Sparky shook off his surprise and moved out of the way.

"Please, stow your bags in this closet and have a seat,"

Sierra said, indicating the forward closet. "We're ready for departure."

She turned toward the cockpit and opened the door, disappearing as Sparky opened the closet door. He placed his bags gently in the remaining space and then walked back to where Woody was still enjoying his evening meal. Woody wiped his hand on his cloth napkin and then shook Sparky's hand.

"How the hell are you?" Woody asked.

"I've been good. Where'd you get that?" Sparky asked, sitting in the seat across the aisle as he eyed what was left of Woody's steak.

"Fully stocked galley in the back, brah. It's awesome."

Sierra returned and took a seat across from Sparky as the Gulfstream started to taxi.

"Excuse me, ma'am, I'll have what he's having, please," Sparky said, pointing to Woody.

Woody belted out a laugh as Sierra's eyebrows furrowed.

"She's not a flight attendant, dude," Woody said, trying not to choke on his water as he laughed.

"I'm terribly sorry," Sparky said, blushing as he held up his hands.

"It's quite alright," Sierra replied.

"That accent. Where are you from?"

"That's none of your concern," Sierra said flatly.

"I did an exchange tour with the RAF," Sparky replied. "I'm just trying to place it. Lancashire?"

"There's food in the back," Sierra said, pointing to the aft galley. "If you're hungry, you can help yourself once we get airborne."

Sparky leaned over and whispered to Woody, "I guess you had a fun flight over here."

"It was great!" Woody said loudly. "I don't ask questions that I don't want the answer to."

"How'd you get wrangled into this?" Sparky asked as the engines spooled up for takeoff.

"Same as you, I'd imagine. Spectre talked me into doing something dumb."

"How do you know him?"

"We flew together in New Orleans."

"New Orleans? You flying Hornets down there?"

"A-10s. I joined Mother Blue a few years ago. Spectre and I deployed together. How'd you know him?"

"Wow. Small world. I didn't know y'all knew each other. Or that you were in the Air Force. I guess it's been a while."

"Well, when you're busy flying every fighter ever made, that stuff happens," Woody said with a grin.

"Spectre and I went to pilot training together. We were good buddies back then, but I guess I did a bad job of keeping in touch with both of you."

"It happens," Woody said, holding onto his tray to keep it from sliding as the plane rotated and took off. "You should really get one of these steaks. It's pre-cooked, but if you heat it up for about ten minutes in the oven back there, it really seals in the flavor."

Sparky looked back at Sierra who appeared to be reading a book or some other document on her tablet and then leaned toward Woody.

"So, any idea what the mission is?" Sparky asked.

Sierra looked up, watching the two pilots as Sparky waited for an answer.

Woody made eye contact with her and then said, "Nope. Above my paygrade. All I know is they'll tell us when we get there."

Seeing Woody's exchange with Sierra, Sparky turned and looked at her. "At some point are you going to tell me who you are?"

"Perhaps," Sierra said with a sly smile as she went back to reading her tablet.

Sparky shook his head and leaned back in his seat, looking out the window as the aircraft climbed through a cloud layer. When they leveled at cruising altitude, the pilots extinguished the seat belt light. Sparky got up and walked to the back.

He made himself a steak sandwich and then returned, this time sitting in the chair across from Woody and placing his food on the table between them.

"So, are you married? Kids?" Sparky asked.

"Married, one little heathen so far."

"How old?"

"Ten months."

"Does the wife know about this?"

Woody shrugged. "She knows I'm going on a short TDY to Nellis."

"*Short*? Spectre made it sound like it could be a pretty lengthy project."

"Depends on what it is. I'm just a TR right now and I have a real estate business. I don't have time for anything lengthy unless it involves aliens attacking and me being the last line of defense."

"TR?"

"Traditional Reservist. I'm a part-timer at the A-10 squadron."

"But if you can't stay for the long haul, why are you going?"

"I told Spectre I'd hear him out first. So that's what I'm going to do. Plus, it sounds like the money might be worth it."

"Yeah, ten million, right?"

"So they say. Like I said, I'm just going to hear him out. Even ten million might not be worth it."

"So, you're going, knowing you might not even do it?"

"Maybe the aliens really are attacking. *I don't know*," Woody said, laughing.

"Maybe I shouldn't have been so eager to agree to it."

"Are you still active duty?"

"Yeah," Sparky replied.

"Well, you probably know Spectre better than I do, but I'm sure it's legit no matter what it is. I'm just not sure it's something you guys will need me for."

"Fair enough," Sparky replied before taking a bite of his sandwich.

As Sparky finished his food, Woody walked to the rear of the aircraft and took a nap on one of the beds.

As the aircraft started its descent, Sierra walked to the back.

She returned with Woody in trail and ordered him to sit. She then walked to the front and came back carrying what appeared to be two black cloth bags.

"Put this on," Sierra said, handing them to both men.

"On what?" Woody asked.

"Your head."

"What?" Woody yelped.

"Sorry, but that's protocol."

"Wait, aren't we going to Nellis?" Sparky asked as he stared at the bag.

"Put them on, or I'm afraid we'll have to divert," Sierra insisted.

"Never mind, I get it," Sparky said as he put the bag over his head.

"Well, will you explain it to me? Because I don't," Woody said. "Are we going somewhere off the books?" Woody asked. "Like Area 51?"

"Something like that," Sparky said.

"So, there might actually be aliens!" Woody said, putting the bag over his head.

* * *

Spectre was sitting in the inner vault of the highly classified black site in the Nevada desert when Kruger walked in.

"You scared me," Spectre said. "I barely recognize you without the beard."

"Believe me, bub, I'm not a fan of it either," Kruger said. "But it's the way this has to go."

"Any word from Woody and Sparky?"

Spectre had been sitting in the vault combing through the highly classified list of possible scenarios trying to come up with the best way to execute the mission without getting his friends killed.

"Your friends are on their way," Kruger said as he walked over to the mini-fridge and retrieved two bottles of beer. He handed one to Spectre and then sat in the chair across from Spectre's corner desk.

Spectre looked up briefly as he accepted the beer and placed it on the desk. He went back to flipping through the various scenario briefings.

"What are you thinking?" Kruger asked.

"That it's a suicide mission," Spectre replied without looking up.

"They'll be on the ground in three hours," Kruger said, looking at his watch. "We'll need some semblance of a plan by the time they show up."

Spectre pulled out one of the documents and placed in on the desk. It had a picture of a Russian fighter jet on it with TOP SECRET classification markings on the top and bottom. He tapped the picture with his finger.

"Can your contacts pull this off?"

"Everything is already arranged," Kruger said. "Just say the word and we'll execute."

"And the other COAs?" Spectre asked, referring to the other Courses of Action.

"We've vetted each of these scenarios, bub. I chose you to make the decision and handle the tactical planning because I think you're best suited for it. Whichever method you decide, we will execute."

"Geez. No pressure, huh?"

"You know what the stakes are, bub."

"We're going to need training."

"*We?*"

"I'll need to get checked out in the aircraft to train them, and it's probably a good idea for me to learn everyone's role so that I can adjust the plan if necessary."

"How much training do you think everyone will need?"

Spectre considered Kruger's question for a minute. "Five sorties, minimum, for a basic aircraft checkout with a qualified instructor. And then we'll need a few weeks to train for the actual mission."

"Let me make some phone calls," Kruger said as he tossed his empty beer bottle into the trash can and stood. "Are you sure you need that many? You didn't have any training to go to Cuba."

"I already knew how to fly that jet. This is a brand new aircraft for both Woody and Sparky. You're asking them to fly a brand new jet and convince the North Koreans that they are experienced demo pilots. This is the absolute bare minimum."

"I'll make it happen," Kruger said. "Are you sure these guys will sign up for this?"

"No," Spectre said. "But they're the two best pilots I can think of for this plan."

CHAPTER FIVE

The Gulfstream carrying Woody and Sparky landed at a remote desert airstrip in Nevada. The runway appeared to be freshly paved, and there were newly constructed hangars lining the ramp, but there were no other signs of life. The field had no air traffic control tower, no fire and rescue, and no other buildings anywhere to be found.

As the plane stopped in front of the western-most hangar, Woody and Sparky were escorted from the aircraft. Once safely inside and the door behind them closed, their hoods were removed.

"Welcome, gentlemen," Spectre said, standing in front of a fold-out table. Next to him were two men neither Woody nor Sparky recognized.

"So where are the little green men?" Woody asked as he looked around the empty hangar.

"Little green men?" Spectre asked with a confused look.

"He thinks we're at Area 51," Sierra responded from behind the two men.

"Not quite," Spectre said with a chuckle. "This is a little different. People actually know Area 51 exists."

"You've piqued my interest," Woody replied. "Go on…"

"First, Woody and Sparky, I'd like you to meet Kruger and Tuna," Spectre said, indicating the men on either side of him. "You've already met Miss Carter, and there are a few others you'll need to meet. But first, let's get the motherhood out of the way. Have a seat."

Spectre motioned to the table and then walked around to the other side. Woody and Sparky each sat in a folding chair. There were documents and pens on the table in front of each man.

"These are your nondisclosure agreements," Spectre said. "Standard boilerplate language. If you say anything about anything you see or hear today to anyone, you'll face ten years in prison and a ten thousand dollar fine per incident."

"Didn't seem to matter to Hillary," Woody joked as he read the document.

"You're not Hillary, bub," Kruger said menacingly.

The smile suddenly vanished from Woody's face as he looked up at the rather intimidating red-haired man standing over him.

"Copy that," Woody said as he went back to reading the agreement.

Sparky immediately signed the highlighted portions and handed it back to Spectre. "When do we start?"

"Dude, did you sign one of these too? How are you going to write a book about this?" Woody asked as he read through the agreement.

"The sooner you sign it, the sooner we can get started," Spectre saying, ignoring Woody's joke.

Woody finished flipping through the document and then signed the highlighted portions. "I feel like I'm buying a house with all these signatures."

Sierra collected the documents and then joined Spectre and company on the other side of the table.

"Sorry for the cloak and dagger stuff, but this is highly classified. What I'm about to tell you is only known by a handful of people, including the President, and the Director of Central Intelligence. It has the ability to severely damage national security in the event of inadvertent or unauthorized disclosure, thus the safeguards. If you decide to help, realize that the mission is strictly need-to-know. So, it may not make sense at first, but trust me, it will," Spectre began.

Woody and Sparky nodded.

"With that said, I'll let Agent Carter give the SITREP," Spectre said before yielding the floor to Sierra Carter.

"Thank you, Spectre," Sierra said as she stepped forward. "General Jon Chang-Ha was the number two scientist in the North Korean Nuclear and Ballistic Missile program. Just over two weeks ago, General Chang-Ha died while attempting to defect during an American Intelligence operation. Although the Americans were unable to question him, Chang-Ha was able to deliver a secure thumb drive to a CIA dead drop and the information we gathered from that is frightening to say the least."

"Wait, I thought the North Koreans weren't the bad guys anymore?" Woody interjected. "Didn't they just declare peace and that their nuclear program was over?"

"What we've learned is that the North Koreans have developed an Electro-Magnetic Pulse weapon capable of reaching and detonating over California and most of the west coast of the United States. They've disbanded their nuclear program because they no longer need it – this would be just as devastating if not worse and, from our estimations, would be much harder to track and stop in time," Sierra answered.

"So, they're not looking for peace?" Sparky asked.

"Kim Jong-Un's number two man, Choe Il-Sung, is apparently much more powerful than we previously understood. Despite Jong-Un's near godlike status within the country, Il-Sung appears to be the 'man behind the curtain' if you will. And from the classified documents General Chang-Ha was able to give us, we believe he intends to attack the U.S. mainland regardless of peace talks," Sierra said. "And soon."

"That's suicide!" Woody said. "Surely they know we'd nuke them into oblivion if they did something like that."

"That's not a risk we're willing to take," Tuna answered. "It would cripple the United States."

"And I'm assuming pre-emptive strikes are off the table to take out this capability?" Sparky asked.

"Based on the information obtained from the thumb drive and other third-party intelligence sources, the President believes that the peace talks are genuine and that the issue lies with Il-Sung. He does not want to risk an all-out war on the peninsula," Tuna said. "This is on us."

"What is on us, exactly?" Woody asked. "We're both just pilots, remember?"

"And that's exactly why we need you," Spectre said with a knowing grin. "To fly airplanes."

"To do what, exactly? Bomb the missile silos? Strafe this Il-Sung dude? Do you have some super stealthy F-45 fighter out here that's completely invisible like Wonder Woman's airplane?" Woody asked.

"Unfortunately, that's as much as we can tell you even with the NDA you signed. This is the point where we need to know if you're in or out," Spectre said. "And if you're in, you're in it until the mission is accomplished."

"I'm in," Sparky said without hesitation.

"Oh c'mon!" Woody said. "You fly me all this way, put a bag on my head, and still tell me nothing?"

"Now you know what the stakes are, bub," Kruger said. "The intelligence is credible and has been vetted through other sources. Everything else will be explained as needed."

"Woody, I know you have a family and real estate business. I have my own family and private enterprise I'm trying to work on, but I wouldn't be here if this weren't a real danger to our freedom and way of life. We may not feel the immediate effects where we live, but within a few months our entire way of life will change, and not for the better. I wouldn't have dragged you all the way out here if I didn't think you could help stop that from happening," Spectre said.

"Is this a suicide mission?" Woody asked softly.

Spectre shook his head. "No. Although we both know Murphy's Law can and will make any plan fall apart on any given Sunday, we're not planning it that way. Everyone comes home. That's the deal."

Woody sighed. "You know NAVY stands for Never Again Volunteer Yourself…but I guess I'm a slow learner. Fuck it, I'm in."

"In that case, follow me," Spectre said as he started toward the door they had entered through.

CHAPTER SIX

They were led out of the hangar and back out onto the ramp. The Gulfstream that had flown them to the remote site in the Nevada desert was gone. There were no other signs of life or human activity.

"I guess our ride is gone," Woody commented, pointing to the empty ramp as he and Sparky followed Spectre and the others.

"I'm sure they'll be back," Sparky replied.

"Hey, what if we had said no?" Woody asked loudly enough for Spectre to hear.

Spectre looked back at Woody without stopping and grinned. "We would have sent you home."

"When?" Woody asked.

"Eventually," Spectre replied.

"C'mon, man!"

Spectre shrugged it off with a laugh as he and Kruger led the way toward the massive hangar a hundred yards from the much smaller hangar they had just come from. It was at least three times bigger and appeared to be all new construction.

Spectre swiped his badge and entered his pin on the keypad next to the door. He then opened it and gestured for everyone to enter. The entry had a short hallway known as a "mantrap" which required the outer door to be closed before the inner door could be unlocked. This time Spectre had to enter a six-digit code and place his hand on a biometric scanner.

Once the lock clicked open and the light above the scanner turned green, Spectre opened the door. The team followed him into another short hallway which opened to a room with several desks and computers.

"This is our daily working area," Spectre explained as he started the tour. "Classified at Top Secret or lower. The other hangar we were in is also cleared up to Secret."

Spectre led them through the cubicles to another door. He stopped and opened a panel, revealing another keypad. This time, the authentication required a retinal scan, fingerprints, and voice analysis.

"Calvin Martin," he said before the system granted him access.

When the lock clicked open, Spectre opened the door and turned back to the group. "Typically, you'll each have to go through the authentication process each time you go in – no tailgating. But for the sake of time and this tour, we'll skip it for now."

"What about her?" Sparky asked, nodding to Sierra Carter. "NOFORN?"

NOFORN or "no foreign nationals" referred to the classification sublevel in which classified information could not be released to non-United States citizens.

"Sierra has been given special access," Kruger answered. "She and her team are cleared to the highest levels of this program."

"I'll explain once we get into the inner vault," Spectre said as he gestured for them to enter.

The inner vault was much smaller. In the center of the room was a conference table with eight chairs. There were two computer stations on each wall and a projector screen on the wall. Once everyone was safely inside and the door was closed, Spectre approached the screen and picked up a remote.

"Have a seat," Spectre said as he turned on the projector.

As he waited for the projector lamp to warm up, Spectre grabbed a bottle of water from the nearby mini-fridge. "Water in here if you guys need one."

"What about beer?" Sparky asked.

"In the hangar," Tuna replied.

Kruger joined Spectre at the head of the conference table, while Sierra and Tuna joined Woody and Sparky at the table.

"This vault is cleared for Top Secret – Sensitive Compartmented Information," Spectre continued. "This is the only place you may discuss OPERATION BLUE CAMARO."

"Blue Camaro?" Woody scoffed. "What kind of name is that?"

"The one the CIA gave it," Spectre shrugged. "Regardless, this place and the vault at Langley are the only two places cleared to discuss it for now. Any questions?"

As Spectre looked around the room, the projector finally came up. He logged into the computer and opened the presentation. The screen showed a classified banner that read TS/SCI-BLUE CAMARO across the top and bottom as the presentation title page opened.

"Alright, so before we begin, I'll explain the ins and outs of what everyone is doing here. Officially, this is an intelligence operation only – nothing more. Sierra is here as an attaché for MI-6 and their counterterrorism division. Unofficially, this is a Project Archangel operation."

"Project Archangel is a covert, unacknowledged task force that partners with Brits to do bad things to worse people while giving the President and his cabinet plausible deniability in the event that things go sideways. Tuna is in charge, along with Sierra Carter, who is the British MI-6 representative. Anything they do is authorized by the DCI and British Secretary of State for Defence, and either briefed or back-briefed to the President directly. No one else knows about it," Spectre explained.

"It has evolved a bit in the last five years," Kruger added. "It used to have a dedicated air wing with close air support capabilities, but we've scaled it back in recent years."

"Sick!" Woody said.

"There's a lot of history there," Spectre said. "But we don't have time to get into that. For now, we have a very tight timeline and you guys need to get up to speed."

Spectre clicked to the next slide. It was a picture of a Russian twin engine fighter jet.

"This is the SU-30MK3NK, a variant of the Chinese SU-30MK2 Flanker-C made specifically for the North Koreans," Spectre said.

"Twin engines, twin tails, twin seats," Woody said. "I like it!"

"One too many seats," Sparky said jokingly.

Spectre switched to the next slide. "The North Korean SU-30 is just finishing its test and evaluation phase but is expected to be the most advanced export version of the SU-30, featuring the upgraded Zhuk-AESA2 active electronically scanned array radar, a passive detection suite, upgraded EO/IR pod, and active jamming capability."

"Why? Why would we let the North Koreans have that?" Sparky asked.

"We're not," Spectre said. "We've already bought out the order and half will be sold to the Malaysians and the other half to the Indians. They will be sold as upgraded versions of the Malaysian SU-30MKM and Indian SU-30MKI respectively. No one will ever know."

"Except the North Koreans?" Woody asked.

"Not yet," Spectre replied. "For now, they must think that they're getting the order and that they will be getting a performance demo in eight weeks as scheduled."

Spectre advanced the slide once more, showing a map of Belarus and pictures of an air base in Minsk.

"Tomorrow, we will fly to Minsk. The Russians are doing on-site training of the initial cadre of the Belarussian Air Force on the first aircraft of their order of SU-30SMs, which are similar enough to the North Korean N3NK variant to work out. We will each get a five-sortie checkout in three days before heading back here, at which point you'll start training for the mission."

"Training for what mission?" Woody asked. "*Now* can you tell us what we're going to be doing?"

"Sure," Spectre said with a knowing grin. "You two are going to become demo pilots."

CHAPTER SEVEN

Spectre handed Kruger a beer and sat behind his desk, kicking his feet up as he popped the top of his own beer and leaned back in the chair.

"Do you still think these are the right guys?" Kruger asked as he sat down across from Spectre. They were alone in the inner vault while the others ate and got settled in to their dorms in the hangar next door.

"I do," Spectre said, taking a long pull from the beer. "They're both great pilots and I'd trust them with my life."

"Even Woody?"

"What about him?"

"He seemed to be unsure of this operation."

"He was active duty Navy to start his career. Those guys are used to getting fucked over. It's just a kicked-puppy routine. He'll be fine. I'm not worried."

"Your show," Kruger said as he tilted his beer to Spectre. "Just tell me what you need."

"Now let me ask you," Spectre said as he put his feet back on the floor and leaned on the desk. "What is the deal with Odin?"

"It's still around," Kruger replied.

"Really?"

"Really."

"So, is that your involvement here?" Spectre asked.

"No, this is 100% Project Archangel and, for all intents and purposes, Tuna is in charge," Kruger said.

"But…"

"But, because of my history with the Russians and the team, Director Chapman invited me to take point on this one."

"You're still with Project Archangel, officially, aren't you?"

"*Officially*, no one is with Project Archangel," Kruger replied.

"You know what I meant," Spectre shot back. "What happened after Helios? You never told me."

"Lyons left me the business," Kruger said, referring to Jeff Lyons, the billionaire that had been in charge of the covert tactical group called Odin before being assassinated.

"And what I didn't donate to wounded warrior groups, I kept to keep Odin running. At first, it worked out pretty well. Tuna and the boys flip-flopped between Odin and Archangel. Whatever they wouldn't or couldn't do because of political bullshit, we'd do. As you know, Archangel became a joint op with the Brits, so there were more opportunities for Odin to intervene because of the red tape," Kruger explained.

"Sounds like a good deal," Spectre responded.

"It was, in theory. But shit started going sideways when we started working in Eastern Europe," Kruger replied.

"For what?"

"To take down the Bratva that tried to steal Helios from the Odin billionaires," Kruger said. Helios was a supercomputer created by the billionaires behind Odin. It was theoretically capable of hacking and manipulating data in any medium, including synthesizing voice and video to create evidence of nearly any crime by any person. They had intended to use it to take down the United States government and "reboot the system" as they called it.

"I've seen their stuff in the news. Didn't one of their bosses get executed in New York not too long ago?"

"That was Wolf," Kruger replied, referring to Alex "The Wolf" Shepherd.

"How is that guy?"

"Back in South Texas, last I heard. I don't think he'll be sending me a Christmas card anytime soon after what happened last time we saw each other."

"With the Bratva?"

"Yeah," Kruger replied as he took another swig and stood. "Want another beer?"

"No, thanks," Spectre said as he watched Kruger walk over to the mini-fridge and grab another beer.

"Long story short on that is I fucked up," Kruger said as he returned to his seat.

"*You?* How?"

"I fell in love," Kruger replied.

"Happens to the best of us," Spectre replied with a grin.

"Yeah, well, it shouldn't happen when you're trying to save the free world."

"Are you kidding? That's when it *always* happens," Spectre said and then laughed. "Ask me how I know."

"Anyway, while working with MI-6 and the CIA, I met an FSB agent named Natasha."

"A Russian *femme fatale*? Nice!"

"She was working deep cover within the Bratva to root out the corruption and the government bureaucrats loyal to the Bratva."

"Sooo…pretty much everyone?"

"Close," Kruger said before taking another pull from his beer.

"So, you fell in love with a Russian spy. Then what happened?"

"The Bratva acquired the names of some of the members of Project Archangel that were involved in killing their boss."

"Holy shit! The most secretive, elite unit on the planet had a leak? How?"

"Because we fed it to them," Kruger replied. "We were working with Natasha and the FSB and wanted to smoke them out."

"You gave them everyone?"

"No, just enough to make them come looking for us. We needed to find the mole in the CIA. We only gave them my name plus Shepherd and Maddie's."

"Agent Tanner? The FBI Agent? And Wolf? Why those two?"

"On paper, they were both dead," Kruger replied. "It was easy to fake Tanner's death since she barely made it out of the safe house alive. And Coolio had given Wolf a new identity in South Texas. That should've been the end of it."

"But it wasn't…"

"No. Shepherd, now Troy Wilson, somehow managed to get tangled up with MS-13, who were trafficking drugs and sex slaves with the Bratva. And they recognized him when he ended up on YouTube."

"And then they wanted revenge. Jesus!"

"Like I said, I fucked up."

"There's no way you could've known that."

"I *should* have. They nearly killed him."

"We all make mistakes, man," Spectre said.

"Not in this business, bub," Kruger replied as he peeled the label off his bottle.

"Well, back to business," Spectre said as he shifted in his chair. "Is any of this going to be an issue in Belarus?"

"No," Kruger said. "The rest of the team is with Natasha in Minsk surveilling the airfield. They will provide security when we get there, but right now there are no known threats."

"So, are the Russians cooperating?"

"Considering we saved their government from a coup by the Bratva? Yeah, I'd say they owe us. So far, they've given us everything you've asked for."

"When you told me they were getting a demo from the factory, I figured that would be the best plan. All of the other options just seemed too risky," Spectre said, referring to the list of possible infiltration options. "Do you think Natasha will be able to do what she says?"

The options had ranged from shooting down Il-Sung's private jet using stolen North Korean MiG-29s, to hijacking the private jet and bailing before ditching it over water, to an outright strike using Russian SU-25 Frogfoot aircraft. To Spectre, none of the options seemed appealing until he learned that the Russians had planned to do a private demo of the advanced Flanker to Kim Jong Un and Il-Sung.

As long as Natasha could get the aircraft, it seemed to be an option that carried the least amount of risk with the best ability to get in and, more importantly, get out. After that, it was up to Kruger and his team to decide how they would carry out the actual assassination of Choe Il-Sung.

"Yes. She and her team are working on it as we speak," Kruger replied.

"Can we really trust the Russians?"

"Natasha is the only Russian I trust."

"I can't wait to meet her, then."

Kruger stood and tossed his empty beer bottle into the trash.

"You'll see her in Minsk. Better get your gear ready. Jenny will be back with the jet in two hours to fly us there."

"Looking forward to meeting her," Spectre said. "And getting back to my own family when this is all over."

"Just get your boys trained and ready and you'll be back to writing your fighter pilot erotica before you know it," Kruger said with a big grin.

"That's actually not a bad idea," Spectre replied. "Maybe I'll name my next character after you."

"Good luck with that, bub."

CHAPTER EIGHT

The team made several strategic stops before landing at Minsk National Airport. As they deplaned, they were met by a team of operators in civilian clothes that Kruger introduced as the other members of Project Archangel. Of the six men, Spectre only knew Reginald "Cowboy" Carter, a former member of the British Special Air Service who had been part of Odin under Kruger.

There were three other Brits and two Americans that Spectre had never met before. Kruger introduced the Brits as Captain Jacob "Ringo" Smith, Sullivan Churchill and Phillip Taylor. The two Americans were "Sledge" Hamler and "Dusty" Hogan. They all had varying levels of facial hair. To Spectre, both Sullivan and Sledge looked like they could've been professional wrestlers in another life. They towered over the others, sporting shaved heads and almost cartoonish physiques.

After brief introductions, Spectre and company were ushered into the mini-convoy of three up-armored SUVs and the teams departed. They were all given fake United Nations credentials as the team headed for the 61st Fighter Air Base in Baranovichi.

"So, what's our cover story here?" Woody asked from the back seat. He was in the middle SUV with Spectre, Kruger, Cowboy, and Sparky.

"Until we get to the airbase, we are representing the United Nations Security Council to inspect various military facilities within the country. Once we get to Baranovichi, you're here to learn how to fly the SU-30 with the others," Kruger replied.

"So, there's no cover story when we get there?" Woody asked.

"No, not once we're on base."

"The Russians and everyone else know we're doing this?"

"The Russians know. The Belarussians don't care. They will do whatever the Russians tell them," Kruger replied.

"I'm confused," Woody said.

Kruger grinned and turned back to Woody. "Good."

"Not cool, brah," Woody replied.

"It'll make sense as we get closer to the mission," Spectre interjected. "Don't worry."

"Will we be learning in classes with the Belarussians?" Sparky asked.

"No," Spectre said. "You're getting the accelerated course. Five flights in three days with academics and then we head back home. You won't interact with the local fighter pilots."

Woody laughed. "Great, it's like a Navy CAT-Other, except worse."

"What's a CAT-Other?" Sparky asked.

"It's a Hornet transition short course. Just ten hours and a checkride. Minimal training. Usually for senior dudes."

"What about emergency procedures and boldface? Will we get that beforehand to study?" Sparky asked, referring to the time critical memory items pilots needed to know and perform verbatim in the event of an emergency.

"The Russians aren't using them. You'll have a quick reference card for your kneeboard," Spectre answered.

"In English?" Woody asked.

"Yes, *in English*," Spectre replied, laughing.

The three-vehicle convoy made it to the airbase uneventfully. They drove straight to the hangar where a woman and two serious-looking men in civilian clothes stood in the parking lot waiting to greet them.

As they exited, the woman walked to Kruger and gave him a hug. They kissed gently on the lips and then said a few words to each other that Spectre couldn't hear. Having known Kruger as the "angry bearded ginger" for so long, it was weird to Spectre to see Kruger showing affection to another human being, but the two appeared to deeply care for each other. He recognized the look from his own relationship with Michelle.

"This must be Natasha," Spectre said as the group waited for Kruger and the woman to finish their chat and then turn to them.

"Nat, I'd like you to meet Cal 'Spectre' Martin, Trent 'Woody' Hardick, and Jonathan 'Sparky' Lynch," Kruger said, introducing her to the trio. The other operators were already at work setting up a perimeter and checking the area for threats.

"It's a pleasure to meet you," Natasha said with a thick Russian accent.

"Likewise," Spectre said, shaking her hand.

"And these two men are Viktor and Anatoly," Kruger said, nodding to the burly men behind them. "They are with Natasha."

"I have heard much about you, Mr. Spectre," Natasha said. "How is Michelle?"

Spectre raised an eyebrow, remembering that Kruger had told him that Natasha was a Russian FSB agent. "You heard about me through work, or…"

"Freddie told me," Natasha said. "Don't worry. We will not kidnap you."

"Kidnap!" Woody yelped. "Dude, what are we doing here?"

Natasha smiled slyly. "Just kidding."

"Wait, you're kidding about not kidnapping him? Or kidnapping him?" Woody asked nervously.

"Relax, bub," Kruger said. "Let's get to work."

"The hangar is clear," Cowboy reported as he approached with Tuna.

Kruger nodded and took the lead with Natasha by his side as the group headed into the hangar. They walked in and Kruger flipped on the lights, revealing two brand new Russian fighter jets.

"Whoa," Spectre said, marveling at the pair of SU-30s in front of him. "These things are huge."

"That's what she said!" Woody quipped as the team fanned out into the hangar.

Spectre rolled his eyes as he walked to the nearest jet. The canopy was open, so he climbed the ladder and looked inside.

Despite being brand new and having large multi-function displays, the cockpit felt dated to Spectre. He wasn't sure if it was the light blue paint on the metal, or the Russian inscriptions, or the analog backup gauges that looked like they were out of a B-17, but for some reason it just didn't seem like a new airplane to him.

"Woody, you fought one of these didn't you?" Spectre asked as he looked down the ladder at Woody and Sparky who were waiting their turn to take a peek.

"I fought the Malaysians a few times," Woody said.

"Do you remember what the backseater could do with the thrust vectoring?"

Woody shrugged. "Beats me. I only looked in the cockpit once, and I only cared about the front seat because that's where all the important stuff happens."

"I'm sure we will find that out during academics, right?" Sparky asked.

Spectre looked around one more time and then stepped down the ladder. Sparky and Woody each took turns exploring the cockpit as Kruger pulled Spectre aside.

"What do you think, bub?" Kruger asked in a low voice so no one else could hear them.

"I think it would be better to have pilots in the backseat who could fly these things if shit starts going wrong," Spectre said.

"Well, we don't have that luxury. I can't train pilots to do this mission with the timeline we have."

Spectre nodded. "I get that, but I'm not sure I can teach you and Tuna to do pilot shit in that timeline either."

"Improvise, adapt, overcome, bub," Kruger replied. "We're just going to have to make it work."

"And you're sure JAX wasn't available?" Spectre whispered. "JAX" had been a Weapons System Officer that had flown backseat for Spectre on several missions with the elite covert unit called Project Archangel. Although he wasn't quite an operator like Tuna or Kruger, at least JAX had some level of special operations training to go along with his expertise in the air as a WSO.

"I'm sure," Kruger replied flatly.

"How sure?"

Kruger sighed softly. "JAX died two years ago."

"What? How?"

"Crashed his Cessna."

"Foul play?"

"None that I could find."

"Well, shit!"

"You just worry about learning the airplanes and getting these guys trained," Kruger said. "I'll worry about the other stuff."

"Who else are you training on your end?"

"Cowboy and Dusty," Kruger replied.

"What's Dusty's story? I've never met him."

"He's a squid. DEVGRU with the teams. He's a good shit, don't worry."

"When we get home, I'll do some backseat rides too just in case."

"In case of what?"

"In case you need someone else to run the OP who can do this without dying in the backseat," Spectre replied.

"We will be fine," Kruger insisted. "And besides, I'm not dealing with Michelle if you have to cross the pond for this."

"Believe me, I don't plan on it," Spectre said. "But I wouldn't want this whole thing to fall apart in the eleventh hour because you don't have anyone else."

"If we're down three out of four guys, we've got bigger problems, bub."

"Fair point."

CHAPTER NINE

The aircraft systems academics were short and to the point. The aircraft had two engines, two tails, and two seats. Their instructor, who went only by the name "Alexei," had said little else with his broken English in their hour-long ground school. At least, that was about all Woody had understood as he struggled to understand due to Alexei's heavy accent.

The team had a quick lunch in the hangar – sandwiches that had been flown in on Kruger's Gulfstream to ensure no chance of tampering. After, they paired up with the Russian instructors for their first flight in the SU-30. Woody was paired with Alexei, which he knew might pose a challenge once airborne due to the language barrier.

"So why you want learn to fly?" Alexei asked as they sat down.

The team had set up four folding tables in the hangar where the instructors and students could brief the mission. Kruger,

Spectre, and Woody were scheduled to go up for the first event while Sparky, Dusty, and Tuna would get their turn shortly thereafter. They would each get two sorties and then follow up with three the next day.

"I just do what I'm told, comrade," Woody said with a shrug.

"You do not know mission?" Alexei asked with a raised eyebrow.

"Look, man, I barely know where I am half the time," Woody said. "I just fly what they tell me to fly. Are you going to teach me?"

Alexei smiled. "Of course. I teach you. No problems."

"Well how the hell do you start this thing?" Woody asked as he picked up the pocket checklist out of his helmet bag.

"Is very easy. I show you," Alexei said.

He briefed the mission for the next twenty minutes. Woody would ride in the front seat and perform all of the checklists. Alexei quickly walked him through the procedures, and reassured Woody that it would all make sense once they were strapped into the jet.

Once started, they would takeoff and fly to the working airspace about twenty miles to the west. Alexei would handle the radios and direct Woody where to go for the departure and arrival. He just wanted Woody to focus on flying the aircraft and learning its handling characteristics.

"Do you have questions?" Alexei asked as he finished his brief.

"More than I'd like to admit!"

Alexei gave Woody a confused look.

"Never mind," he said as he realized Alexei didn't understand his dry sense of humor. "I'm ready when you are, sir."

"Da," Alexei said. "We go now."

Woody nodded as he grabbed his notes and helmet bag. He headed to the corner of the hangar where their gear had been hung on wooden pegs.

"All of your gear from home," Spectre said as he suited up alongside Woody.

Woody leaned over and whispered to Spectre. "Dude, this is nuts! Are you sure it's safe?"

Spectre laughed. "You paid attention to the ejection seat brief, right?"

"Yeah." Woody replied as his voice jumped an octave.

"Just make sure it's armed before you taxi," Spectre replied with a wink.

"Seriously, dude, this is worse than the Navy. Five rides in two days with a guy that barely speaks coherent English? And while I appreciate the Woody-level academics involving counting engines and tails like The Count on Sesame Street, I'm not sure that's really the best way to learn an airplane."

Spectre put his hand on Woody's shoulder before turning to walk out. "I have faith in you, buddy."

Woody laughed nervously. "Not helpful!"

Woody finished zipping his G-suit and put on his harness. He stuffed his helmet into his helmet bag and headed toward the hangar door. Some of the operators that he had been introduced to before were standing guard in various locations of the hangar, carrying rifles and wearing earpieces. They seemed to at least be taking security very seriously. He just wished they were a little more in depth when it came to learning the airplanes.

Woody found Alexei just outside the hangar and they walked side by side to the row of jets a few hundred feet from the hangar.

"Not to be nervous," Alexei said. "We will not die."

"What makes you say that?" Woody asked.

"Your friend say you are nervous. Like little girl."

"No way, man! I'm just trying not to kill myself. That's not nervous. I'm just not suicidal!"

Alexei laughed. "Relax. Is good."

"Relax," Woody mimicked under his breath as he shook his head.

They made it to the aircraft and Woody shadowed Alexei for the preflight. As with everything else, it seemed rushed and incomplete to Woody. When they climbed up the ladder and Alexei showed Woody the ejection seat preflight, he made sure to slow Alexei down to be certain he understood every detail. He then thoroughly checked the seat a second and third time before climbing into the front seat.

Woody suddenly felt like he was back in Ohio learning how to fly for the first time. He felt exactly like he had the first time he crammed into the little Cessna 150 with his slightly overweight instructor. Both then and now, everything in the cockpit looked foreign and he wasn't entirely convinced that his instructor would safely bring them back home alive.

But the difference was, that back then his fears were unfounded and he had no real experience in flying to know any better. His instructor ended up being a great pilot and teacher. He was a big farm boy from Alabama who had spent much of his life flying crop dusters and subsequently was a great stick, despite the weight and balance issues his size posed.

Now, he really was in a foreign aircraft. Although someone had used stickers to placard over controls and instruments in English, the readouts and displays were still either in metric or Russian. And Woody wasn't entirely sure Alexei wasn't a spy, or drunk on vodka, or both. He just hoped the seat worked if it came down to it.

Woody turned on the battery and established communications with Alexei. He stumbled through the startup checklist with Alexei trying to talk him through it like a nervous Air Force pilot training student on his dollar ride in T-6s.

After thirty minutes, they were finally ready to taxi. Alexei called for taxi and the controller responded in Russian. Woody had no idea what the two said and did nothing until Alexei translated.

"Go straight. Turn left at Taxiway Alpha," Alexei directed.

Woody pushed up the power, noticing that it took a lot more throttle to get moving than the A-10 he had most recently been flying. He tried to set up the radar display as they turned onto Taxiway Alpha, but soon realized it was a wasted effort since he understood none of the menus.

The controller gave them further taxi instructions to the runway that Alexei translated for Woody once more. As they reached the end of runway holding area, they pulled up to the other three aircraft and were fourth in line for takeoff.

He saw Spectre in the front seat of the third aircraft and flipped him off. Spectre laughed and returned a thumbs up before going heads down, seemingly setting something up with the avionics.

Woody looked back down at the takeoff and abort speeds he had scribbled onto the card on his kneeboard. The numbers were in kilometers per hour and made no sense to Woody whatsoever.

One-by-one, the three aircraft took the runway individually and took off. The ground shook as their afterburners lit and they accelerated down the runway to take off.

"Line up and wait," Alexei prompted from the backseat as he and the controller exchanged another radio call.

Woody taxied onto the runway and held position. Another brief exchange between Alexei and the controller led Alexei to say, "Cleared takeoff."

Watching the engine indications, Woody pushed the throttles to the military power stop and watched the engine instruments. He looked for the gauges to settle within the operating limit numbers he had highlighted on his checklist. Once he was satisfied, he released the brakes and pushed the throttles through the afterburner gate.

The afterburners lit, gently pushing Woody into his seat as the aircraft accelerated down the runway. The airspeed accelerated rapidly in the HUD as Woody struggled to crosscheck them with the numbers he had written.

Within seconds, the SU-30 lifted off the runway. Woody raised the gear and climbed at a shallow angle. It accelerated like a rocket. It felt more powerful than anything he had ever flown before.

The aircraft accelerated and he suddenly felt Alexei on the controls. "I have aircraft," he said abruptly.

Woody let go of the stick. Alexei lowered the nose and accelerated just over a hundred feet off the ground. When they reached the end of the runway, Alexei violently pulled the stick back into a seventy-degree climb.

"Whoa! Low tranny!" Woody said.

As Alexei checked in with the departure controller and the controller rattled off instructions to him in Russian, Woody looked over his shoulder at the runway and airfield disappearing behind them. It was the most impressive unrestricted climb he had ever experienced.

For the first time all day, Woody smiled behind his mask. Despite the feeling of impending death, it was still a lot of fun.

Maybe this wasn't such a bad idea after all.

CHAPTER TEN

Spectre was exhausted after the first sortie. It had been a long time since he had pulled Gs in an aircraft, and even longer since he had gone over 8Gs. It was a lot harder on his body than he remembered. Maybe he was just getting old.

His last flight at the controls had been in a 737-800 for an ultra-low-cost carrier out of New Orleans. Before that, he had flown an A-10 for the Air Force Reserve with Woody and before that, an A-29 Super Tucano. It had been nearly a decade since Spectre had last flown an F-16 and pulled high Gs.

A lot had changed for him since then. Although Spectre was physically still in peak condition, he was nearing forty. His body had been through a lot, having been shot, stabbed and losing a kidney as he and his wife fought to save the country from a despotic madman occupying the office of the Vice President of the United States.

His neck was already starting to get sore as he sat on a bench outside the hangar watching the next group land from their introductory flights. As he gently turned his head, he saw Woody approaching in his red Folds of Honor t-shirt with the top of his flight suit wrapped around his waist. Spectre nodded gently as he saw that Woody was carrying two bottles of water.

"Stay hydrated," Woody said as he handed one of the bottles to Spectre and sat down.

"How'd the flight go?" Spectre asked.

"Not bad. The airplane is all metric! Woody doesn't speak European," Woody replied laughing. "If knots and feet were good enough to put a man on the moon, it's good enough for me."

"Yeah, the numbers are way out of whack from what we're used to, but I'm told the jets we're getting will have Lynch avionics so it'll be Imperial units and easier to understand."

"My instructor was asking why we were wanting to learn how to fly these jets during the brief."

"What'd you tell him?"

"Everything that I know, which is that I have no idea."

Spectre laughed. "Good job."

"Alexei takes a little getting used to, but he is a good instructor," Woody said. "I had fun. That airplane is incredible."

"Did he do the heavyweight demo?" Spectre asked.

"No, what's that?"

"Don't try to do any of the high alpha stuff when you're heavy," Spectre warned. "The jet drops like a rock and takes almost fifteen thousand feet of altitude to recover if you depart controlled flight. My IP put it in a flat spin at twenty-five thousand feet to show me and I was pretty sure we were going to bust through the ten-thousand-foot floor. Recovered right at eleven-five. It was pretty violent and eye-opening."

"No, we didn't do any of that, but I'll take your word for it. No need to show me."

"Fair enough," Spectre said.

He looked to the flight line as the first of the second wave of aircraft taxied back in. The aircraft pulled to a stop as a lineman chocked the wheels and the engines spooled down. The canopy opened and the frontseater hopped over to the backseat ladder to assist the backseater.

He appeared to talk briefly to the backseater and then the two slowly descended their ladders. Spectre saw that the backseater was Tuna right before he doubled over and started vomiting toward the aircraft. The Russian instructor jumped back out of the field of fire and appeared to be laughing.

"That's not good," Spectre said as he watched Tuna drop to his knees and vomit some more.

Spectre put the bottle of water on the ground next to the bench and started toward Tuna. Sparky taxied in and gave Spectre a huge grin and thumbs up as Spectre jogged across the flight line. His flight had obviously gone very well – or at least better than Tuna's.

Spectre reached Tuna just as the instructor helped him stand. Tuna was still coughing as he pulled out a bottle of water from his helmet bag and tried to drink.

"You okay, buddy?" Spectre asked.

"Fuck no I'm not okay!" Tuna yelled between coughing. "That shit sucked!"

The instructor let out a hearty laugh and then said, "I make man out of you yet!"

"Fuck off!" Tuna said.

The instructor laughed again and then headed back toward the hangar, leaving Spectre to assist Tuna.

"I'm not made for this shit, dude," Tuna said as he tried to steady himself. "Flipping and spinning and doing all of that bullshit. I'm a grunt."

"I understand," Spectre said. "It's not for everyone."

Tuna took a sip of water and then started another coughing fit.

"It's okay, man. Let's get your gear off and you can lie down for a bit," Spectre said as he turned Tuna toward the hangar.

"I can't do this, dude. You're going to have to make Dusty a primary or pick someone else or something," Tuna said. "I'm sorry."

"We'll figure that out when we get there," Spectre said. "Let's just get to the hangar first."

"Okay," Tuna said as he wiped his mouth with his sleeve.

Spectre helped Tuna to the hangar where Sierra and Ringo intercepted them and helped Tuna with his gear. Kruger had just finished briefing with his instructor for his second flight when he saw them enter the hangar. He excused himself and walked over to Spectre.

"He looks like shit," Kruger said.

Spectre nodded. "Do you have a backup to the backup in mind?"

Kruger gave Spectre a quizzical look.

"Tuna is out. That now just leaves Dusty and you. We're going to need a backup in case someone else falls out."

"Tuna will be fine," Kruger said. "He'll shake it off."

Spectre shook his head and looked at his watch. "We don't have time. The next flights are already briefing. We have limited time here to get acclimated before we take delivery. There's no room for error."

"C'mon, bub."

"Who did you have in mind?" Spectre pushed.

FINI FLIGHT

Kruger scanned the hangar. The members of Project Archangel were either milling about or actively performing security sweeps.

"What about Jenny?" Spectre asked, nodding to the Kruger's chief pilot who was curiously examining a SU-30 that had been taken apart for maintenance in the hangar.

"She would've been my first choice, but no way does that cover story fly," Kruger said.

"Okay, well that leaves Cowboy or one of the other Brits," Spectre said. "I don't really know any of them, so you tell me."

"Cowboy!" Kruger yelled across the room.

Cowboy had been one of the ones milling about. He heard Kruger and jogged to where he and Spectre had stopped to chat about Tuna.

"What is it, boss? Is Tuna okay?"

"Suit up. You're the next man on deck," Kruger said.

"You mean...flying?"

"Have you ever had any issues with motion sickness?" Spectre asked. "Flying, rollercoasters, etc.?"

"Not that I know of. My friend used to take me up in his little aerobatic plane all the time. It was a load of fun, actually."

"There's your man," Spectre said to Kruger.

"What's the mission?" Cowboy asked.

"Learn everything you can about flying in the backseat. Your instructor is Yuri. He's over there," Spectre said, pointing to the instructor standing off to the side watching Tuna being assisted by Sierra and company.

"Get moving, bub," Kruger ordered.

"Right. Cheers, then," Cowboy said as he nodded and started toward the instructor.

"I'd better get going too. Time for my brief," Spectre said, rubbing his sore neck.

"Sucks getting old, doesn't it?" Kruger asked as he watched Spectre.

"You're telling me."

CHAPTER ELEVEN

The team finished their last sorties and debriefs just after sunset. They ate more sandwiches from the galley of the Gulfstream and settled in for their night sleeping in the hangar. Those that weren't flying set up rotating guard shifts to stand watch over the quiet hangar.

"Dude, this jet is awesome and all, but I almost died today!" Woody said as he opened a bag of chips.

He was sitting at one of the tables that had previously been used for flight briefings and debriefings with Spectre, Sparky, Cowboy, and Dusty. As far as anyone knew, Kruger, Tuna, and Sierra were on the Gulfstream doing a secure teleconference with CIA Director Chapman and the U.K. Secretary of State for Defence Nigel Williams.

"What do you mean you almost died? How?" Sparky asked.

"The TVC can be a little touchy," Woody said.

"What's TVC?" Dusty asked.

"Thrust Vectoring Control," Spectre answered. "It's what controls the movable nozzles in the back."

"Ah," Dusty said. "My guy didn't show me that."

"You'll probably get more tomorrow," Spectre said. "Today was just a fam flight."

"So, you departed controlled flight or what?" Sparky asked Woody.

Woody nodded as he took a bite of his sandwich. "Alexei thought it was hilarious. Me? Not so much!"

"Well, you'll have three more flights tomorrow to figure it out before we go home," Spectre said.

"Dude, there's no way," Woody protested. "Maybe a few days, but five sorties in two days with minimal academics?"

"Not like we can understand anything they're saying anyway," Sparky added.

Spectre held up his hands. "Look, guys, I get it. But this is a high-risk environment and we're trying to minimize exposure. You'll get plenty of seat time once we get back to the States."

"In all fairness, I guess this is more seat time with an instructor in the back than we get with the F-35. And it's pretty easy to takeoff and land," Sparky said.

"Yeah, if you can get past the commie metric readouts," Woody added.

"There you go. Just like the F-35 and A-10. No sweat," Spectre said.

"But we get a ton of academics and sims before we ever touch an airplane," Sparky said. "Not quite what we're getting here."

"We'll get you spun up back home. We just needed to get you some seat time before the aircraft arrive," Spectre said.

"And when is that?" Woody asked.

"Classified," Spectre said with a grin.

"Of course it is!" Woody replied sarcastically.

"Is there anything specifically we should be focusing on for this mission?" Sparky asked.

"Nope," Spectre said flatly. "Need to know until we get to that point."

"Do I even need to know how to work the TVC?" Woody asked.

Spectre smiled, seeing Woody's obvious attempt to dig for more information. "Learn everything you can about the aircraft from your instructor."

Woody threw up his hands. "Oh, come on!"

"Cowboy, you've been awfully quiet," Spectre said as he tried changing the subject. "How'd the flight go?"

"Pretty fun ride, mate," Cowboy said. "Looking forward to tomorrow."

"See?" Spectre said. "That's the spirit!"

"Just sucks that I'm going to have to shave this amazing beard," Cowboy added.

"*See?*" Woody said.

Before Woody could complain some more, Spectre looked up to see Kruger and Sierra approaching. They both appeared to be unhappy, presumably about something from the teleconference.

Spectre made eye contact with Kruger who motioned for him to come over. Spectre excused himself and met Kruger near one of the disassembled SU-30s.

"Bad news?" Spectre asked.

"Change of plans," Kruger said.

"Oh?"

"The timeline for the delivery of the assets has changed," Sierra said, referring to the SU-30s that were to be shipped to their off-site location.

"How soon?"

"Pickup tomorrow," Kruger answered.

"Shit!" Spectre hissed. "How's that going to work?"

"Tuna and I are going to take Ringo and Churchill and we're going to meet Natasha to facilitate the transaction with the Russians," Kruger whispered. "You and the others will stay here and go home tomorrow as planned."

"But what about the three sorties tomorrow? Don't you think you'll need them?"

"I've got it, bub," Kruger said. "I'll figure out the rest when I get home. This is more important."

"Surely you could send one of the others instead," Spectre said.

"Getting the assets is the most important part of this plan," Kruger said. "If that falls through, we're fucked. I'm going to be there."

"Are we still driving back to Minsk after our flights tomorrow?" Spectre asked.

Kruger nodded.

"So, we're losing half of our protective detail?"

"Threat assessment is low," Sierra said. "We've determined that it's unlikely that you'll need the contingent we had coming here."

"Look, lady, I realize you and I don't know each other," Spectre said to Sierra before turning to Kruger. "But *you've* met me. You know that's not how my life works. We're just asking for trouble."

"It'll be fine, bub," Kruger reassured Spectre. "Taylor and Sledge are perfectly capable. And Cowboy and Dusty will still be with you. That's a four-man team."

"I want a rifle," Spectre said.

"I'll be there as well," Sierra added. "I assure you, I'm quite proficient."

"I'm well aware," Spectre said. "But I want a rifle and gear. In fact, I think we should all be armed."

"Won't happen, bub," Kruger said dismissively. "If you get stopped at a checkpoint, that won't fly. Only the security teams get weapons or our cover is blown."

"Then have Coolio change my identity to a member of the security team. You know I can handle myself, and I've trained with you before. These pilots are just as important as the assets. Without them, you still have nothing."

Kruger turned to Tuna. "It's your show, bub. What's the verdict?"

"Better safe than sorry," Tuna answered. "I'll have Coolio start working on the new documents."

"Thank you," Spectre said.

"And there's another small problem," Kruger said.

"Jesus, what else?" Spectre asked.

"We could only get one Russian heavy transport aircraft," Kruger said.

Spectre frowned. "Wait, that's only like two aircraft! What about spares? We can't run training and an op relying on just two jets!"

"Relax, bub, we managed to get an Air Force transport reassigned to help. You'll have three jets."

"Three? C'mon, Kruger, that leaves us no margin for error."

"That's the deal, bub. We work with what we have. Improvise, adapt, overcome."

"Goddammit. I don't like this, Kruger. It's a house of cards."

"Just make sure your boys get through tomorrow without any issues," Kruger said. "Don't worry about the assets."

"Not a problem. They have a busy day ahead of them. And they're already complaining about not getting enough seat time."

"Realistically, do you think they'll be on timeline?" Sierra asked.

Spectre nodded. "Pilots bitch. That's what we do, but these guys are professionals. They'll be ready."

"Alright then. Well, we'd better get going," Kruger said. "See ya in the land of freedom."

CHAPTER TWELVE

Zhukovsky International Airport
Moscow Oblast, Russia

Darlene "Jenny" Craig taxied the Gulfstream to the Gromov Flight Research Institute ramp on the north side of the Zhukovsky International Airport. It was just after 1 AM, but two marshallers were there with glowing orange wands to guide her in and chock the Gulfstream's wheels before she shut the engines down.

The Russian equivalent of Edwards Air Force Base, the Gromov Flight Research Institute was home to Russia's state-run research, test, and development center. It had been used during the Cold War to reverse engineer American aircraft like an Iranian F-14A Tomcat, and aircraft shot down over Vietnam like the F-111 and F-4.

More recently, however, it served as Russia's test pilot school and was home to many fighter test platforms to collect and analyze aerospace engineering data. With the world's second longest runway at nearly eighteen thousand feet, it also served as a backup landing site for the defunct Shuttle Buran test program – a near clone of the American Space Shuttle program that became the first shuttle to make an unmanned space flight.

The stairs of the Gulfstream lowered. Kruger exited followed by Tuna, Ringo, and Churchill. They were all wearing tactical pants and long sleeve polo shirts. The custom-made Dragon Silk Body Armor that had been developed at Odin was concealed beneath their shirts. They carried suppressed Sig Sauer MPX rifles chambered in 9MM and had Sig X-Five handguns holstered on their hips.

Natasha met Kruger at the aircraft. In the distance, he saw Viktor and Anatoly standing and chatting with an older man in a three-piece suit. Natasha gave Kruger a hug and they shared a short kiss.

"I am sorry the timeline has changed, my love," Natasha said.

"It's okay," Kruger replied. "We'll manage."

"What time will your American Air Force transport be here?" Natasha asked.

Kruger looked at his watch. "Should be landing in ten."

"Good," Natasha said. "Our contractor's aircraft will be towed from the cargo ramp within the hour. I hope to have both airborne before sunrise."

"The sooner the better," Kruger said.

Tuna joined the couple as he eyed the man in the suit. "Do we get to meet him?"

"It is better if you don't," Natasha said. "He is very high-ranking official in the UAC."

"UAC?" Tuna asked.

"United Aircraft Corporation," Kruger answered. "That's the parent company for the Russian manufacturers of these jets."

"Da," Natasha said.

"But doesn't the government know about this operation?"

Natasha smiled and shook her head. "Only few people within the FSB know. Is better that way."

"What about the cash?" Tuna asked.

They had a pallet of cash in the cargo hold of the Gulfstream, a combination of bribe money and a down payment for the aircraft. The rest of the money would be wired through off shore banks, dummy corporations, and other CIA instruments that Kruger neither knew nor cared to know about.

"Leave it," Natasha ordered. "When the aircraft are loaded, Viktor will handle it."

"Fair enough," Tuna said.

Kruger looked up and saw landing lights in the distance. He could barely make out the silhouette of a massive transport aircraft in the moonlit sky. He looked at his watch. The Air Force C-5 Galaxy out of Ramstein AFB in Germany was right on time.

"Eyes open. Stay sharp," Kruger said, tapping his rifle. He looked back at Ringo and Churchill who were standing watch near the Gulfstream. He gave them a thumbs up and pointed to the arriving C-5 as it crossed the runway threshold.

As the C-5 touched down, Kruger saw an amber flashing light in the distance. Across the ramp, a large hangar door slowly opened. The vehicle with the light entered the hangar. Moments later, it emerged, dwarfed by the massive Russian Antonov AN-124 cargo transport as it towed the plane out of the hangar.

"Where are the assets?" Kruger asked as he turned back to Natasha.

"In that hangar," Natasha said, pointing behind the man in the suit still speaking with Anatoly and Viktor.

"How long will it take them to load?" Kruger asked.

"They say two hours," Natasha said. "Perhaps less."

Kruger nodded. The Russian transport was towed across the ramp slowly. The operator did a masterful job of maneuvering the massive aircraft into position right in front of the hangar storing the assets. As the tug driver disconnected from the nose wheel, the C-5 taxied toward them. Although it too was massive, it seemed small compared to the Russian aircraft.

The C-5 stopped a few hundred feet from the AN-124 and the same marshallers that had chocked the Gulfstream assisted with the C-5. When all of its engines were shut down, the nose opened and the loadmaster exited.

Tuna jogged over to him, intercepting the loadmaster before he could make contact with the man in the suit.

"I think we're the ones you're looking for," Tuna said.

"Buzz," the young loadmaster said, using the challenge word.

"Window," Tuna replied.

The loadmaster nodded. Tuna had replied with the correct challenge word.

"So, what are we hauling?" the loadmaster asked.

"An aircraft and spare parts," Tuna said, pointing to the hangar behind the AN-124. "Wings and tails have been removed. You're transporting them."

"Where are we taking them?" the loadmaster asked.

"You'll find out when airborne," Tuna replied. "Need to know basis."

FINI FLIGHT

"We're going to need to know a little bit more than that," the loadmaster said.

"You're filed to the east coast. Once you get there, you'll get the rest of your clearance. Don't press the issue."

The loadmaster held up his hands defensively. "Just asking. No problems, sir."

"Let me know if you need anything," Tuna said as he turned to walk to the AN-124.

The first of the aircraft was towed out of the hangar. The nose, wings, tails, and horizontal stabilizers had been removed. They were in separate containers to be loaded into the C-5. The aircraft were nothing more than fuselages with landing gear and engines.

The Russians went to work loading and securing their cargo. They were contractors, hired by Natasha and the FSB. They were to fly their cargo to Vandenberg Air Force Base in California where their cargo would be offloaded and eventually assembled. Their manifests simply indicated they were flying empty to pick up rocket components for their space program and the International Space Station. They were paid for their silence, backed up with threats by the two FSB agents standing in the distance with the man in charge.

As the two SU-30s were loaded, the crews went to work loading the C-5. Its mission was slightly different. It would initially fly to Dover AFB in Delaware where it would sit for two days under armed guard. After, it would fly to Nellis Air Force Base in Nevada where the aircraft would be assembled and flown to the black site. The remaining parts would be flown to Vandenberg Air Force Base and the two SU-30s would be assembled and flown to the black site to join.

The entire operation would take four days, giving Spectre and his team down time to review what they had learned and for Spectre to train them in armed and unarmed combat. Kruger just hoped there were no further complications.

It was just before 4 AM when the aircraft were finally loaded and secured. Kruger and Tuna checked the manifests a final time. Everything was as they had planned.

Kruger kissed Natasha goodbye and then he and Ringo joined the crew on the AN-124. They would be acting as security for the entire trip. Churchill and Tuna would stay with the C-5.

As the two transports taxied out, Natasha said goodbye to Viktor and Anatoly and then boarded the Gulfstream. She would accompany Jenny back to Minsk and then continue with her part of the operation after Spectre's team finished its training and headed back to the United States.

CHAPTER THIRTEEN

"You guys doing okay?" Spectre asked as he approached his team. They were sitting around one of the briefing tables drinking water and Gatorade. Woody and Cowboy had wrapped the top half of their flight suits around their waists. They all looked exhausted.

"Woody is a four G kind of guy. Eight is a bit much," Woody moaned, referring to the G-forces he had pulled in his previous two sorties so far that day in the SU-30.

"Just one more and we can all go home," Spectre said. "Then you'll get a couple of down days before we start training again."

"You still haven't told us what we're training for," Woody said.

"The most important mission of your career," Spectre said with a grin. "Now let's go. Time to brief."

"Goddammit," Woody said with an exaggerated groan as he slowly stood and untied the flight suit from his waist so he could put it back on.

"C'mon, mate, it's not so bad," Cowboy said as he also put his flight suit top back on. "It's fun."

"I miss the A-10," Woody replied. "Much more gentlemanly."

"Learn as much as you can," Spectre said. "You can have a steak tonight on the flight home as your reward. The jet is supposed to be catered this time."

"Now you're talking!" Woody said as he turned and saw Alexei. "C'mon, Lexi. Let's do this!"

Alexei smiled at his student's newfound enthusiasm and slapped Woody on the back. "Is good!" he yelled.

Spectre looked at Sparky. They were both tired too, but neither said anything. They just had one more flight to muscle through and then they'd be on their way home.

"How are you feeling about this jet?" Spectre asked.

"It's not bad," Sparky said. "The Russians built a sturdy airplane, but the avionics integration sucks. Hopefully you're not expecting us to go out and employ this thing with any level of proficiency."

"Learn what you can," Spectre said cryptically. "We'll fine tune what you need to know when we get back home."

"Copy that," Sparky replied.

Spectre nodded and then turned to find his instructor. They briefed and stepped for his last flight in the front seat of the SU-30. From here on out, he would be riding in the backseat as the instructor for Woody and Sparky as they honed their skills for the upcoming mission.

The flight went uneventfully. Despite his fatigue, Spectre enjoyed every minute of it. The Flanker was an incredible aircraft. They worked on high angle-of-attack and slow speed maneuvering as well as recovering from departures from controlled flight. After finishing their work in the airspace, they came back and flew two instrument approaches for practice and then landed.

After climbing out of the front seat for the last time, Spectre shook hands with his instructor and returned to the hangar. He watched Sparky and Dusty finishing their briefs with their instructors as he took off his gear and stowed it.

"That was fun. Let's eat!" Woody said as he approached with his helmet in hand.

"Better flight?" Spectre asked, unzipping his G-suit.

"Alexei took me out for a quick low level. It was a lot more fun than pulling until the lights go out," Woody said, referring to the loss of vision pilots often experienced at high Gs when their Anti-G Straining Maneuver (AGSM) was insufficient. "Besides, hunger is a powerful motivator."

"Sparky and Dusty should be going out now. When Cowboy gets back, we'll get all our bags loaded and get ready to move out," Spectre said.

"And then we eat?"

"And *then* we eat," Spectre said.

"Perfect! But don't forget the ice cream!"

Spectre laughed as he finished putting away his gear. As he closed the black Pelican Case, Sierra walked up to him and handed him a bottle of water.

"You look like you've had a long day," she said.

"I'm going to sleep like a baby on the flight home," Spectre said.

Sierra pulled a folded envelope from her back pocket "Your new documents, sir."

Spectre opened them and read the passport and official papers. "Security detail. That was fast."

"Mallory and Coolio work well together," Sierra replied, referring to her own computer analyst back at MI-6.

"Thanks for doing this," Spectre said, holding up the documents.

"Sledge will issue your weapons and uniform," Sierra said before pointing to Spectre's flight suit. "You won't be able to wear those pajamas."

"Fair enough," Spectre replied. "Any news on the asset pickup last night?"

"Kruger and Ringo touched down about an hour ago," Sierra said. "So far, so good."

"What about the others?"

Sierra frowned. "Diverted to Lajes in the Azores."

"Diverted? For what?"

Sierra shrugged. "I'm no pilot or mechanic, but I think it had something to do with oil. Maybe oil pressure?"

"Can they fix it? Or get another aircraft?"

"They're assessing that right now," Sierra replied. "I'm waiting for an answer."

"So, what do we do? Are we going to fly to Lajes from Minsk?"

"Absolutely not."

"Why not?"

Sierra looked around them to ensure no one was listening.

"It's bad enough we're flying everyone on one jet back to the states. There's no reason to mix assets with people. That's how state intelligence agencies start putting pieces together. I cannot allow it."

"And they can't put it together with us here?"

"It's a calculated risk we've had to take," Sierra replied. "Unless you would've preferred to learn to fly the aircraft on your own?"

"Fair enough," Spectre said. "So how many assets does that give us?"

"Without the one in Lajes?"

"Yeah."

"Zero."

"Zero? How? Why?"

"From what I understand, they had to load key components on the Air Force aircraft to make room."

"Can't they send a C-17 in to get those pieces? So we'll at least have what Kruger and Ringo brought back?"

Sierra seemed to consider it for a moment. "I'll have Mallory and Coolio look into it. I don't like the idea of involving more people than we have to. And another aircraft and crew just adds to the risk."

"I get that," Spectre said. "But these folks are professionals. They deal with this sort of stuff all the time. I think you can trust them."

"I trust no one."

"Well, it's either that or we have no mission at all. That C-5 could be stuck there for weeks."

"I'll make the call."

CHAPTER FOURTEEN

The last training sorties went uneventfully. They debriefed with their instructors, thanked them for their help, and then packed up their gear. They took two armored SUVs with Spectre, Cowboy, Woody, and Sierra in the lead vehicle. Sparky, Dusty, Sledge, and Taylor followed close behind in the second SUV.

It was just after sunset when they cleared the base and started on their way to Minsk. Because of the time of night, they opted to take the most direct route to the airport. Their route would take just under two hours and avoid population centers where they were most at risk of being ambushed.

Sierra drove while Spectre took shotgun. His suppressed Daniel Defense MK18 rifle chambered in 5.56 NATO was within easy reach next to his right leg. He was dressed in tactical clothes along with Sierra and Cowboy as part of the security detail. Woody was in a suit he had been given, posing as a United Nations dignitary.

"So, you're sure I can't have a gun?" Woody asked, breaking the silence as they sped down the desolate highway.

"What?" Spectre asked.

"Everyone here has a gun. What about me?"

"We've been over this," Sierra replied impatiently. "You are a dignitary. Dignitaries don't carry weapons."

"I'm just saying. Alexei seemed a little sketchy when we left," Woody said.

Spectre turned around in his seat to face Woody. "Sketchy how?"

"He just seemed really interested when we were packing up," Woody said. "And when I went to find him to thank him for the training, he was gone."

"And you're just telling us this now?!"

"I thought I was just being paranoid because I was…and still am…hungry!"

"Bloody hell, mate," Cowboy interjected. "You have to tell us about things like that."

"It might have been nothing," Woody argued.

"We're in a foreign country dealing with the Russians. There's no such thing as *nothing*," Sierra piled on.

"I thought the Russians were our friends now," Woody said.

"Friends today, enemies tomorrow," Spectre said. "You know better than that."

"So, about that gun…"

"Still a no," Spectre said as he turned back around.

Sierra looked at Spectre and said, "You may want to alert the others."

"Already on it," Spectre said as he started to key up his secure radio.

"Alpha One to Bravo," he said.

"Bravo One," came the reply from Sledge.

"Keep your eyes open," Spectre said. "One of the pilots took an interest in us as we were leaving and then disappeared. We're going to pick up the pace."

"Copy that," Sledge replied.

Sierra accelerated the SUV down the empty highway. They were the only ones on the road, but Spectre nervously kept a lookout.

"Aren't Russian intelligence agents helping us, though?" Woody asked. "Who would be after us?"

"The Russian government is fractured," Sierra said. "Although we are receiving help from the FSB, the Bratva still has influence in many places. There are too many factions at play right now."

"Did you tell Alexei anything about our mission?" Spectre asked.

"No, because I don't even know what we're doing...*still*," Woody said.

"And now you know why," Spectre said.

"Very funny," Woody replied.

They cut the drive to Minsk down to an hour and a half, arriving just outside the city well ahead of schedule. They bypassed the city and headed straight for the airport on the eastern side of the city.

"I called Jenny," Spectre said as he stuffed his phone back in his pocket. They were nearing the China-Belarus Industrial Park just outside the airport. "The jet is ready to go early. She amended the flight plan."

"What about the steaks?" Woody asked anxiously.

"You can heat them up once we're airborne."

"Reheated steaks, I-"

Before Woody could finish, there was a flash of light from their left. Sierra swerved, narrowly missing a dump truck coming from the industrial park attempting to T-bone them.

"Jesus!" Sierra yelped as she wrestled the wheel to maintain control.

There was a loud crash behind them. Spectre looked back to see that the second SUV hadn't been as lucky, hitting the right front of the dump truck and bouncing off it. The back end spun around and it rolled several times before coming to rest in a nearby ditch.

Seeing the crash unfold in her rearview mirror, Sierra slammed on the brakes and made a U-turn. The dump truck came to a stop just short of the ditch and two men with rifles got out.

"Shit!" Spectre said as he saw the armed men and readied his weapon.

Spectre saw a second pair of headlights speeding toward them from the industrial park. As it neared, he saw that it was a panel van. It appeared to be heading straight for the crashed SUV.

"We've got company!" Spectre yelled.

Sierra stopped short of the crash scene as the two men from the dump truck opened fire at them. The bullets peppered the bullet-resistant glass, causing it to splinter.

"Woody, get down and stay in the vehicle!" Spectre barked.

"What? Give me a gun!"

"Just do it, mate," Cowboy said as he pushed Woody down to the floor by his shoulders.

As the bullets ricocheted off the armored panels, Spectre and Sierra opened their doors and returned fire. They both managed to drop the attackers with well-placed shots.

Cowboy exited behind Spectre and the trio moved toward the panel van in a V formation with Sierra in the lead. The panel van stopped between them and the crash, as its occupants exited and tried to get to the second SUV.

FINI FLIGHT

Spectre saw the driver door of the SUV open and Sledge attempting to crawl out. He watched as Sledge saw the men approaching him and drew his handgun. One of the attackers opened fire. Sledge returned fire before pulling the door shut.

The driver of the panel van exited in an attempt to engage Spectre and company but was immediately dispatched by Sierra who didn't miss a step as they continued toward the crash. As they reached the edge of the panel van, one of the attackers saw them and opened fire.

They took cover behind the panel van and then returned fire. The three attackers were out in the open and apparently not well trained. They were easily dispatched as Sierra and company continued toward their teammates.

When they reached the overturned SUV, Sierra set up a watch position as Cowboy and Spectre went to work attempting to extract their teammates. They opened the driver door first, finding Sledge bleeding and barely conscious. His handgun was held loosely in his hand and he appeared to have been shot through and through between his vest and collarbone.

As Cowboy started first aid, Spectre reached in and unlocked the rear door. He saw Taylor unconscious in the front passenger seat and Dusty in the backseat attempting to release Sparky from his seatbelt as he hung precariously upside down in his seat.

Spectre opened the rear door. "Sparky!"

"He's unconscious, but the belt is stuck. I didn't want to cut it without a way to lower him," Dusty said.

"You okay?" Spectre asked, seeing blood on Dusty's face and neck.

"I'm fine. Just a few scratches. Help me get him down," Dusty said.

In the front seat, Cowboy did his best on Sledge's wound, using the Quik-Clot from his Individual First Aid Kit to slow the bleeding. He helped Sledge out of the driver's seat and onto the side of the road where Sierra was standing and then raced to the other side where Taylor was still unconscious against the roof of the vehicle.

Taylor hadn't been wearing his seatbelt. Cowboy checked for a pulse and noticed that he was still breathing. He pulled Taylor out into the ditch and then went to the rear passenger door to help Spectre and Dusty with Sparky.

They cut him free from his seatbelt and lowered him gently, careful to support his neck as they brought him down. He was breathing and had a pulse but had a gash on his forehead from where he had apparently hit his head during the crash.

As they carried him out of the vehicle, Sparky suddenly came to. Disoriented, he tried to get up but Spectre calmed him. "It's okay, buddy, we're going to get you out of here."

"What happened?" Sparky asked groggily.

"You were in an accident," Spectre said as he tried to keep Sparky from moving too much.

"What about the others?" Sparky asked.

"We need to get moving," Spectre said. "That van is still running. Let's load Sparky, Sledge, and Taylor and get to the plane. We can divert to Germany en route."

Dusty nodded and ran toward the panel van. He got in and turned it around, backing it up to allow them to load the casualties in the back. Cowboy ran to their remaining SUV.

"Is everyone okay?" Woody asked nervously as Cowboy got in and threw it in gear.

"Just stay down, mate," Cowboy barked.

They loaded the casualties into the van. Sierra stayed with them to continue first aid while Spectre joined Cowboy in the SUV. They sped to the airport where Jenny was waiting with the Gulfstream.

"Jesus, what happened?" she asked as they opened the panel van.

"We were ambushed," Spectre said as he went to help unload the injured.

"I'll have to change the flight plan," Jenny said.

"No, don't," Spectre said. "Let's get airborne. We can divert once we assess everyone airborne."

"You got it, boss. I'll get ready for an immediate departure," Jenny said as she returned to the aircraft.

CHAPTER FIFTEEN

Kruger sat down at the secure video teleconference station deep inside the Sensitive Compartmented Information Facility (SCIF) in the Command Post at Edwards Air Force Base. He was still jet lagged from the flight, having been awakened from a deep sleep in his room at the High Desert Inn by Coolio with news of the attack on the team.

Ringo sat down next to Kruger and handed him a cup of black coffee. "Where are they?"

"They diverted to Warsaw. Sierra is staying with Sledge and Taylor. The rest of the team is airborne. Just waiting for Cowboy and Tuna to ring in," Kruger answered.

"What a bloody mess," the former British Special Air Service commando replied.

The video teleconferencing software suddenly displayed a popup that other users were ready to join. Kruger accepted the requests and was connected to Cowboy on the Gulfstream and Tuna in Lajes.

"Hello, gents," Ringo said as the connections established.

"Cowboy, what the hell happened?" Kruger asked impatiently, skipping any semblance of pleasantries.

"Taylor was hurt pretty badly," Cowboy said solemnly. "Sledge is hanging on, but he's not looking good."

"What happened specifically?" Kruger asked.

"We were ambushed at the industrial park by the airport. A dump truck tried to T-bone us but Sierra managed to evade it. The second vehicle was hit and rolled into a ditch. Taylor was injured during the crash. Sledge was shot during the ambush. We managed to neutralize the attackers. Six men in total."

"Who was in the rear vehicle?" Kruger asked.

"Sledge, Taylor, Dusty, and Sparky," Cowboy answered.

"Shit," Kruger hissed. "Was Sparky injured?"

"He was knocked unconscious during the crash, but the docs checked him out and said he should be okay. He's with us now," Cowboy said.

"Any idea who did it?" Ringo asked.

"Woody said one of the Russian instructors was acting squirrely when we left," Cowboy answered.

"Does he know which one?" Kruger asked.

"Alexei," Spectre answered as his head popped into frame over Cowboy's shoulder. "Hey, Kruger, busy night over here."

Kruger turned to Ringo. "We need to pick Alexei up and have a chat with him."

Tuna overheard Kruger and said, "Send someone to pick us up and we can do it. It's not like we're going anywhere anytime soon. They're saying they're going to have to fly a part in to fix this POS plane."

Kruger shook his head. "No, you need to stay with the asset. The C-17 will be there in a few hours to pick up the parts to bring here."

"C'mon, Kruger, we don't need to sit here to babysit an empty cockpit," Tuna argued.

"We're not doing anything until we find out who these people work for and whether the mission has been compromised," Kruger said.

"You're not thinking of scrubbing the mission, are you?" Spectre asked.

"All options are on the table at this point," Ringo answered.

"And then what? What about the threat?" Spectre asked.

"We will pursue other options," Kruger said. "For now, just focus on getting everyone back to base and do your training as scheduled."

"Sparky is going to need some time to recover," Spectre said. "I know the docs said he's okay, but he doesn't need to be grappling and shooting guns until he's 100%."

"Do whatever you think is best," Kruger said. "That's your show."

"Kruger, what do you want me to tell Director Chapman?" Tuna asked.

Despite Kruger's authoritative nature, Tuna was still in charge of Project Archangel and technically leading the operation. He had direct reporting responsibility to the Director of Central Intelligence while Ringo reported to the U.K. Secretary of State for Defence. It was part of the new Project Archangel organizational structure since it had become a joint U.S. U.K. unit.

"Let him know the status of the assets and that we're working to have two ready. Everything else is on schedule," Kruger answered.

"And the ambush?"

"You can let him know that we are working on getting our boys treated and then they'll be back on their way to London," Ringo answered. "It shouldn't affect the mission."

"Any other questions?" Kruger asked.

Kruger waited for a response. When there were no questions, he said, "Okay, then, we'll figure out who was behind this and come up with a plan of attack from there. Let me know if there are any other changes."

He ended the video teleconferencing session and turned to Ringo who stood and pushed in his chair.

"I will talk to Natasha and we will find out who did this."

"Look, Kruger, I know you two are in a relationship and everything, but are we sure this wasn't done by the people she works with?"

"I'm sure," Kruger said flatly.

"What does the Russian government even know about this operation?"

"Only what they need to. The only people within the FSB that know about it are Natasha, Viktor, and Anatoly."

"And there's no chance their bosses asked questions?"

"Sure, there's a chance. I doubt it, but there's a chance."

"I just question whether the entire mission has been compromised by the Russians. They are not our friends."

"That's what I'm going to find out, bub," Kruger replied. "But until then, we continue as planned."

"What does Natasha know?" Ringo asked.

"What do you mean?"

"Beyond the acquisition of the assets and the North Korean threat, what does she know?"

"That's it."

"You're sure?"

"What are you getting at, bub?"

Ringo shook his head. "Look, I'm not trying to point fingers, but you've known this woman – what – maybe a year? And she's FSB? I'm sorry, but it just gives one pause to ask questions, especially when the mission goes sideways and good men get hurt."

Kruger's jaw clenched as he stood, causing Ringo to step back defensively.

"You're right," he said with a soft sigh.

"I am?"

"Yeah, you're right that I've only known Natasha for a year and that what happened tonight is a great reason to stop and ask questions."

"But?"

"But I trust her. And I've been given no reason not to since we met. The Russians have the same intel on North Korea as we do about their EMP program. They reached out diplomatically to help, remember? Just because they don't know the full plan doesn't mean they're not willing to help. Until I see concrete evidence that we've been compromised, I'm not pulling the plug on this yet," Kruger said.

"I am just advising caution," Ringo replied. "That's all."

"And we will be cautious. But unless you're ready to send a team in country to do this the old-fashioned way, this is the best we have for now. And the clock is ticking."

"That's what I'm afraid of," Ringo said dejectedly. "That may just be our only option."

CHAPTER SIXTEEN

It was just after five A.M. when the alarm clock in the small visiting officer's quarters room started to beep. Alexei rolled over and hit the snooze button as he tried to get a few more minutes of sleep. *Just five more minutes*, he thought. His first brief wasn't until seven A.M. and the student was an experienced MiG-29 pilot transitioning to the SU-30.

Alexei drifted back to sleep. Ten minutes later, the beeping started once more. Before he could roll over to silence the alarm, it suddenly stopped. He wasn't sure if he had dreamed it or not, but he didn't really care. He kept his eyes closed as he drifted in and out of sleep.

As he debated whether to check his alarm, Alexei suddenly felt something cold and hard pressed against his forehead. He slowly opened his eyes and saw a dark figure standing over him.

Alexei was suddenly wide awake as his adrenaline surged.

"Get up," a female voice said in Russian.

Alexei shot up in the bed, pushing himself backward until he hit the headboard. The woman tracked him with the suppressed handgun as he desperately looked for an escape path. His heart raced as he squinted to see the woman in the darkness.

"Who are you?" Alexei asked. "What do you want?"

"Put your clothes on," the woman ordered. He was wearing only a pair of boxers.

"What is the meaning of this?"

The woman fired a round into the bed next to his leg. Alexei jerked away, curling up against the headboard as his eyes darted between the woman and the handgun.

"Do it now," she ordered.

Alexei held up his hands and slowly swung his legs around to the other side of the bed. He stood and walked to the closet where his flight suit had been hung the night before. As he grabbed it off the hanger, he looked back and saw the woman watching his every move with the weapon pointed at him.

"Hurry," the woman said.

Alexei put on the flight suit and then sat on the bed with his boots and socks. He put them on one at a time. As he stood, he slowly drew his boot knife from its sheath and prepared to face his attacker.

Before he could turn to face her, she shot him in the side of his left knee, causing him to collapse and drop the knife. He screamed out in agony as he rolled to his side clutching his wound.

The woman casually walked to him, picking up the knife and tossing it aside before she drove her heel into the fresh wound.

"Imbecile," she said.

"Who are you? What do you want?" he cried out.

"Fine," she said with an exasperated sigh. "Answer my questions and I may allow you to live."

"Anything! I'll tell you the truth. I swear!"

"The Americans. You remember them, yes?"

"Yes! Of course I do!"

"You were on your phone when they left. Who did you call?"

"I didn't-"

Before he could finish the lie, the woman shifted her weight onto her heel, driving his blood-soaked knee into the carpet.

"We have video," the woman said as Alexei grunted. "No more lies."

"Sergei! I called Sergei Asminov!"

"Bratva?" she asked.

Alexei nodded as he grimaced. "Minsk Bratva."

"Why? What did you tell him?"

"Please…"

"Please?" the woman put the warm barrel of her suppressed CZ P10C handgun against Alexei's temple. "Do you wish to end our chat?"

"No! Please don't kill me! But you don't understand. He will torture and kill me if he finds out I talked."

"And what do you think we will do?"

"We?" Alexei asked.

She sidestepped as the lights suddenly came on. Two burly men were standing by the door, dressed in suits. They appeared uninterested in Alexei's current state of distress.

"You are FSB!" Alexei said as he realized what was going on.

"Why did you call Asminov?"

"I was just trying to make some extra money for my family, that's all. I swear!"

"What did you tell him?"

"I told him that there were Americans here. I put a tracker on one of the vehicles when they left and called him to let him know that they were leaving. That's it! I swear!"

"What does Asminov want with them?"

"I have no idea. I met his men in a bar. They told me if I saw anything worthwhile, to give them a call and they would pay me handsomely. I thought the fact that Americans were flying our fighter jets would be something he might be interested in. He was!"

"You were warned about discussing the Americans with outsiders, yes?" the woman asked angrily.

"Yes," Alexei replied like a scolded child.

"And yet you did it anyway."

"Yes."

"Do you know what the Americans were here for?"

Alexei looked up at the woman, knowing that she was seconds from pulling the trigger and splattering his brain matter all over the closet.

"Please…"

"Answer the question," one of the burly men said with his booming voice.

"To learn how to fly the Advanced Flanker," Alexei answered.

"Do you know why?"

Alexei shook his head slowly. "I only know what I was told."

"None of the pilots told you anything?"

"No!"

"You are sure?"

"I swear!"

"How much were you paid?"

"Five thousand."

"Where is it?"

"In the nightstand."

She nodded and one of the men walked over to the nightstand. He opened the top drawer and retrieved an envelope full of cash. He nodded to the woman as he stuffed it into his coat.

"That's for my family!"

"They will get it," the woman said. "Goodbye."

Alexei's eyes widened. The woman squeezed the trigger, killing Alexei at point blank range. As his body fell limp, she unscrewed the suppressor and holstered her weapon.

"Clean this up and then we will find Asminov," she said as she stepped over Alexei's body and headed to the door.

Natasha pulled out the encrypted satellite phone that Kruger had given her and dialed his number as she stepped out of the room.

"I found the source," she said in English. "I will have an answer for you by the end of the day."

"I love you," Kruger replied.

"I love you too," she said as she ended the call.

CHAPTER SEVENTEEN

Spectre walked out of the vault and into the hangar where Sparky and Woody were waiting by a large box fan. They were both in shorts and a t-shirt, sweating in the hot hangar.

"What did Kruger say?" Woody asked as he saw Spectre approaching. Spectre had been on a secure VTC with Kruger trying to find out whether the mission would be scrubbed or not after the ambush in Belarus.

"Alexei sold us out to the Bratva thinking the government would pay a ransom. Natasha's team picked up the Bratva boss. He didn't know anything about what we were doing out there, other than we were Americans and probably with the government. So, the mission is still a go."

"What happened to Alexei?" Woody asked.

"I didn't ask," Spectre said.

"It's probably better that you don't know," Sparky interjected. "The Russians have their own methods of dealing with people. It's not all that friendly."

"Alexei was weird, but he seemed like a nice guy. I actually liked flying with him," Woody said.

Spectre clapped his hands. "Alright, let's get to work. Sparky, how are you feeling?"

Sparky rubbed the top of his head. "Other than this knot, I'm fine."

"No headaches or blurry vision?" Spectre asked.

Sparky shook his head. "Nope. Been doing fine."

"Excellent. Well, let's get the mats out and get started. Today I'm going to teach you how to defend yourself."

"Against what?" Woody asked.

"Anything," Spectre replied.

"Russian gangsters seem like a good enough reason," Sparky added, tapping his head again.

Spectre led them to a storage closet where they found mats, punching pads, and sparring gear. Woody and Sparky went to work setting the mats up while Spectre retrieved a box of rubber Glocks, knives and a fake AK-47.

Spectre had learned Krav Maga while flying and living in South Florida. He had reached the rank of black belt and become an instructor. He had also been trained by Kruger and the other instructors when he joined Project Archangel. The covert paramilitary organization had trained him in both armed and unarmed combat, demanding that its pilots be just as capable in combat as its Tier One operators.

He started them off on a few warm-up drills. He had them work on their punching and kicking technique, using the air in front of them as a target. After a few minutes of warming up, he made them stretch before handing them the pads to practice punching and kicking.

They went through the various strikes including knee and elbow strikes and then took a ten-minute water break. Spectre paid close attention to Sparky, who seemed to be grimacing a little more each time Woody would strike the pad.

"You okay, Sparky?"

"Yeah, I'm fine," Sparky replied catching his breath and then downing the rest of his water.

"No headaches or anything?" Spectre asked. Despite the flight docs at Nellis clearing Sparky when they returned to the States, Spectre was still worried. Sparky had lost consciousness in the accident. In any other scenario, that would've grounded him for at least six months. But because of the nature of the mission, they were taking chances and pressing ahead. Spectre just wanted to be sure.

"Doing great, boss," Sparky said as he forced a smile.

"Alright," Spectre said, clapping his hands. "Let's work on blocking drills."

Spectre had Woody turn the pads in his hands and swing at him. He demonstrated the proper technique to block the various strikes and then had them take turns practicing. They both seemed to be picking it up quickly, but he was still worried about Sparky. The longer they practiced, the more he seemed to fade.

"Alright, let's work on unarmed defenses against firearms," Spectre said, cutting the practice short. Defenses against weapons were technically more complex, but physically easier and would give Sparky a break.

He started by demonstrating defenses against the knife with the blade up. "You're going to get cut," he said as he demonstrated the block for a knife attack from above. "Just accept that fact now when dealing with a knife. That's why we use forearm blocks and never grab the blade."

Spectre had Woody and Sparky practice the blocking drills at half speed, one attack variation at a time. When he was satisfied that they were getting the hang of it, he had them increase speed and vary the attacks.

"Very good," he said. "Now, let's talk about firearms."

Once again, Spectre demonstrated before having his duo practice. He had them practice disarming each other from various positions and distances. "Always move out of the line of fire," Spectre instructed as he critiqued them.

When they were finished, Spectre held up the AK-47 to show them how to disarm a guard. But before he could, Cowboy walked in and interrupted.

"Telephone, mate," Cowboy said, pointing back toward the door to the vault.

"Kruger?" Spectre asked.

Cowboy nodded and Spectre handed the wooden AK-47 to him. "Show them how to disarm someone," he ordered.

Cowboy reluctantly accepted the fake weapon as Spectre jogged back to the vault. He went through the various security protocols and found the video teleconferencing software up and running on the desk in the back of the vault.

"Kruger, what's up?" Spectre asked.

"Jets are ready," Kruger said. "Jenny will fly Woody and Sparky here tonight."

"I should probably go with them," Spectre said. "I'll ride in the back of Sparky's jet."

"Why Sparky?"

"Just to be safe," Spectre said. "I'm still a little worried about his head injury."

"Is he okay? How'd he do in training?"

Spectre shrugged. "He said he was fine, but he seemed to be fading toward the end. I had to throttle back."

"Are you sure that's not due to conditioning?"

"Could be," Spectre admitted. "But given everything that's happened and the jet lag we all have, I'd rather be safe than sorry."

"What about Woody?"

"He's doing fine," Spectre said. "No issues today."

"Good," Kruger said. "Get some rest and I'll see you here."

"What about the other jet?" Spectre asked. A C-17 had picked up the parts and brought them along with Tuna to Edwards to meet Kruger. Churchill had stayed behind as the lone man responsible for the security of the aircraft.

"Still waiting on parts for the C-5. They're thinking maybe tomorrow."

"So, we're not that far off timeline."

"We've been off timeline since the beginning, bub."

"And you're sure the threat in Belarus is no longer a factor?"

"Absolutely," Kruger replied.

Spectre paused for a moment and then asked, "What happened to Alexei?"

"He's no longer a factor," Kruger said.

"Dead?"

"Don't worry about it," Kruger said. "I'll see you later tonight."

Kruger ended the conversation, leaving Spectre staring at the VTC conferencing software logo on the screen. He sat back and sighed. He didn't like the way the mission was unfolding already. He only hoped there were no further complications.

CHAPTER EIGHTEEN

The team landed at Edwards Air Force Base in California under the cover of darkness. There was no welcoming party when Jenny taxied the Gulfstream to the remote Defense Advanced Research Projects Agency (DARPA) hangar and shut down both engines. It was after midnight and everyone had gone home for the day, except for the armed security detail watching over the classified facility.

The large hangar doors opened as Spectre exited the aircraft followed by Sparky, Woody, and Cowboy. Kruger and Ringo walked out to meet them as ground personnel went to work hooking up tugs to the recently reassembled SU-30 fighter jets.

Kruger walked right to Sparky and shook his hand. "How are you feeling?"

"Fine," Sparky said. "Just a little bump on the noggin. I'm good to go."

"Hey, I'm fine too," Woody said as he leaned in between them to shake Kruger's hand. "In case you were wondering."

"I wasn't," Kruger responded gruffly. "But I'm glad you boys are doing okay. You've got a lot of training to do in a short period of time. The mission timeline has been advanced."

"Advanced?" Spectre asked.

"I'll brief you in the vault back home," Kruger said, frowning.

"Bad news?"

"Very."

"Awesome," Spectre said.

"Maybe now we'll finally get to find out what's going on," Woody said. "That'd be nice."

Spectre nodded toward the two fighters that were being positioned by the ground crews on the ramp. "Might want to go get your preflight done. We're not hanging around here."

"Sure thing, brah," Woody said, rolling his eyes. "Far be it for me to know what's going on."

"C'mon, let's go," Sparky said.

"I'll meet you at the jet, Sparky," Spectre said. "Thanks."

"No worries."

"I guess I'd better get to it too, then," Cowboy said. They had decided to let him ride in the backseat of Woody's aircraft to give him more seat time since he had been thrown in at the last minute. With the recent events and apparent timeline shift, it was even more important that he get all the seat time he could just in case.

When the three were gone, Spectre turned to Ringo and Kruger. "You don't have to tell me the details, but tell me this – how fucked are we?"

"Rightly fucked," Ringo answered, shaking his head. "It's a bloody disaster."

"How soon are we talking?" Spectre asked.

"A week," Kruger said grimly.

"A *week*? As in a week earlier?" Spectre asked.

"A week as in *a week*. From now," Kruger said.

"Jesus!" Spectre said. "No fucking way. We need to pull the plug on this now."

"I don't think that's going to happen, bub," Kruger said.

"Well then, you just signed your own," Spectre said before turning and pointing at the men preflighting the two jets, "and *their* death certificates. There is no way they can be trained to the level of proficiency required for this mission in a fucking week!"

"Lower your voice," Kruger warned. "We're not talking about this out in the open, got it?"

Spectre threw up his hands. "Alright, dude, whatever. I'm going to get these jets to *the oasis* and then we can chat. But I'll tell you right now, it ain't happening."

The Oasis was the code name they had given to their isolated base of operations in the Nevada desert. Spectre knew that once there he could hash it out with Kruger, but as far as he was concerned the mission was a scrub. They'd need to go to plan B, or C, or whatever else they had in store. The crews were barely proficient enough to fly the jets back to base after two days of training, much less to employ the aircraft after a week. *A fucking week!*

Spectre stormed toward the aircraft. The ground crew had hung his G-suit, helmet, bag, and harness on one of the pylons. He put on his gear as Sparky and company gathered by the nose of the aircraft and watched him.

"Everything alright, brah?" Woody asked. "You look super pissed."

"It's fine," Spectre lied. "Are the jets okay?"

"I didn't find any missing rivets or important bolts," Sparky said. "But that's not to say there weren't any before they disassembled the jets. The Russians build in a safety factor anyway, don't they?"

"Good," Spectre said. "Still feeling okay?"

"Feeling great!"

"Alright boys, let's get out of here," Spectre said as he zipped the last zipper on his G-suit.

The two crews saddled up and went through their checklists. The DARPA ground crews assisted them through their startup procedures and then each crew chief rendered a crisp salute as they taxied out.

At the late time they had chosen to depart, the tower was unmanned. There was no one to call for taxi or takeoff clearance. Their plan was to fly low, getting safely away from Edwards Air Force Base to the south before turning east and contacting Los Angeles Center for an instrument flight rules clearance pickup. It was the aerial equivalent of a surveillance detection route to make sure no one was tracking them.

Sparky and Spectre took the lead as Woody and Cowboy followed in the second SU-30. They held short of the runway. Woody flashed his position lights to indicate that he was ready. Sparky took the runway and lit the SU-30's afterburner, gently pinning them both back in the seat. Fifteen seconds later, Woody and Cowboy took the runway and followed.

"Heathen One-Two tied," Woody called as they were airborne, indicating that they were locked on to Spectre's aircraft with their radar.

With Woody and Cowboy two miles in trail, the two-ship flew south for two minutes at a thousand feet over the terrain. When they were outside of the Edwards operating areas, they turned east and climbed to eleven thousand five hundred feet.

"Heathen One-Two, goggled, visual," Woody called over their interflight frequency, indicating he was wearing his night vision goggles and had the lead aircraft in sight.

"Cleared in," Spectre said. Since it was a short flight, they opted to fly in close formation to only give one radar return as a single aircraft.

"Good evening Los Angeles Center, Learjet November Six-Niner-Eight-Delta-Charlie," Spectre called.

"November Six-Niner-Eight-Delta-Charlie, go ahead," the female controller responded.

"Six-Niner-Eight-Delta-Charlie is a Lear 60 at eleven thousand, five hundred, twenty miles southeast of the Hector VOR looking for an IFR pickup to McCarren International," Spectre said. As part of their deception, they were using the real registration of a Lear 60 that Coolio had confirmed was undergoing repairs and not operating that night. They had chosen the Learjet because it was closest in performance to the cruise speeds they planned to use.

"November Six-Niner-Eight-Delta-Charlie, squawk One-Four-Zero-Two and ident," the controller said.

"One-Four-Zero-Two with the flash, Eight-Delta-Charlie," Spectre replied.

"You sure they're gonna buy that, dude?" Sparky asked over the intercom.

Before Spectre could answer, the controller replied, "Eight-Delta-Charlie, you're radar contact one-five miles southwest of the Hector VOR. You're cleared to the McCarren International Airport via direct Hector and the CRESO FOUR arrival. Climb and maintain Flight Level Two-Four-Zero."

"Direct Hector for the CRESO FOUR. Climb and maintain Two-Four-Zero," Spectre replied.

"There ya go," Spectre said over the intercom. "So far so good."

"I stand corrected," Sparky replied as he started to climb.

They leveled off at twenty-four thousand feet and were given a descent down to twelve thousand less than five minutes later for the arrival. The SU-30's avionics were in English, but it wasn't equipped to fly any of the Standard Terminal Arrivals (STAR) as a real Learjet would be. Spectre used his iPad to read the STAR plate and he manually entered the coordinates of each fix into the navigation system.

As they continued toward Las Vegas, Spectre heard Jenny check in behind them. Their plan was to fly to Nellis for a quick approach and then continue to *The Oasis* a few minutes behind Spectre's flight.

As Spectre checked in with approach, he cancelled their clearance to McCarren International. "Approach, November Six-Niner-Eight-Delta-Charlie would like to cancel IFR."

"IFR cancellation received, say intentions," the male controller replied.

"We're going to head southeast to Kingman. Boss's orders," Spectre said, doing his best imitation of a corporate pilot.

"And you want to proceed VFR?" the controller asked with a hint of confusion in his voice.

"It's a nice night," Spectre replied. "Affirm."

"Do you want flight following?"

"Negative, sir, that won't be necessary. Thanks for all your help."

"Okay…November-Six-Niner-Eight-Delta-Charlie, squawk One-Two-Zero-Zero and remain clear of the Class Bravo airspace. Good night."

"Squawking VFR and we'll stay clear, Eight-Delta-Charlie, goodnight."

Sparky started a shallow bank and descended. They headed toward the uncontrolled Kingman airport eighty-miles to the south, gradually descending into the dark abyss below them. Spectre donned his Night Vision Goggles to assist in terrain clearance, but was using the SU-30s radar to paint the terrain as well.

When they reached five hundred feet a few miles from the airport, Sparky cleared Woody to take spacing and then entered a hard turn. Woody fell back to a mile in trail and Sparky dropped down to one-hundred feet.

They doubled back and flew into the Nellis Airspace at a hundred feet off the desert floor, squawking the appropriate code as they entered the military airspace so the controllers would know it was them. The military controllers had been briefed on their expected arrival and were used to classified missions operating in the area.

Sparky led the formation to their secret base on the western half of the area and the two fighters landed uneventfully on the unlit runway.

"Well, that's a first for me," Woody said as the planes were towed into the hangar and they took off their gear.

"What's that?" Spectre asked.

"I've landed on pitching aircraft carriers at night and in bad weather, but I've never come into the overhead at a hundred feet and landed on an unlit runway with night vision goggles and no moon. That was pretty sporty."

Spectre smiled. "Welcome to Project Archangel, my friend."

CHAPTER NINETEEN

Spectre was waiting at the desk in the inner vault when Kruger and Ringo walked in. He held up the beer he had been sipping on and said, "Cold ones in the fridge."

Kruger diverted to the mini-fridge and grabbed two beers. He handed one to Ringo and twisted the top off his as he sat down. He took a long pull and then belted a frustrated sigh.

"So, back to how fucked we are," Spectre said as he watched Kruger start to unwind.

"Peace talks with the North Koreans are stalling. Intel analysts at Langley think the EMP launch will happen much sooner," Kruger said. "It's a shit show."

"So, why not go in and do a pre-emptive strike?" Spectre asked.

"We take this little asshole out and Washington thinks they can salvage the talks. He's currently the one interfering," Kruger answered.

"What's Plan B?" Spectre asked.

"There is no Plan B," Ringo said.

"Oh, come on," Spectre said with a look of disbelief. "There *has to be* a Plan B."

"Sure. They'll launch their ICBM. We'll knock it down. We'll have no choice but to retaliate and within twenty-four hours Seoul and Osan will be leveled by the artillery at the DMZ. The Chinese will intervene and then the Japanese will join in to defend their own interests and World War III will have officially kicked off," Ringo replied.

Spectre knew Ringo was right. The North Koreans were estimated to have in excess of twelve thousand pieces of artillery and twenty-three hundred pieces of multiple-launch rocket launchers. Between artillery, ground forces, and air strikes in the initial hours of the war, everything near the border of South Korea would be decimated. And that didn't even take into account the chemical and biological weapons the North Koreans were thought to possess. It was one of the many reasons the stalemate between the North and South had gone on as long as it had. All-out war was simply not an option.

"What you're asking the guys downstairs to do is not going to happen in a week, Kruger," Spectre said after a brief silence. "It was already a stretch with the timeline we had."

Kruger shrugged. "They're the guys you picked. I would've preferred you to do it."

Spectre shook his head. "It doesn't matter who's in those jets. No one's learning curve is that steep."

Kruger looked at his watch. "Well, then you'd better get some sleep so you can get an early start."

Spectre rolled his eyes. "We don't have the airspace reserved until the afternoon. It's not that easy."

Kruger downed the rest of his beer and set the empty bottle down on the desk. "I'll go make some phone calls."

Spectre looked at Ringo as Kruger got up and walked out. "Is he serious?"

"I would assume so."

"What isn't he telling me?"

Ringo shrugged. "You know the drill, mate. Need to know."

As Spectre considered his response, Kruger suddenly reentered the vault. "You have the airspace all day tomorrow and whatever you need for the rest of the week."

"What? How?" Spectre asked.

"Don't worry about it, bub. It's done. What else do you need to make this happen?"

"A miracle," Spectre replied.

"I can't help you with that, but in the meantime, get some rest. I told the ground support guys 0800, which is in six hours," Kruger said.

"You really think we can make this work without everyone, *including you*, dying in North Korea?" Spectre asked as he stood and faced Kruger.

"We don't have a choice, bub."

CHAPTER TWENTY

Spectre was dragging ass and the coffee wasn't helping. He had gotten up early with the rest of the team and flown the first of three scheduled training missions. It was going to be a long day.

The first flight had gone well. Spectre had briefed it and flown as the instructor pilot sitting in the backseat of Sparky's airplane while Cowboy rode with Woody. They had started out slow, working on the basics to allow Sparky and Woody to get familiar with the aircraft.

So far, Sparky and Woody seemed to be adapting quickly. They had done various canned drills, practicing things like short-range radar, targeting with the helmet-mounted sight, and using the captive-carry training version of the AA-11 Archer infrared missile with its extremely lethal high-off boresight capability.

Mentally, the mission had been demanding, but physically it wasn't much. The set-ups were all cooperative to give the students solid sight pictures. They never pulled more than four or five Gs. In a fighter that could easily pull nine, it was a walk in the park.

But despite the relatively low-key start, Spectre was tired. He was still jet-lagged from their trip to Europe a few days earlier, and had only slept four hours the night prior. The stresses of planning and training for a mission that was becoming more and more impossible by the second had started to take its toll. The bags under his steely-blue eyes were proof of that.

Spectre put his coffee cup down on the briefing room table as he sat down. Unlike the folding tables and chairs in the hangar in Belarus, this facility had actual briefing rooms with whiteboards, computers, and furniture inside the vault in the hangar that was next door to the hangar with the SCIF.

He was all alone in the room as he reviewed his notes from the flight prior. He had already debriefed Sparky, Woody, and Cowboy on their performance. Now he had ten minutes to integrate those notes and come up with a quick plan for the next flight.

As he finished coming up with a lineup card, Woody walked in and handed Spectre a Red Bull. "You look like you could use a pick-me-up."

Spectre accepted it and put it next to his now-empty coffee cup. "Thanks. Where's everyone else?"

Woody looked at his watch. "They still have five minutes. Sparky was getting a snack and Kruger is in the other vault talking to some big wig."

Spectre stopped writing and looked up at Woody. "How do you feel in the aircraft right now?"

Woody sat on the briefing room table and considered the question. "Flying this jet is easy. The Russians built a solid airplane. *Employing it* is another story. If you're asking if I would go out and defend the Straits of Taiwan with it, the answer is no. But as a wingman it's not that difficult. It helps that this version of the aircraft is in English."

Spectre nodded. That was one of the first requirements he had for this operation. The demonstrators that they were using had to have the same software that the actual aircraft would use. Luckily that meant mostly Lynch avionics like the Malaysian SU-30 MKM and Indian SU-30 MKI.

Sparky walked in followed by Kruger. "Everything okay?" Spectre asked Kruger as he and Sparky took their places around the table.

"Fine," Kruger grumbled. "Just getting an update on Churchill in Lajes."

"How is he?" Spectre asked.

"As frustrated as anyone would be in that situation," Kruger replied.

Spectre stood and turned toward the whiteboard behind him.

"Alright, let's get started," he said.

Spectre briefed the second mission in just under thirty minutes. The plan was very similar to the first mission. They would start out with basic exercises to get sight pictures and work on the switchology drills necessary to employ the weapons. It would allow Sparky and Woody to hone their skills while giving Kruger a fresh look since he hadn't been in the airplane in a while. This time, Spectre would be riding in the backseat of Woody's aircraft to work on any issues he had been having.

After the warm-ups, Spectre intended to move from *crawl* to *walk*. They would do basic fighter maneuver drills called "perch setups" in which one aircraft would start out offensive and the other defensive. This would allow them to practice entering the adversary's imaginary "turn circle" which was the imaginary arc it traced across the sky, and then close in to the control zone to employ the simulated gun.

On the other side, the defender would practice defensive maneuvers, starting with the initial break turn and then recognizing the offender's weapons employment zones. Once the attacker was inside the control zone, the defender would then practice his guns defense until Spectre determined that the training objectives had been met.

They took off and climbed to the working airspace above the top-secret airfield. After a brief "G-warmup" in which they made sure their bodies and systems were ready to pull g-forces by making two hard, 180-degree turns, they set up for the first exercise.

Spectre coached Woody through the guns tracking drill as Sparky provided a stable target. After three iterations, Sparky added a jink and spoiled Woody's gunshot, taking advantage of the super-maneuverability of the Advanced Flanker.

"Sparky's pretty damned good," Woody commented over the intercom as they recovered and leveled off.

"Yeah, he's doing well," Spectre said. "Just remember to give yourself an out because you can easily end up with a face full of jet if he swings the nozzles and you're not ready for it."

"Copy that," Woody said.

They switched roles and allowed Sparky to practice his gun work. Woody tried to spoil Sparky's shot on the last setup but was unsuccessful.

"You have to go earlier," Spectre coached. "Use the thrust-vectoring."

"Got it," Woody replied.

After completing the warm-up drills, they set up for their first high-G exercise. Sparky moved into the appropriate position two miles off Woody's wing.

FINI FLIGHT

"Next set will be 9K offensive for number two," Spectre called over the radio.

"Two," Sparky replied crisply.

"One's ready," Spectre called.

"Two's ready," came the reply.

"Check right," Spectre said.

Woody initiated a hard turn to the right.

"One point nine," Sparky called, indicating he had a good radar lock and was at just under two miles away.

Woody reversed his turn back into Sparky and set up an easy left-hand turn, looking over his shoulder to help set the appropriate aspect angle for the setup.

"One point eight," Sparky counted down. He was nose-on to Woody and Spectre and the range was steadily clicking down.

"One point seven…one point six… Fox Two!" Sparky called, indicating the simulated launch of his air to air missile which also served as the "Fight's On" call.

Woody started a hard break turn into Sparky as Sparky rolled wings level. If Sparky kept his pursuit course, it would create a high aspect pass or overshoot. Sparky had to be patient and "drive" toward Woody's imaginary turn circle.

But Woody had other plans. Instead of a level break turn as briefed, he rolled into a split-s, reefed back on the stick, chopped the throttles to idle in order to bleed speed, and then went full afterburner while using the thrust-vectoring to minimize his turn radius. The aircraft responded almost instantly, turning to face their attacker.

Spectre started to call a knock-it-off to reset the fight since that wasn't the point of the engagement, but decided to let it go as he saw Sparky's aircraft respond. Sparky climbed and the aircraft rolled onto its back, trading energy for altitude since he knew Woody's maneuver was a one-trick pony.

As the two aircraft crossed high aspect, Woody reversed into another split-s toward Sparky who responded by using the thrust vectoring to create a single-circle fight downhill. The nose of Sparky's Flanker started to come to bear but then suddenly stopped and the aircraft seemed to point straight at the ground.

"Banshee, knock it off, Banshee One knock-it-off," Spectre called as he saw Sparky's aircraft no longer maneuvering in relation to them.

There was no response as the aircraft continued zooming toward the ground. Woody reversed to follow and get a better look.

"I think he G-LOCed," Woody said, referring to a G-induced Loss of Consciousness in which a person loses consciousness under G-forces due to blood pooling in the lower extremities under high g-forces.

"Sparky, pull up!" Spectre yelled over the radio.

"He's not responding," Kruger called out over the radio.

"Pull back on the stick!" Spectre yelled.

As the jet screamed toward the ground, Spectre's heart sank. He knew he was close to watching two of his best friends die in a fireball. Just as he was about to call for them to eject over the radio, Kruger finally complied and the nose of the aircraft started to track upward.

Woody gave chase as the aircraft leveled off. He rejoined on Sparky's left wing. Spectre could see Sparky slowly come to and try to shake it off.

"You okay, Sparky?" Spectre asked over the radio.

"Yeah…yeah, I'm okay," Sparky slurred.

"Alright, fence out, we'll take you home," Spectre said.

CHAPTER TWENTY-ONE

Woody and Spectre led Sparky and Kruger back to the secret base and then acted as a chase aircraft for him as he landed. Despite having lost consciousness, Sparky was lucid and seemed to be okay. They followed him down to seventy-five feet and watched him touch down uneventfully, before executing a go around and landing.

By the time they taxied to the ramp and parked next to Sparky's jet, Sparky and Kruger were already in the hangar removing their gear. Spectre and Woody hurried through their shutdown checklists and quickly took their off their gear. Spectre ran to join Sparky as Kruger escorted him to the waiting Gulfstream.

"Really, I'm fine," Sparky said as Spectre caught up with them. "I just wasn't on top of my G strain."

"It's just a precaution," Spectre said. "Let the flight docs at Nellis check you out. This is standard procedure."

"I'm fine," Sparky insisted, shaking his head.

Kruger and Spectre exchanged a look as Jenny stepped out of the aircraft to help Sparky up the stairs. He shrugged off her assistance and made his way into the forward-most executive leather chair and fastened his seatbelt.

Kruger and Spectre took their seats as Jenny returned to the cockpit and finished her preflight checks with her co-pilot. A few minutes later, they were airborne for the short flight to Nellis Air Force Base.

Spectre called ahead and coordinated for an appointment with the chief of aerospace medicine. After the quick fifteen-minute flight, they landed and found the Wing Executive Officer waiting with a car to take them to the appointment.

The three men piled out of the Ford Fusion and walked right into the medical clinic to see the flight surgeon. To the untrained eye, they looked like any other fighter pilots stationed on base. They were wearing combat patches that gave no specific unit and major's rank on their shoulders.

"You'll have to wait outside," a nurse told Spectre and Kruger as they tried to go into the exam room with Sparky.

There was a small secondary waiting room inside the flight medicine section of the clinic. It was empty as Spectre and Kruger took their seats while Judge Judy blared on the TV above them.

"You know he's done, right?" Kruger asked in a low voice.

"What do you mean?" Spectre asked. He knew exactly what Kruger was getting at, but didn't want to admit it.

"We almost became a smoking hole in the desert today," Kruger whispered. "Something's not right with him. He's not coming back."

"GLOC could happen to anyone," Spectre argued. "We just flew across the world and then asked these guys to flip their body clocks and fly three sorties in one day. He was probably just tired."

"Woody didn't seem to have a problem."

Spectre shrugged. "Everyone is different. Hell, I started to gray out a little in the backseat when he did his break turn."

Kruger shook his head. "He didn't just gray out though. He was lights out. Hell, I saw him have a seizure or something in the front seat before he finally came to."

"Ahh...The funky chicken."

"Funky chicken?"

"Yeah, that's what they call it during the centrifuge training when you GLOC. You lose blood flow to your brain and when it comes back, everything just kind of resets. It causes muscles to spasm and flail."

"Well, whatever it was, he'd be dead right now if I hadn't been in the backseat with him. And that won't work *in country*. You *know* what this means, bub," Kruger said.

"It means we need to wait and see what the doc says and then we can talk about what it means."

Kruger grunted, folded his arms, and pretended to watch the TV. It was thirty minutes after Sparky first entered the exam room, before the flight surgeon finally walked out.

"I'm Colonel Wynn," the flight surgeon said as he approached carrying Sparky's patient chart. "Based on the phone call I received, I understand this is a pretty high priority case. Which of you is in charge?"

"It is," Kruger answered. "And we're both in charge."

"Fair enough, well, I'm afraid we're going to need to do more tests on Major Lynch. He told me he was involved in an automobile accident and I'd like to rule out intracranial hemorrhaging."

"How likely is that, sir?" Spectre asked.

Colonel Wynn frowned. "I'd say it's more likely than not, based on my initial exam. But I can't say for certain without doing imaging."

"When can he do it?" Kruger asked.

"Right now, actually," Colonel Wynn replied. "He's being prepped as we speak. Based on the priority that the general gave me, I put it in as a Tier One request. I should have the results within the next two hours."

"So, do we wait here, or can we go with him, or what?" Spectre asked.

"There's nothing you can do for him," Colonel Wynn said before looking at his watch. "You may want to go get lunch somewhere on base and be back in an hour. You have time."

"We'll wait," Kruger said.

Spectre nodded in agreement.

"Suit yourself," Colonel Wynn said. "Wait here, and I'll have the nurse come get you when we have a definitive answer."

"Thank you," Spectre said.

They returned to their chairs in the waiting area. Spectre looked at Kruger. "He's going to be fine."

"Doesn't sound likely, bub," Kruger said. "But, we'll wait for the results. And then…"

"And then what?"

"And then we need to talk about Plan B."

"There is no Plan B," Spectre said. "You said so yourself, remember? Five days and all that. Without Sparky, we're done. We are fucked."

"No, we're not," Kruger said.

"What do you mean? These guys are the only ones I trust. Who are we going to find to do this in less than a week?"

"I think you know, bub."

Spectre's eyes widened. "Absolutely not. No fucking way. No. That wasn't part of the deal."

Kruger slouched in his chair and let his head rest against the wall behind him as he closed his eyes. "Well, then you're right. We're fucked and so is everyone else in this country."

"Goddammit!" Spectre belted out as he stood and kicked over a nearby chair in frustration.

CHAPTER TWENTY-TWO

Spectre had a little under twenty-four hours to make a decision, but deep down he knew there was no decision to be made. It had already been made for him and he was just going through the motions.

When he walked through Bear's front door, Michelle was holding Cal Jr. and immediately read the look on Spectre's face. Without a single detail, she knew what was about to happen. Spectre's expression had said it all.

"They're making you go," she said softly as she walked up and hugged him.

Spectre kissed her and then kissed his son on the forehead. Cal Jr. smiled and laughed before trying to hand Spectre the stuffed airplane he had been holding.

"Thank you, buddy," Spectre said, graciously accepting it.

"How did you know?" Spectre asked Michelle.

"You wouldn't be here otherwise," Michelle replied. "Unless they scrubbed the mission."

"Those are the options, yes," Spectre said. "Where's Bear?"

"They're out back," Michelle said.

"Good. You and I should talk," Spectre said as he took Cal Jr. from her and walked to the living area. While he was gone, Michelle had been staying with Bear and his wife to help with Cal Jr. so she could continue her private practice as a lawyer.

They sat down on the couch. "So, which is it? Are you done?" Michelle asked.

"I think so," Spectre said. "I don't think there's any way to make it work at this point."

"What happened?"

"There was a car accident when we were in Europe. One of the pilots hit his head. Turns out, he has an intracranial hemorrhage and they're going to need to go in and relieve the pressure. He lost consciousness during a flight, but we should've found it earlier. That's my fault."

"How is it your fault?"

"I let Kruger and his team push him through the medical stuff instead of doing a full evaluation. He should never have gotten back in a jet until he had a full workup. They would've caught this much sooner. Jesus, he may never fly again."

"Cal, you can't blame yourself for that."

"The pilots are my responsibility. And now one of them is in the hospital. Doesn't matter anyway, Kruger told me the timeline moved up," Spectre said.

"How soon?"

Spectre looked at his watch. "Three days from now we have to be operationally ready to go. There's just no way, even if I could find someone to take his place."

"Do they have a backup plan?"

"Yeah. *Me*."

"And you don't want to do it?"

"That wasn't part of the deal," Spectre said. "I signed on for training only. Nothing else."

"So, that's it? You're home now. What are they going to do?"

Spectre shrugged. "Not my problem."

Michelle frowned. "Cal, it is *our* problem. You know what the stakes are."

"Haven't we given enough?"

Michelle rubbed Spectre's shoulder. "We have, but that doesn't mean we can sit back now just because we've already given. You have a skillset that the country needs right now to avert a world war."

Spectre shook his head. "There's no way I can get myself or Woody ready for this in just a few days. We really needed months to prepare."

"You planned an operation to go to Cuba to rescue a girl and recover an F-16 on a bar napkin, didn't you?"

"We were only supposed to go to Cuba and gather intel, remember?" Spectre replied. "It just kind of fell apart from there."

"And you improvised, right?"

"That was different," Spectre replied. "The Cubans didn't quite have the military we're talking about here."

Michelle kissed Spectre. "You know I'll support any decision you make, but I think you should at least strongly consider it."

Spectre sighed softly. "I know, but I was kind of hoping you'd tell me to stay home."

"Why?"

"Because Kruger and Jenny are waiting for me at the airport right now anyway," Spectre said, wincing as he waited for Michelle to react.

"So, you're going?"

"I don't think I have a choice. If I don't, they're going to send Woody in alone. And you know he can't be trusted by himself," Spectre said with a chuckle.

"So, why didn't you just say that from the beginning?"

"Because I really was hoping you would say no. I told Kruger I needed to talk to you about it first and see my son before I made a decision. But we were on the same page, which is why I love you so much. If I don't go, this whole mission falls apart and a lot of people will die. But I didn't want to influence your decision. And if you had said no, I would've stayed home."

"Please, be safe," Michelle said as she kissed Spectre.

"I will," Spectre said.

He hugged Cal Jr. and kissed him on the forehead before kissing Michelle again. "I'd better get back to the base. We have a lot of training to do in a short time."

"Will I see you again before you go?" Michelle asked.

"I'll try to Skype you guys," Spectre said.

He kissed them both again a final time and then walked out the door as he choked back a tear. He hated saying goodbye, but this time was especially hard for him. Something was nagging at him.

Something deep within his gut told him to just enjoy the last few moments. That same voice was screaming at him to stay home and forget any of this had ever happened. He had said goodbye so many times before and always made it home safely. He had been through hell and back with Michelle, but this time was different.

He had never had this feeling before. As he turned and looked back at his wife and son a final time before walking out the door, he could feel the dread building inside him. He had to go through with this mission because it was his duty, but deep down he felt it was a one-way mission.

He felt like this was the last time he would ever see either of them. And although his inner voice was now screaming for him to stay home, he waved goodbye and walked out the door. It was time to go save his country.

CHAPTER TWENTY-THREE

The third aircraft had been delivered and assembled by the time Spectre and Kruger returned from their field trip to Louisiana. Woody and Cowboy had driven to Nellis and picked it up during the night while Tuna and Churchill drove the armored SUV back to their secret base.

When they arrived at the hangar, the team was eager to find out if the plan was going forward. They all gathered under one of the Flankers as Spectre and Kruger carried their bags in.

"How's Sparky?" Spectre asked Woody. He and Cowboy had stopped by the hospital on the way to the base to check on him after his surgery to relieve the pressure from the hemorrhage.

"He was still sedated in ICU when we went by. His family was there, so we didn't bug him," Woody said. "But I saw the flight doc, and he said that Sparky may never fly again. Waivers for stuff like that are really hard to come by."

"Goddammit," Spectre hissed. "I shouldn't have pushed him."

"So, what's going on, man? Are we doing this or not?" Woody asked.

"Come with me," Spectre said.

Spectre motioned for Woody to follow as Kruger stayed behind to update the rest of the team. They walked through the hangar and went to the inner vault to talk in a secure location.

The two walked into the inner vault and Spectre poured himself a cup of coffee before sitting across from Woody at the table in the center of the room. He took a sip from his mug as Woody impatiently waited for answers.

"Well?" Woody asked.

"With Sparky out, it's just you and me now," Spectre said before taking another sip. The caffeine was desperately needed. He was still tired with no end in sight. He would have to push through on caffeine and adrenaline if they had any hopes of being ready for the mission in the next few days.

"No shit, brah."

"Okay, so here's the deal," Spectre said. "We're going to pose as demo pilots for the Russians. The North Koreans are interested in buying the SU-30s and have requested a demo for the top brass."

"Dude, I don't look Russian," Woody protested. His father had been an American fighter pilot and his mother was Vietnamese.

"No, but the Russians often use pilots from other countries in the region to demo their aircraft if they think it'll help with the sale," Spectre replied. "And yours is not a speaking role anyway. All we're going to do is fly."

"What kind of flying?"

Spectre shrugged. "That's the hard part. We don't know, and won't know until we get there. In the past, they've wanted airshow-style demonstrations. Sometimes they've asked for demos against their current fleet. And there's even a chance Kim Jong-Un will want a ride. That's why we're training for everything."

"But Kruger and Cowboy and those other guys are not WSOs. What are they going for?" Woody asked.

"They're only there for the ground mission," Spectre said.

"Which is…"

"To kill Choe Il-Sung."

"An assassination mission? In *North Korea*?"

"Relax. They have a plan for the specifics that even I'm not privy to. All I know is that we fly them in, help them gain access to this asshole, and fly them out."

"Fly them out on a flight plan or under hostile fire?"

"Could be either," Spectre said. "That's why we're training for everything."

"Great, so I need to learn how to SAM weave in this jet too?"

"It's not ideal," Spectre admitted.

"None of this is ideal. Are you sure we're the best option the U.S. military can come up with, dude?"

"Believe me, I wouldn't be here if I weren't absolutely positive that this is it," Spectre said. "We're what stands between a chance at peace and World War III."

"*Great*," Woody said.

"You good?" Spectre asked.

"I'm good," Woody replied. "I just hope you know what you've gotten us into."

"Just fly the plane like you've been doing and we'll be fine. Today, we'll go out and work on a few more perch setups and then start doing high aspect BFM."

"Are you sure you can handle me? The last guy that tried ended up in the hospital," Woody said with a grin.

"I'll manage," Spectre replied.

"Hey, so, quick question – how long are we going to actually be in country?"

"Why do you ask?"

"Well, I saw on the news that they're moving ahead with denuclearization and all of that. If that falls apart, will we be there long enough for them to turn on us?"

"Since we're going with a Russian envoy, I doubt it. They have nothing to do with this. I'm hoping just a few hours. Maybe an overnight at most."

"Russian envoy?"

"Kruger's girlfriend. She's posing as an executive for the guy we got the jets from at the Sukhoi factory. They're working the ground mission with Kruger. That's seriously all I know. They've kept it pretty compartmentalized."

"Why?"

"In case we get captured."

Woody's eyes widened. "Captured? You think that's a real risk?"

"Anything could happen at this point," Spectre said with a shrug. "But if we train well and do our part, I don't think there will be any problems. They're all professionals."

"With the way this mission has gone so far, I'm not so sure about that."

CHAPTER TWENTY-FOUR

It was their last training sortie before the big show, and Woody felt like he and Kruger were finally starting to become a cohesive team. All he had to do was get to the merge with Spectre unobserved, get a quick simulated missile shot, and they'd be finished with training and on their way to North Korea. For whatever that was worth.

After the meeting in the vault, Spectre had come up with a solid game plan to get the most out of their last few training sorties. Kruger was paired permanently with Woody while Spectre alternated between Dusty and Cowboy, now acting as a mission critical pilot instead of just an instructor in the backseat.

For their final training sortie, Cowboy occupied the backseat of Spectre's SU-30. They had started sixty miles away – at the edge of the designated restricted airspace – with a plan for Woody to intercept while Spectre and Cowboy assumed the role of an unaware bogey.

When both aircraft were set at their respective sides of the airspace, Spectre called "Fight's On" and they turned toward each other. Woody and Kruger worked together to use the SU-30 Advanced Flanker's Phazotron N010 Zhuk-27 Active Electronically Scanned Array Radar. Once they had the target and were in range, Kruger switched to tracking Spectre's aircraft with the Infrared Search and Tracking System (IRST) to allow for passive tracking without exciting the Radar Warning Receiver (RWR) in Spectre's aircraft.

At twenty miles, Woody turned hard right to start working the offset. It was a move to test awareness of the bogey and then to set the merge geometry. If the bogey pointed its nose at them, that would be evident on their display and would mean the bogey was looking for a fight. If Spectre and Cowboy continued on their current heading, it meant that they were unaware. In that case, the turn would also build space and angles so that Woody could end up at Spectre's 9 o'clock low where it would be harder for them to see him as he made the visual identification up close and took the shot.

They weren't sure intercepts were something the North Koreans would need to see as part of the demonstration, but Spectre wanted them to be prepared for anything. They needed to look and act the part of Russian demo pilots down to the smallest detail.

Woody was watching Spectre's aircraft continue on its heading on his display when he heard Kruger say, "Oh shit!"

"Nah, brah, he's unaware," Woody said reactively as he looked out through his helmet mounted cueing system and found the circle over Spectre's aircraft in the distance.

"No!" Kruger yelled over the intercom. "Bogey…err…Bandit… Fuck! There's an asshole on our six!"

"What?" Woody asked as he looked over his shoulder and suddenly saw a giant gray jet rolling in on them.

Instinctively, Woody deployed a string of flares and ripped the throttles to idle as he started a hard break turn into his attacker.

"Woody!" Kruger protested under the G-forces.

Even at idle thrust, the SU-30 gave Woody everything he was asking for and more, almost instantaneously giving their unsuspecting attacker a face full of Woody's aircraft.

The F-22 pilot that had intercepted them had misjudged the range and closure rate due to the size of the SU-30 and had given himself no path of escape as the spine of Woody's aircraft filled his HUD. He tried to turn left and away from Woody but the closure was just too great and the two aircraft collided over the desert.

As the airspeed bled down and Woody continued the turn, he felt the impact from the F-22's right wing clipping his left wing. The aircraft suddenly rolled violently and then started to spin.

"Uh oh," Woody said as he struggled to regain control.

As he had been trained, Kruger started calling off altitudes as the world tumbled around them. "Fifteen thousand!"

Time seemed to stand still as Woody struggled to stop the spin and regain control. He had no idea what control surfaces even worked after the impact, but he was determined not to lose the aircraft.

"Twelve thousand!" Kruger yelled.

"Cobra One-Two, status?" Spectre asked over the radio as he and Cowboy noticed that Woody and Kruger were no longer maneuvering in relation to them.

"A little busy!" Woody managed to get out over the radio as he continued to fight the aircraft.

"Ten thousand!" Kruger warned. They were descending like a brick and had less than two thousand feet to go before reaching their designated "uncontrolled ejection altitude" below which it would be unsafe to punch out.

In a last-ditch effort, Woody split the throttles and put in a full boot of rudder. With one throttle in full afterburner and the other at idle combined with the rudders, he hoped to at least slow the spin and get the aircraft flying again.

"Nine thousand!"

"Woody?" Spectre asked over their radio frequency. "You guys okay?"

"Standby!" Woody yelled.

Woody's plan started to work. The tumbling of brown and blue started to slow.

"Eight thousand! We gotta go!" Kruger said over the intercom.

"Negative! I got this!" Woody said.

"Seven thousand!" Kruger said.

"I got it!" Woody reassured him.

"Five thousand!"

The tumbling slowed to a wobble. Woody ripped the lone throttle to idle as they exited the spin and the ground rushed toward them.

"Four thousand!"

Woody tried to pull back on the stick, but as he did the aircraft tried to roll. He fought it with rudder and decreased his pull.

"Three thousand!" Kruger warned.

"She's flyable. I got it!"

"Cobras knock it off, Cobra One-One knock it off," Spectre called over the radio. "I'm heading to your position.

"Still busy!" Woody replied. He was fighting the jet as it continued to descend. They were still fifteen degrees nose low and pointed at the rocks beneath them. He tried to deploy the speedbrake but it only made the rolling motion worse.

"Two thousand!" Kruger warned.

"We're recovering," Woody replied calmly. He continued easing back on the stick as he managed the throttles and rudder to keep the wings level.

"Fifteen hundred," Kruger said.

"We're leveling off," Woody said as the nose finally tracked through the horizon and he breathed a sigh of relief.

He looked over at his left wing. Half of it appeared to be missing and it was streaming a fluid.

"Woody, are you guys down at fifteen hundred?" Spectre asked.

Regaining his composure, Woody said, "Yeah, we just had a midair with a Raptor. Not sure what happened to him though."

"He's at our left, seven O'clock low," Kruger said over the intercom.

Woody looked over his shoulder and saw the billowing smoke from the crash site. His stomach turned as he realized the Raptor had crashed. He only hoped the pilot flying had been able to make it out.

"I see it," Woody said. He looked up and saw another Raptor orbiting above the site. "Looks like his wingman is overhead."

Woody keyed up the radio. "Spectre, heads up, one of the Raptors crashed and his wingman is playing on-scene commander at ten thousand feet. I'd avoid the area."

"I see him," Spectre said. "And I'm visual with you at two miles. I'll rejoin and we can get a battle damage check."

"Cleared in," Woody replied. "I'm putting home plate on the nose."

Spectre moved to within a few feet of Woody's aircraft. Starting on the right side he climbed up to check the top and then descended to cross underneath, slowly inspecting the damage until he reached the left side and climbed up once more. After he finished the check, he returned to Woody's left wing.

"Looks like the tip of the left vertical stab is gone and at least a quarter of your wing. There's hydraulic fluid and fuel streaming out of the wing but it doesn't appear catastrophic, how's the controllability?" Spectre asked.

"Shitty!" Woody replied. His leg was starting to get tired from the pressure on the rudder pedal.

"Let's climb up and get a controllability check and see if we can get it configured," Spectre said. "You may have to jettison the aircraft."

"Not after all we went through!" Woody shot back. "This jet is going home."

"We've got another jet, bub," Kruger said from the backseat. "Just saying."

"We're twenty miles from the field," Spectre said. "Let's climb up to at least twelve thousand and configure."

"Copy," Woody replied as he slowly added power and raised the nose.

When they leveled off just above twelve thousand feet, Woody gave Spectre the visual signal that the landing gear was coming out. Spectre configured with him and the two aircraft lowered their landing gear. It was important that Spectre be in the same configuration to give Woody a reference for angle of attack and airspeed values of a normal aircraft.

As the gear lowered, the rolling tendency actually decreased slightly. "So far, so good," he said over the radio.

He started slowing to the approach angle of attack. As the jet slowed below two-hundred knots, the rolling tendency grew more pronounced. At a hundred and seventy knots, the aircraft started to roll.

"Looks like no slower than one-eighty," Woody said over the radio as he added power. He had taken the minimum controllable airspeed and added ten knots as a safety factor.

"Copy that," Spectre said. "The field is one o'clock and twelve miles."

"In sight," Woody said. "In the descent now."

Spectre moved to a chase position and followed Woody down. He chased the crippled aircraft down to fifty feet and leveled off as he watched the landing. Woody touched down fast but had no issues slowing down on the massive thirteen-thousand-foot runway.

Satisfied that Woody was safely on the ground, Spectre retracted the gear and entered the overhead pattern. He and Cowboy landed just as Woody's aircraft was being towed back to the hangar, dripping fuel and hydraulic fluid.

"So, what does all this mean now?" Cowboy asked as they taxied in.

"We're fucked," Spectre replied solemnly. "Again."

CHAPTER TWENTY-FIVE

Kruger and Spectre were flown to Nellis by Jenny an hour after they had landed in their SU-30s. They were wearing the same non-descript flight suits as before, although this time Kruger wore Colonel rank on his shoulders. As Jenny taxied the Gulfstream to a stop on the transient ramp, the Wing Executive Officer was once again waiting to escort them.

They were taken to the Red Flag building, processed through security, and given visitor badges. They were escorted into the vault where pilots from multiple countries were rushing about. The Wing Exec explained that they had been in the middle of an international Red Flag and all aircraft had been recalled and the exercise terminated for the day in the wake of the Class A mishap.

Spectre had been there once before while flying the F-16. He had participated in a Red Flag shortly before his second deployment to Iraq. It had been an eye-opening experience to see all of the various aircraft come together in such a massive exercise, simulating the first week of a major conflict. He wondered if these aviators would soon be putting their training to the test in a war with North Korea. It was starting to seem more and more likely.

The Wing Exec took them upstairs to yet another inner vault and walked them into a briefing room where two men were sitting and talking. The older pilot was a Lieutenant Colonel and his nametag simply read "Dawg" while the younger pilot was a Captain who went by "Blade."

Dawg turned and faced Kruger and Spectre as they walked in behind the Wing Exec.

"Sir, I'd like you to meet Lieutenant Colonel Young and Captain Willis. Captain Willis is the mishap wingman from today's event," the Wing Exec said to Kruger before turning to the two pilots. "Gentlemen, this is Colonel Kruger and Major Specter, Air Force liaisons to DARPA."

The pilots shook Spectre and Kruger's hands. They were using cover identities given to them through the CIA to allow them full access to the base and its aircrew.

"Were you one of the pilots that flew into Restricted Area Sixty-Nine-Oh-One?" Kruger asked the Lieutenant Colonel.

"No, sir," Dawg replied.

"Then you are excused," Kruger replied gruffly as he nodded to the Wing Exec.

"Sir, I'd like to sit in on this meeting," Dawg replied.

Kruger looked at the young captain sitting at the table. His eyes were bloodshot and he had the all-too-familiar thousand-yard stare Kruger had seen a hundred times before. "You okay, son?"

"I'm fine," Blade replied.

"Sir, with all due respect, this is my squadron," Dawg protested. "I have a pilot in critical condition from being hit by what I can only assume by your presence is your aircraft. I think I deserve answers."

"You *deserve* answers?" Kruger asked angrily.

Spectre could see the rage building in Kruger and intervened. "It's fine. We'll debrief both of you when this is done. Let's start with why two Raptors were in the restricted area in the first place."

"Is this safety privileged as part of the Safety Investigation Board?" Dawg asked.

Before Kruger could reach across the table and strangle the irritating squadron commander, Spectre motioned for him to sit. Dawg reluctantly complied and they all sat at the table.

"Look, we're not here for anything other than to find out what happened and protect our program. We're not part of the SIB or AIB or anything like that. We just need answers because what we're doing is vital to national security," Spectre said as they sat.

"I wasn't asking you, *Major*," Dawg replied and looked to Kruger. "Sir, I just want to protect my people. That's all."

"Alright, bub, I've had enou-"

Spectre suddenly slammed his hand down on the table and pointed at Dawg. "Hey, dipshit, look at me."

"Excuse me?" Dawg asked as both he and the captain jumped.

"You need to check your ego for a second and listen very carefully," Spectre said in a low growl. "You have no idea who or what you're dealing with right now. We're trying to do this the easy way, but if you keep this up, we're going to have to resort to alternative means. And I don't think you want to piss off the good colonel any more than you already have."

Dawg ran his hand through his hair and exhaled. "I'm sorry," he said, looking at Spectre. "It's been a long week and today has been a nightmare. My guy is in surgery and we're all a little on edge right now. I shouldn't have said that."

"Look, I get it," Spectre said. "We all want the same thing here. Just answer the questions and we'll be on our way so you can go deal with this mess. Fair?"

"Fair enough," Dawg replied.

"Good call, bub," Kruger said ominously.

"Blade, what happened?" Spectre asked the captain.

"We were escorting the strikers into the target area and Taco's nav system dumped," Blade replied.

"Taco was your flight lead?" Spectre asked.

Blade nodded.

"Major Dave Lory," Dawg added.

"Then what happened?" Spectre asked.

"We set up our CAPs and Taco said he was going to reset the system," Blade replied. "A few seconds later, he came back and said it was up and he was targeting a bogey, but the bullseye position he gave was out of the airspace."

"And for the rules of engagement, a *bogey* was…"

"Unknown aircraft without hostile intent," Dawg said.

"Continue," Spectre said.

"I tried to tell him that he was targeting something outside the airspace, but our comms were being jammed and it was intermittent."

"So, he went to visually ID it?" Spectre asked.

Blade nodded. "I left my CAP to support him."

"Did you also pick up the aircraft with your sensors?" Spectre asked.

Blade nodded. "A few minutes later he called a visual ID over the fight frequency that he had ID'd a hostile Flanker and then the next call was that they had run into each other and he was punching out."

"He said *Flanker* over the radio?" Spectre asked.

"I think so," Dawg replied. "It all happened so fast, but I remember being confused because we weren't fighting any Flankers. I figured he was just confused or it was a red air F-15 painted to look like a Flanker or contract red air or something."

Spectre and Kruger exchanged a look.

"Did you see the aircraft?" Spectre asked.

Blade shook his head. "No, by the time I got there, Taco had ejected. I assumed the role of on scene commander and started working search and rescue assets to go get him. I never saw anything else."

"How many aircraft were on frequency when he called the ID?" Spectre asked.

"All of the blue players plus the AWACS…Geez, I dunno. Thirty?"

"Can you give us the room for a second?" Kruger asked abruptly.

"Sure," Dawg said. "We'll be right outside."

"Thank you," Kruger said.

He waited for the two pilots to leave and then turned to Spectre.

"We're done," Kruger said. "There's no way to salvage this."

"Well, not necessarily," Spectre said. "It sounds like the only guy that actually saw us was the flight lead."

"And he called it out on the radio for everyone to hear," Kruger replied. "Right before he ran into us. They're going to investigate that. Not to mention, Woody was pretty shaken up after. I don't think there's any way to put the genie back in the bottle."

Spectre shook his head. "This is the Air Force. The investigation will take weeks and the initial investigation is safety privileged anyway. By the time anyone knows about it, we'll be long gone. Besides, we can blame it on contract red air."

"Contract red air?"

"Yeah, the government is spending money to have contractors act as adversaries. We could easily come up with a cover story that we were testing these aircraft for the Lyons Group Aviation Consultants. Coolio could make that happen with a few keystrokes, and I'm sure we can get the CIA to help create the paperwork to make it look legit," Spectre said.

Kruger considered it for a moment. "If you're wrong and this gets out, don't cry to me when you're rotting in a North Korean prison, bub."

Spectre smiled. "I don't know why we didn't do this sooner. I'm sure it will work."

CHAPTER TWENTY-SIX

"So, what does this mean for Woody?" Woody asked as he sat in the inner vault discussing the next steps with Spectre and Kruger. "Am I fired?"

"No, you're not fired," Spectre said before taking a long pull from his beer.

"Am I in trouble?"

"You're not in trouble," Kruger said.

"I broke your jet and a really expensive Raptor, though."

"You saved our airplane and prevented an even bigger mishap," Spectre replied. "But you *should have* ejected. You know that, right?"

Woody shrugged. "I had it saved, brah. How is the pilot?"

"When we left the base, they said he was just out of surgery and expected to make a full recovery," Spectre said. "It could have been a lot worse."

Woody shook his head. "That guy came out of nowhere. Should never have happened."

"You're going to have to put it behind you, bub," Kruger said. "Are you going to be able to do that?"

"Do I have a choice?" Woody asked.

"You always have a choice," Spectre replied. "This operation is completely voluntary."

"I know, but what I'm asking is whether there's a backup plan or not. If I say no, is America fucked as we know it?"

"We'll go to our backup plan," Kruger said gruffly.

Spectre looked at Kruger. "I thought there *was* no backup plan."

"There's always a backup plan, bub. But it's a limited probability of success option."

"So, basically, if I don't go, we're fucked," Woody replied.

"Pretty much," Spectre said.

Woody suddenly flashed a knowing grin. "Good. I just wanted that to be on the record for when you write your book about us saving the world, Spectre."

"Shut the fuck up!" Spectre said as they all started laughing.

"But seriously, what's next?" Woody asked.

"The techs will start tearing down the aircraft tonight for shipment," Kruger said. "Tomorrow, we're going to do a refresher course in resistance and interrogation and then take the jet to meet them."

"Whoa, whoa…*Resistance training*?" Woody asked.

"Better than average chance that one or all of us ends up in a North Korean prison," Kruger said flatly. "Time to brush up."

"In that case, I'd like to change my previous answer!"

"Too late," Spectre replied. "Your book is already written."

"Shit!"

FINI FLIGHT

"It'll be fine, Woody," Spectre said. "It's just in case."

"Spectre, if I end up in a North Korean prison, I'm gonna kick you square in the jimmy."

"Fair enough," Spectre said, still laughing.

"On that note," Kruger said as he stood. "Gentleman, if you'll give me the room for a few minutes, I need to make a secure call back to Langley."

Spectre finished the rest of his beer and tossed the bottle in the trash as he and Woody stood. "I'm starving, what's for dinner?"

"Hopefully it's Thai food," Woody replied.

Kruger waited for them to walk out and then walked to the desk in the corner. He opened the laptop and logged in, setting up the secure video teleconferencing system. He entered in the information for the direct connection to Director Chapman and then waited for it to connect. A few seconds later, the Director of Central Intelligence appeared on screen.

"What the hell is going on over there, Kruger?" Chapman barked.

"I'm gonna need you to check your tone, bub," Kruger warned. "I don't work for you."

"I'm sorry," Chapman said as he rubbed his temples. "What do you have for me?"

"The mission is a go," Kruger replied.

"What about the fallout from the mishap?"

"As long as the paperwork we discussed gets taken care of on your end, I think we have a good enough cover story to get us through the exhibition," Kruger said.

"It's been taken care of as you requested. DOD was completely on board."

"And my other request?"

"Citizenship for Natasha?" Chapman asked. "That's a bit tougher."

"It's non-negotiable."

"I get that, but that's something the President will have to weigh in on, and he's been a little bit preoccupied lately trying to make sure these peace talks don't fall apart. Believe me, I want to help you on this."

"She won't be able to go back to Russia when this is all over."

"I know that, and we will take care of her," Chapman said. "But citizenship is a bit more difficult."

"Tell the President that I will make a healthy donation to his reelection campaign if that will help."

Chapman waved his hand. "You don't need to do that, Kruger. What you're doing for us outweighs any campaign contribution you could make. I'm going to get you everything you're asking for, but some of it will take time. Trust me, I'm on your side."

"Never trust someone who says, 'Trust me.'"

"Kruger, you saved my life. I trust you and you know you can trust me. We will make it happen. But the other side of this, too, is that if the North Koreans get word that we're working on citizenship for Natasha, the whole operation might be compromised."

"Look, bub, she's all that matters to me."

"I will take care of it personally," Chapman said. "In the meantime, is there anything else you need before you head out? You have every asset available to you in order to make this operation a success."

"We're good, bub," Kruger said. "We will make it happen."

"Good. I can't stress enough how high the stakes are here. If you fail, a war with North Korea supported by the Chinese is almost a certainty. It will be a third world war with nuclear and EMP weapons. No one will come out a winner."

"Copy," Kruger said. "I'll be in touch once we're boots on the ground. Kruger, out."

CHAPTER TWENTY-SEVEN

The team's Gulfstream business jet landed at Vladivostok International Airport in Russia and taxied to the remote hangar on the south side of the field. The massive Antonov AN-225 transport was parked in front of the isolated hangar.

The team quickly disembarked and went inside the hangar where technicians were working to reassemble the two Advanced Flankers. Kruger and Spectre met with Natasha and Anatoly, while Cowboy and Woody wandered through the hangar, inspecting the progress of the crews.

Kruger and Natasha shared a quick hug and kiss. Spectre could tell the couple deeply loved each other, but both were too focused on their respective missions to let their relationship interfere.

"Everything is ready for tomorrow," Natasha said. "The meeting is set."

While Natasha and Kruger discussed Kruger's chat with Director Chapman, Spectre joined Cowboy and Woody as they stood next to one of the jets and watched the crews reattach the wings.

"So, this is how the bologna is made," Woody commented, gesturing to the partially assembled aircraft as he saw Spectre.

"This is a good team. The jets will be fine," Spectre said.

"Are you sure? I tried talking to them, but they just ignored me. I don't think they even speak English!"

"They're with DARPA," Spectre said. "And they've been instructed not to talk to anyone, just as *you* were before we left. Everything is strictly need-to-know."

"I wasn't going to talk to them about what we're doing. Just shooting the shit about the airplane."

Spectre gently grabbed Woody by the shoulder and turned with him to walk away from the jet. Cowboy followed, laughing to himself as he watched the chatty pilot struggle with the concept of not being able to make new friends.

"Come on, Woody," Spectre said. "Don't worry about them. Let's get our bunks set up for the night. We have a big day tomorrow."

As they started toward the back of the hangar, they suddenly heard someone yelling Natasha's name behind them. Spectre turned to see Viktor running toward Natasha and Kruger. He couldn't hear what Viktor told him, but he appeared frantic.

"I'm going to go see what this is about," Spectre told Woody. "Go ahead without me."

"Oh, here we go again," Woody said, shaking his head. "What could go wrong?"

"Relax," Spectre said with a grin. "You'll be very popular in Russian prison."

"That's what I'm worried about, dude!"

Spectre laughed as he walked toward the side door that Natasha, Kruger, and Viktor exited. He heard shouting in Russian just outside and his smile suddenly vanished. Something very bad was happening.

He slowly opened the door to find a half dozen armed Russian soldiers standing behind a Russian officer. He was angrily saying something to Kruger in what sounded like Russian as Spectre approached.

The soldier standing nearest the officer raised his rifle and pointed it at Spectre as they turned to see him. Spectre held up his hands and said, "Easy there. What's going on?"

"Who are you?" the officer asked in English.

"I'm just a janitor," Spectre replied. "Who are you?"

"This is Colonel Miron Ilyech," Kruger said before turning to the officer. "Did I say that right?"

"Do you think this is a joke?" Colonel Ilyech asked angrily. "I will have you all arrested."

"You are interfering with an FSB operation, Colonel," Natasha said in Russian.

"I checked with Moscow, my dear. There is no such operation occurring on my airfield. You are in violation of the law," he replied in Russian.

"What did he say?" Kruger whispered to Natasha.

"I said you are all under arrest," Colonel Ilyech replied in English. "Along with everyone in that hangar."

"Not gonna happen, bub," Kruger said calmly. "I recommend you get back in your vehicle and pretend you never saw us."

Colonel Ilyech laughed and then suddenly turned serious as he drew his handgun and pointed it at Kruger. The soldiers all pointed their rifles at Spectre and company in response.

"Do you dare mock me?" he asked. "You are in Russia!"

Kruger slowly raised his hands as Spectre, Natasha and Viktor followed suit.

"Colonel, I implore you," Viktor said in Russian. "There is a mistake in Moscow. This is an official operation and you are interfering with matters of national security."

"We will see about that," Colonel Ilyech replied in Russian.

"Can we do this in English, please?" Kruger asked. "Also, put down your weapon before I take it from you."

"Your arrogance is laughable," Colonel Ilyech said as he kept the weapon pointed at Kruger's forehead.

"I don't think so, bub," Kruger said before nodding toward the colonel. "Why don't you take a look at your chest?"

The colonel's eyes widened as he looked down to see the red dot of a laser trained on his chest. He looked to his left and saw that the men standing next to him also had them on their foreheads.

Seizing the opportunity, Kruger disarmed the colonel, flipping the gun around as he pointed it at him instead.

"Here's the deal, bub," Kruger said as the untargeted guards kept their weapons raised. "You're outgunned here. By a lot."

"This is an act of war!" Colonel Ilyech cried.

"Stop talking for a second and let me finish," Kruger said as he lowered the gun. "This can go one of two ways for you – if you lose the attitude, you and your men walk away with a little more cash in your pockets and the peace of mind of knowing that the world will be a safer place after we finish our operation. Although, you'll just have to trust us on that one because we won't tell you what it is."

"And if I refuse?" Colonel Ilyech asked. "Would you dare start a war with the Russian Federation?"

"Of course not," Kruger replied. "Because that would never happen. You see, everyone in that building works for me. And I don't work for anyone. We don't exist. No one will hear your cries. No one will find your bodies. Your families will never know what happened. Is that what you want?"

"Well, no, but…"

"Dude, he's offering you money and your life versus death. Are you seriously having trouble making that decision?" Spectre asked.

"I am a man of honor," Colonel Ilyech replied.

"C'mon out, boys," Kruger said over his in-ear transmitter.

Moments later, the rest of the team appeared wearing their body armor with their weapons trained on the soldiers. Tuna and Churchill took point while Sledge, Ringo and Dusty emerged from the flanks. Cowboy walked out from the hangar dressed in his armor as well, escorting Anatoly with a large suitcase.

"Tell them to lower their weapons and get on their knees," Kruger ordered Colonel Ilyech.

The colonel gave the order in Russian and the men did as they were instructed. Anatoly left his escort a few dozen paces behind and handed the suitcase to Kruger.

"One million U.S. dollars to distribute any way you see fit," Kruger said as he tossed it onto the ground in front of the colonel. "All we ask is for you to peacefully return to wherever you came from and forget you ever saw us."

Before the colonel could reply, Natasha pulled out her phone and unlocked it. She swiped to a surveillance photo of the colonel's daughter and bent down to show him.

"Consider carefully before you think of speaking of this to anyone, colonel," Natasha warned in Russian. "The consequences will be severe."

"Da," the colonel replied as he nodded nervously in agreement.

He slowly reached for the handle of the suitcase and looked up at Kruger. "I am sorry to have bothered you. Please have a good evening."

"Thank you," Kruger replied. "Good choice."

CHAPTER TWENTY-EIGHT

Spectre barely slept that night. It was a problem he had suffered his entire military flying career. He almost never slept before checkrides, first missions in combat, or important sorties. His mind just wouldn't shut down. He was always running through every possible scenario, chair flying it over and over in his mind.

He guessed he had gotten about four hours total by the time he rolled out of his cot and headed toward the small kitchen and break room next door. Kruger was already up, brewing the first pot of coffee as Spectre stumbled in.

"You look like shit, bub," Kruger said as he poured a cup and handed it to Spectre.

"I'll be ready," Spectre replied, accepting the cup. "But this will help."

"I know you will be. It's not you that I'm worried about."

"Woody?" Spectre asked after taking a long sip.

Kruger nodded as he turned back to the stove where he was making eggs and bacon for the team. "He sure complains a lot."

Spectre laughed. "That's just Woody. He's been kicked a lot in his military career. He's a good pilot. He'll be fine."

"What about Woody?" Woody asked as he stumbled in, rubbing his eyes. "Also, I smelled bacon."

"It'll be ready in a second," Kruger reported.

"I was just telling Kruger about your bad luck with the military," Spectre said.

"Dude, I'm just happy to be here," Woody said as he walked to the coffee pot. "Well, not *here* exactly, but you know what I mean."

The rest of the team made their way into the kitchen as Kruger served the eggs, bacon, and toast. They all seemed focused, but relaxed. Spectre had always been impressed with how professional the men and women he worked with could be.

The team ate breakfast together and then headed into the hangar for the mission briefing. The plan was for Spectre to fly with Cowboy and for Woody to fly with Kruger. They would fly formation with Natasha, Anatoly, and Viktor in the FSB's Global 8000 business jet. Once they were all safely airborne, Tuna and company would load up into the Gulfstream and fly to Osan Air Base to meet Coolio and Sierra to monitor the mission and coordinate the exfil mission if things went sideways.

When Kruger was finished briefing the group, the tactical teams led by Tuna and Churchill broke off to set up security and assist with the Flankers being towed out of the hangar. Kruger, Spectre, Woody, and Cowboy stayed behind to brief their mission.

"This is the easy part," Spectre said. "Our only goal is to get to Sunchon. If we make it that far, the mission has a chance."

Spectre briefed the takeoff and join-up with their Russian escorts and then continued into what they would do once in country. They had been through this dozens of times before during training, but this time it was live. They would only have one shot.

After finishing the "motherhood" and "meat of the mission" Spectre moved on to the most important part of the brief – contingencies. Unlike most training missions, this mission had a ton of them. He briefed what they would do in the event they were jumped by North Korean fighters, what they would do if targeted by North Korean surface to air missiles, and their plan for mutual support if one of the aircraft was damaged and had to limp to South Korea.

The worst-case scenario was ejection. They had an evasion plan of action, but depending on where they actually bailed out, their chances of escape ranged from not likely to *no fucking way*. Their best bet was to try to make it to the ocean where a SEAL team could hopefully pick them up.

In the event that only one crew ejected, the other couldn't loiter to provide support. They were unarmed, and the chances of losing the other aircraft too were high. They all understood that ejection meant they were on their own. It was a risk they all knew and accepted.

"Any questions?" Spectre asked as he completed the brief.

"When do we get the kimchi?" Woody asked.

"Sierra will have as much as you want waiting for us when we get to Osan," Spectre replied as he looked at his watch. "Let's get going."

The crews suited up and stepped to the aircraft. The two Flankers had been towed out of the hangar and parked next to the Global 8000. Spectre and Woody both completed their walkarounds, paying special attention to the pods that DARPA had installed on the left wing of each aircraft. The pods were designed to look like AA-12 air to air missiles but were actually highly advanced electronic attack pods.

With the walkaround complete, Spectre fastened his harness and climbed up the ladder. A crew chief followed him up and helped him strap in. Spectre shook his hand and the crew chief nodded. They hadn't spoken a word to each other the entire time he'd been in country, and Spectre didn't even know the man's name. It was all part of the compartmentalization of the mission.

Spectre did a preflight sweep of the switches in the cockpit, moving from left to right, and then turned the battery on. He turned the intercom on to establish communications with Cowboy in the backseat.

"Test – test. How do you read?" Spectre asked.

"Loud and clear, mate. How me?"

"Got you same. You ready back there?"

"Let's do it!"

Spectre gave the crew chief the signal and started the Auxiliary Power Unit (APU). It whirred to life just as Woody started his. As he went through the startup sequence and preflight checks, Spectre realized it might be the last time he ever started a jet. From this point on, they were playing for keeps.

Both crews went through their preflight checks and the Global 8000 crew started their aircraft. When his before taxi checklist was complete, Spectre looked over at Woody who gave him a thumbs up.

"Empire check aux," Spectre said on the secondary radio.

"Two!" Woody replied.

"Empire One-One, check," Spectre said over the primary frequency.

"Two!"

"Empires are ready," Spectre said, letting the Global 8000 pilot know that they were ready to go.

"Da," came the reply from the male voice. The Global 8000 began its taxi just as the orange glow of the sun peaked over the hangars.

Spectre and Woody turned their taxi lights on and followed. They were immediately cleared for takeoff as the Global 8000 reached the end of the runway, and one by one they took off.

Spectre rejoined on the Global's right wing as Woody rejoined on its left. They turned southwest and climbed. In just a few minutes, they would be entering North Korean airspace.

Spectre said a small prayer to himself as the Global checked in with the North Korean controllers, requesting permission to enter the airspace. He prayed that if he didn't make it out alive, that Michelle and Cal Jr would be taken care of and live happy and healthy lives without the threat of world war.

"Cleared into North Korean airspace," the advanced DARPA software translated the controller's words into Spectre's headset.

There was no turning back.

CHAPTER TWENTY-NINE

The radio was eerily quiet as they flew down the North Korean peninsula at thirty-two thousand feet. There wasn't much air traffic, and when they did hear other aircraft, the transmissions were extremely short.

DARPA had equipped their aircraft with a small computer that hooked into their communications systems that could translate both incoming and outgoing transmissions. It took a little getting used to, but it seemed to be working just fine so far.

The system would change the voice depending on who was talking, to allow the crews to more accurately decipher who was talking. It attempted to mimic the speaker as best it could, while still being comprehensible.

There seemed to be two controllers on frequency. One male controller spoke Russian to the FSB Global 8000 pilot leading their formation while a female controller spoke Korean to everyone else. So far, Spectre had only counted an Air Koryo flight and what sounded like a flight of two MiG-21s on a combat air patrol, but he suspected the military aircraft had their own air traffic control system entirely separate from the frequency they were on.

There was a bit of an undercast as they approached Sunchon. Spectre switched to the Automated Terminal Information System (ATIS) on the auxiliary radio. The airbase was reporting a broken ceiling of four-thousand feet and visibility eight miles with light winds out of the south.

Spectre switched back to the interflight frequency on the aux radio. "Looks like it'll be the low show, Woody. Four-thousand-foot ceiling."

"Copy you," Woody replied over the interflight freq. "Sounds like an adventure!"

"He's a sarcastic one, isn't he?" Cowboy asked over the intercom.

"Just remember, we're going to stay flat," Spectre said, reminding Woody of the demo profile they had briefed for their arrival. With a four thousand foot ceiling, they wouldn't be able to do the vertical maneuvering demo, which wasn't a bad thing since the vertical maneuvers had a decent chance of departure from controlled flight and impact with terra firma.

"Roger," Woody replied.

They started their descent toward the airfield. The Global 8000 was given a handoff to the Sunchon approach controllers. The pilot acknowledged and checked in as the formation approached the Sunchon Airport on the southwest side of the city of Sunchon in South Pyongyang. It was the home of the 55th Fighter Regiment consisting of MiG-29 and SU-25 jets and had a single eight-thousand-foot paved runway.

They stayed on the Global 8000's wing until they were safely below the cloud deck. It was a bit higher than four-thousand feet, but still not high enough to do any vertical maneuvering. The pilot of the Global 8000 advised the controller that the two Advanced Flankers would require a separate clearance and vectors before clearing Spectre and Woody to detach. The DARPA system perfectly translated the Russian pilot's command and Spectre raised the Flanker's big speedbrake to create separation.

As the Global 8000 continued toward the field, Woody rejoined on Spectre's right wing. "Empire One-One, turn right heading two-seven-zero," the North Korean controller said in Russian.

Spectre repeated the clearance, hoping the translator did its magic as he complied with the request. The controller was attempting to create spacing so that the Global 8000 could land well before Spectre and Woody arrived, which would allow them to put on a quick demonstration before landing. They had to do everything as if they were Russians trying to sell their fighter jets, which meant showmanship was everything. A key aspect of mission success meant making a good first impression that was credible to the North Korean dignitaries.

The controller vectored them around Sunchon while the Global 8000 landed at the air base. From the higher altitude, the city looked like any other he'd seen from the air. But, as the controller cleared them to lower altitude, Spectre saw that the buildings were outdated, worn, and falling apart in most cases. It looked worse than he had expected – almost post-apocalyptic.

The controller turned Spectre's flight back toward the field and asked Spectre if he had the field in sight. With the diamond in his HUD on the end of the runway, Spectre acknowledged that he did and the controller handed him off to Sunchon Tower.

"Sunchon Tower, Empire One-One," Spectre said, still wincing as he spoke in English, half-expecting them to realize the ruse and shoot him down at any moment with an KN-06 surface to air missile.

"Empire One-One, cleared to commence maneuvering," the controller replied.

So far, so good.

"Alright, Woody, push it up, let's make it loud," Spectre said over the interflight freq.

They accelerated to four hundred knots and lined up on Runway 15. Spectre took the flight down to five hundred feet as they approached the numbers of the dilapidated runway. As he looked down, Spectre wondered if they would blow a tire on the busted asphalt, a contingency he hadn't even considered in their pre-mission planning.

Spectre found the brightly-colored observation tent near the southeastern part of the field. It was on the ramp next to a half dozen MiG-29s parked in a row and he watched the Global 8000 pull to a stop next to it. Spectre banked slightly to the left and aimed for it as their show center.

"Standby," Spectre said as they approached. "3…2…1…ACTION."

On Spectre's command, they both lit their afterburners and turned away from each other. They each completed two-hundred and seventy degrees of turn, easing the pull so that they would create a head-to-head pass.

"Left to left," Spectre called, reminding Woody of their deconfliction plan.

"Left to left," Woody repeated.

As they merged, Spectre turned left across Woody's tail and Woody turned right, creating a single circle fight toward the viewing stand. They bled off airspeed, reversing direction each time they subsequently merged and crisscrossing in a flat scissors fight.

As they passed over the viewing stand, Spectre called, "Empire, knock-it-off. Empire One-One knock it off."

"Empire One-Two, knock it off," Woody repeated.

"Empire request left downwind," Spectre said over the primary tower frequency as Woody maneuvered to a trail formation behind Spectre.

"Cleared to land Runway One-Five," the controller replied.

"Cleared to land," Spectre repeated.

They turned downwind and Woody took spacing behind Spectre's aircraft. Unsure of the radio calls, Spectre resisted the urge to call "Left base, gear down, full stop," as he would've in his Air Force days.

Instead, he just lowered the gear and flaps and landed just past the numbers about five hundred feet down the runway.

"You think they bought it?" Cowboy asked over the intercom as they rolled out and Woody landed behind them.

"We're about to find out," Spectre replied.

He slowed the Flanker to taxi speed as he headed toward the viewing area. The runway looked even worse up close, filled with potholes and loose asphalt. It was evident that the North Koreans didn't believe in sweeping the runways for foreign object debris as the U.S. military did.

"Uhhh…boss, we may have a problem," Woody said suddenly over the aux frequency as Spectre turned onto the taxiway in front of the viewing stand.

"What's up?" Spectre asked.

"I think the jet might've sucked up a piece of this shitty runway on landing. I got a compressor stall indication on rollout and had to shut down the right engine," Woody said. "Sounded pretty bad."

"Fuck me," Spectre said as he dropped his mask.

"What does that mean?" Cowboy asked.

"It means that jet isn't flying anywhere anytime soon," Spectre replied over the intercom and then keyed up the interflight radio. "Copy. We'll deal with it after we shut down."

"Bloody hell!" Cowboy said.

"You got that right," Spectre said. "We might be fucked."

CHAPTER THIRTY

Woody taxied off the runway and limped the Flanker down the taxiway behind Spectre's aircraft. The number two engine had been successfully shut down and the Exhaust Gas Temperature (EGT) indication had come back down to within limits. There was no indication of fire or any other abnormalities.

"I knew we'd end up in a North Korean jail!" Woody said over the intercom.

"We're not going to end up in jail, bub. Just stick to the plan," Kruger replied from the backseat.

"How are we going to do a demo with only one engine?" Woody asked nervously.

"You won't have to. Just stick to the plan, don't say anything, nod, and smile," Kruger replied.

"Right," Woody said.

"How bad did the EGT spike?" Spectre asked over their aux frequency.

"I saw 980 before I shut it down," Woody replied.

"So, it's toast," Spectre said.

"Affirm!"

"Copy," Spectre said. "I'm going to take the spot in front of the viewing stand and you can park in the spot next to me. Do a quick post flight, but don't be obvious about it."

"Wilco," Woody replied.

He turned left to follow Spectre as they taxied by the row of SU-25s and MiG-29s. Some of the aircraft didn't even appear flyable, missing engines or seats. Woody wondered where the North Koreans were going to get the money for Advanced Flankers, but that wasn't his problem. He just wanted to kill the bad guy and get the hell out of there.

Spectre turned right into the poorly marked spot in front of the viewing stand. Woody continued forward for a few feet and then turned to line up on his mark. There were no marshallers or wing-walkers to guide him in, but he could see he had plenty of room.

He set the parking brake and shut down the good engine. "Canopy's opening," Woody announced as he hit the switch.

Two men ran in from the left and chocked the wheels of Woody's aircraft. They then ran back to where they had been standing, grabbed two ladders and returned to attach them to the side of the jet. Woody took his helmet off and pulled the Acces ear plugs out of his ears as he put the helmet on the canopy rail. He pulled a case out of his pocket and inserted the communicator he had been given. It was another gift from DARPA, specially designed to translate foreign languages and also had a two-way line of sight communicator with the rest of the team.

Woody wormed out of his harness and descended the ladder to where Kruger was already on the ground taking off his G-suit. "Remember, get an initial assessment, but don't bring any attention to what you find," Kruger warned in a low voice.

Woody nodded and quickly took off his G-suit and hung it on the ladder. He walked under the nose of the aircraft, quickly looking over it as he eyed the number two intake. He made his way down the fuselage and peered into the intake. As his eyes adjusted, he immediately saw the damage – a least four blades were completely mangled and two were partially bent. The motor had been completely fragged by a chunk of asphalt kicked up by Spectre's aircraft on landing.

He caught himself lingering and then quickly moved to the right main landing gear and continued his post flight inspection. The tires and brakes were in good condition, and there didn't appear to be any other damage to the intake. *They had that much going for them at least.*

Woody checked out the right wing and then moved down the fuselage. He stopped at the tail of the aircraft and did his best to hide his reaction as he saw the nozzle on the right side. It was heavily damaged and charred. It only confirmed what he already knew, but now he was worried that the North Koreans might also catch on sooner rather than later.

He finished the post flight inspection and then nodded to Kruger as he joined him at the ladder. "Totally screwed," Woody whispered.

"Nod and smile," Kruger said under his breath.

The two walked around the nose of the aircraft and joined Spectre and Cowboy at attention in between the two Advanced Flankers. He saw Natasha standing with Viktor, Anatoly and a group of North Korean generals. There was a camera crew filming them as Natasha gave them the sales pitch for the aircraft.

A group of soldiers approached as they waited. The men frisked Spectre and company for weapons and then went to the aircraft. They each climbed up the ladders, inspecting the cockpits for bombs or weapons before descending and returning to the group of dignitaries. The leader nodded and the group approached.

"Look sharp, boys," Spectre mumbled.

Woody immediately recognized Kim Jong-Un and then saw the target, Choe Il-Sung, walking next to him. They were followed by two other generals and an attractive female officer who appeared to be taking notes. A camera crew trailed as Kim Jong-Un approached Spectre at the far right of their formation.

As Kim Jong-Un smiled and shook their hands, Natasha began introducing the pilots by their codenames. Kim Jong-Un appeared to be uninterested in the background of the others, but stopped in front of Woody and pointed casually.

"This one is from where?" Woody heard him ask through the translator ear piece.

"Vladivostok," Natasha replied in Korean. "His mother is Vietnamese."

Kim Jong-Un appeared pleased by the answer, but Choe Il-Sung remained unconvinced. He walked up to Woody as Jong-Un walked away.

"He is pilot?" he asked in Korean.

"He is a great pilot," Natasha replied. "Of course, not as good as Dear Leader."

"Good flying," he told Woody in Russian. The translator ear piece worked almost too well. Had Woody not recognized that it was in Russian, he never would've known the little man was testing him.

"Spasibo," Woody replied, using the limited Russian he had learned in their crash course.

Choe Il-Sung seemed pleased by the response and nodded before rejoining Jong-Un. The team remained in place as

Natasha followed Jong-Un and company on a cursory walk around of the aircraft.

When they were out of earshot, Woody looked down at Kruger's gloved hands and whispered, "Did you do it yet?"

"It's done," Kruger replied without looking at Woody.

"Good, now let's go turn dinosaurs into hot air and get out of here."

CHAPTER THIRTY-ONE

It wasn't the first time ricin had been used in an assassination. On September 7th, 1978, dissident writer Georgi Markov was injected by a ricin pellet while walking in London. It was believed to have been shot from a modified umbrella carried by a Bulgarian KGB operative. The pellet injected 0.2mg of ricin directly into Markov's leg and he died four days later.

The gloves Kruger and Cowboy were wearing had been specially designed with micro-injectors that deployed when pressure was applied. A tiny, almost invisible spike would emerge from the forefinger and inject the victim with 0.1mg of a specially develop compound of the toxic substance. Within hours, the victim would begin exhibiting signs of illness.

The enhanced ricin compound would prevent the victim's cells from making the proteins needed for survival. The symptoms would initially appear to be gastrointestinal and then become more serious as kidney and liver failure set in.

Eventually, the victim would begin suffering from respiratory distress and death would occur within twelve hours. It was plenty of time for them to make their escape, provided everything went according to plan.

Kruger stared straight ahead at attention as the procession of dignitaries approached them. He immediately recognized Kim Jong-Un followed by Choe Il-Sung. All he needed was for the two of them to do exactly as they had done for every photo op the intelligence community had of them with fighter pilots, and the mission would be a success.

Although they were impossible to tell apart from normal gloves, only Kruger and Cowboy wore the specially designed gloves. There was no time for the pilots to change gloves while taxiing in, and the risk was just too high to wear them while flying. The team determined that having both Kruger and Cowboy wear them would be sufficient. They had also considered having Natasha or Anatoly wear them, but given the climate and time of year, they determined that there was no easy way to justify it if asked.

The smiling North Korean dictator started with Spectre and shook his hand. He thanked Spectre for the magnificent display and then said, "I'm a pilot too. Top pilot in North Korea."

Spectre smiled but said nothing as he shook Dear Leader's hand. Jong-Un moved on to Cowboy standing to Spectre's left and shook his hand. Kruger resisted the temptation to look down and watch the handshake as he hoped Cowboy wouldn't inadvertently deploy the micro-needle and kill the leader of North Korea.

Not that the little fat kid didn't deserve it for what he had done to his people, but that wasn't the mission. Jong-Un was at least making an attempt at peace talks with the President, and for those to continue unabated, he needed to stay in power. The only objective was to remove the wildcard from the deck by eliminating Il-Sung.

"This is Captain Rostov," Natasha said, introducing Kruger in Korean as she walked in front of Jong-Un introducing each pilot. "He is very experienced."

Jong-Un quickly moved to Kruger after shaking Cowboy's hand. Kruger made sure not to tap his forefinger. Two taps and a long press was all it took to deploy the micro-needle and inject the ricin.

"You fly great," Kruger heard Jong-Un say through his in-ear translator. Kruger forced a smile as he shook the dictator's hand. Jong-Un then seemed distracted by Woody and pointed at him.

Kruger didn't pay attention to what he was saying as Il-Sung moved to him. As Il-Sung reached out, Kruger shook his hand with both hands, double-tapping his forefinger on the back of the man's much smaller hands and then squeezing gently.

Kruger felt the micro-needle deploy and the small amount of ricin inject into the victim, but Il-Sung didn't seem to notice. He looked Kruger in the eyes and then turned his attention to Jong-Un's sudden fascination with Woody.

They asked about Woody's background, but Natasha managed to answer to Dear Leader's satisfaction and they continued to look at the aircraft.

"Did you do it yet?"

"It's done," Kruger replied without looking at Woody.

"Good, now let's go turn dinosaurs into hot air and get out of here."

Kruger looked at Cowboy who nodded in reply, indicating he had also been successful in injecting the poison.

Anatoly broke ranks from the group as they walked around Spectre's aircraft. He walked up to Kruger and said, "Jong-Un wants to sit in the cockpit."

"So? Let him," Spectre answered.

"He wants a pilot," Anatoly said.

"He knows we don't speak Korean, right? What good will that do?"

"One of you needs to be there," Anatoly insisted.

"Spectre, you go," Kruger said. "He's asked too many questions of Woody."

"Fine," Spectre said reluctantly. "But they need to get the fuel trucks out here and power carts going so we can get the hell out of this shithole."

Spectre left Anatoly with the others and went to join the crowd at the base of the front cockpit ladder. Kim Jong-Un nodded and then climbed up the ladder, plopping himself onto the seat. Spectre was frisked once more by one of Jong-Un's bodyguards and then allowed to follow him up.

He stood on the ladder as Jong-Un turned to his right and posed for pictures by the ecstatic camera crew. As Jong-Un started to flip switches, Spectre waved his hand, hoping to grab his attention. The man was like a toddler, trying to touch every display and switch he saw.

As Spectre waited for Jong-Un to lose interest and come back down, the dictator suddenly looked at Spectre and the smile on his face vanished. "I want to fly."

Spectre wasn't sure his in-ear translator was working correctly. *Did he just say he wants to fly?*

"I want to fly," Jong-Un said again.

Seeing Spectre's puzzled look, he made a flying motion with his hand. "Fly," he said in Korean as he simulated an aircraft taking off.

Spectre just nodded and smiled, not sure what to do. Jong-Un seemed thrilled with that response and excitedly started to get out of the seat, causing Spectre to descend the ladder to stay out of his way.

Jong-Un was helped down the ladder by one of the generals as Spectre stepped back. He overheard him tell Il-Sung and the others that he wanted to ride along in the airpower demo they had planned.

Spectre made eye contact with Natasha and shook his head. He overheard her tell Jong-Un that she would discuss it with her superiors, but Jong-Un insisted. He would have to go for a ride in the aircraft in order for the sale to go through.

Natasha excused herself and walked with Spectre back to where Kruger and the others were still waiting.

"What's going on?" Kruger asked.

"The little fat kid wants a ride," Spectre answered. "We need to tell him no."

"Well, he can't ride with me," Woody said. "I've only got one engine, brah."

Natasha looked back over her shoulder. Jong-Un was posing for pictures in front of the aircraft with the general. She shook her head as she looked back at Kruger. "We have no choice."

"What do you mean, *we have no choice*?" Spectre asked. "Of course we do!"

"I'm afraid not," Natasha said. "It will be seen as a sign of disrespect and may prompt a call to Moscow."

"Well, we can't take him with us across the border," Spectre said and then looked at Kruger. "Can we?"

"We're not kidnapping the North Korean dictator, bub," Kruger said. "But this could work out for us."

"How?" Spectre asked. "And how long before....*you know what* happens to *you know who*?"

"Relax, bub," Kruger said before turning to Woody. "But you may not like the plan."

"Oh, great!"

CHAPTER THIRTY-TWO

The refueling trucks had just pulled away from the aircraft as Natasha walked back to the group with Anatoly. Despite Woody's protests, the team had just finalized their plans to fly with Kim Jong-Un.

"Good news," Natasha said. "He doesn't actually want to fly."

"What?" Spectre asked. "I heard him say it – or, at least, I heard him translated."

Anatoly shook his head. "It was poorly translated, my friend. We spoke to Choe Il-Sung directly. It is merely a photo-op. He will not leave the ground."

"Speaking of," Woody said as he looked at his watch. "How's our buddy feeling? Shouldn't we be getting the hell out of Dodge soon?"

"He is not showing symptoms yet," Natasha said. "But we are running out of time."

"So, what is their plan?" Spectre asked.

"They will tow the aircraft with Kim Jong-Un in the front cockpit for propaganda purposes and then tow it back," Anatoly said.

"How long will that take?" Kruger asked. "Woody is right. We are on a timeline here."

Anatoly shrugged. "They did not say."

"What about the second demo?" Spectre asked. "Are they still wanting that?"

"We will find out when they return from their photo session," Natasha answered. "But I have heard that Kim Jong-Un may be leaving for Pyongyang shortly after his photo op."

"What does that mean? Can we go home?" Woody asked.

"We don't know yet," Natasha said. "It could mean asking us to stay until he returns. Or it could mean continuing without him for the tactical demonstration."

"Or it could mean going home?" Woody pressed.

"Woody, c'mon man," Spectre said.

"What? I'm a glass half full kind of guy!" Woody replied.

"When will you know?" Spectre asked Natasha.

Natasha turned to the jets. Kim Jong-Un, in full flight gear and helmet, was climbing the ladder into the front seat of Spectre's aircraft as film crews tracked his every move. She turned back to the group and said, "I'll go talk to them while he's filming and let you know."

"I can't believe what I'm seeing," Spectre said as he watched Kim-Jong Un with the rest of the group.

The little dictator climbed the ladder and was assisted with strapping in by one of the North Korean aircraft maintainers. He put his helmet on and posed for a picture before sliding the smoke-tinted visor down over his eyes. His oxygen mask hung loosely by his face as he smiled at the camera crew that were now standing on the ladder to get a close-up.

In the backseat, one of the base's pilots strapped in. "Why do you think he needs a backseater?" Spectre asked.

"It's all about appearances, man," Woody said. "Shows he's in charge."

They watched as they finished taking pictures and the camera crew descended back down the ladder. The ground crew removed both ladders and used the external canopy close switch to close the canopy.

"Dude, they're going to be roasting in there without the engines running and no AC," Woody said."

"All for appearances, right?" Spectre asked.

When the canopy was closed, Kim Jong-Un gave a thumbs up. The tug that had been hooked to the aircraft earlier began pushing the aircraft back as men with orange wands walked alongside each wing. They turned the Flanker around and began towing it down the taxiway toward the runway.

"I would almost feel bad for them if they weren't such a despotic regime," Woody said. "This is sad."

The Flanker reached the end of the runway and was positioned as if it was about to take off. The tow bar was disconnected and the tug moved away so that they could get multiple angles of Dear Leader at the controls, preparing to take off.

Natasha left the group and walked over to the group of generals standing with Choe Il-Sung and Viktor as they watched the photo-op take place.

"I've got a bad feeling about this," Woody said as they watched Natasha join Viktor.

"Relax, bub," Kruger said. "She knows what she's doing."

"She is very convincing," Anatoly added. "She will do what is best."

The photoshoot concluded and the canopy was opened as they hooked up the tow bar and the tug towed the jet back to where it had been parked. Kim Jong-Un was helped out of the aircraft. Spectre could see that he was sweating from being in the hot aircraft for the fifteen-minute ordeal. He took pictures with the pilot that had accompanied him in the backseat.

It wasn't until she took off her helmet that Spectre realized it had been a female fighter pilot. They posed together for several pictures and then Kim Jong-Un was ushered away by the entourage of generals.

Natasha returned, leaving Viktor with the group as she walked back to Spectre and company. "Okay, they are returning to Pyongyang," she said.

"What did they say about the tactical demonstration?" Spectre asked.

"They would like it to proceed," Natasha said. "And then they would like to escort you to Pyongyang for a demonstration there."

"With one engine?" Woody asked.

"They don't know that," Natasha replied. "I have not told them."

"Well, we can work with that, I think," Spectre said."

"Work with that?" Woody asked. "How? How am I going to shake a fighter escort with a single engine? I'm good, but not *that* good!"

"You won't have to," Spectre said with a knowing nod to Kruger.

"What? What did you guys do?" Woody asked nervously.

"Remember that plan that I said you wouldn't like all that much?" Kruger asked.

"Yeah…"

"Well, that's the plan we're going to roll with," Kruger said.

"I told you I had a bad feeling about this!"

CHAPTER THIRTY-THREE

Spectre wasn't a huge fan of the new plan, but after talking with Woody and Kruger at length about it, he agreed it was the only way. Their original plan to use the DARPA EA pods to cloak themselves and run away together during maneuvering was no longer valid. The single engine performance of the Flanker had put them at an extreme disadvantage.

It was a shortcoming he was about to experience firsthand. As part of their plan, they had swapped aircraft to give Spectre the wounded bird with Kruger in the backseat. It was the only way Spectre would approve such a risky mission – he wanted to personally fly the bad aircraft and assume the higher level of risk.

Spectre had more training than Woody from his time at Project Archangel and would be better suited to handle himself if they were shot down and had to evade North Korean forces to get back to South Korea. Besides, Spectre reasoned, he had talked Woody into this mission. He wouldn't be able to live with himself if something happened to him.

He taxied his Flanker behind Woody as they held short of the runway and two MiG-29s thundered down the runway doing a formation takeoff. They would serve as the adversaries for the tactical trials.

The North Koreans wanted proof of the SU-30's Active Electronically Scanned Array (AESA) and Infrared Search-Track Pod (IRST) capabilities before buying the specially designed Flanker. To test it, the two MiG-29s would accompany them to the working airspace just off the west coast of North Korea. They would each take a corner of the airspace and then turn toward each other for the simulated fight.

The engagement would be recorded through North Korean surveillance radar, video on all aircraft, and GPS data gathered from the participating aircraft. After the long-range engagements, another flight of two MiG-29s would replace the first two, and Woody and Spectre would be expected to demonstrate the Advanced Flanker's dogfighting capabilities against a formidable foe like the Fulcrum.

"Just relax, bub, everything is going to work out," Kruger said over the intercom from the backseat. "The plan will work."

As they had briefed, Kruger had decided it would be best for him to personally chaperone Spectre in case something went wrong and they ended up evading in country. He knew Cowboy would also do a good job, but Kruger believed it would be better for him to assume the risk since it was mostly his plan.

"This ain't my first rodeo," Spectre said. "I just hope the water is warm if we have to jump out."

The Sunchon Tower controller cleared Empire 11 flight for takeoff. Woody taxied onto the left side of the runway and pulled forward slightly. Spectre followed and continued to the right side, lining up next to him before looking over Woody's jet and giving a thumbs up.

Woody flipped Spectre off and then lit the afterburners. The earth shook as the Flanker accelerated down the runway. Spectre counted to five and then pushed the left throttle to afterburner. Typically, he would've waited ten seconds, but on one engine they had decided that five would be sufficient spacing. They were in uncharted waters and making up rules as they went.

The aircraft felt like it was taking forever to get up to speed. Impatiently, Spectre rotated slightly early, which caused the takeoff roll to increase even more. As they reached the midpoint of the runway, they finally went airborne and Spectre retracted the landing gear.

Spectre used the aircraft's datalink to follow Woody's aircraft through the overcast layer. When he emerged at just over three thousand feet, he called "visual" and Woody cleared him to rejoin.

"This thing is a pig," Spectre said over their aux frequency. "I'm crossfeeding the tanks but the fuel imbalance in blower is getting pretty massive."

"How much?" Woody asked.

"Four hundred pounds," Spectre said, indicating that his right fuel tank was four hundred pounds heavier. Without the right engine operating in afterburner, the left engine was siphoning off fuel faster than crossfeeding from the right fuel tanks would allow.

"Keep me posted," Woody replied. "FENCE in."

"Two!" Spectre replied as he completed his "FENCE" check to ensure his systems were setup for the mission.

Woody checked in with the Ground Control Intercept (GCI) controller. The controller gave him a heading and told him that the MiG-29s were seventy miles away on the west end of the airspace. They reported that they were ready to engage.

"Empire One-One is ready," Woody replied.

The controller gave them a vector to the west to begin the intercept. Spectre flew a mile off Woody's wing as they pointed at the two radar contacts on his screen. The Advanced Flanker's AESA was already tracking them, ready to hand off to the IRST for passive detection.

As they climbed through twenty-thousand feet, Woody called, "Action," over the aux radio.

"Good luck, brah," he added.

"C'ya!" Spectre replied as he rolled inverted and began a 5G pull.

He kept the burner lit as he put the first waypoint on their egress route to South Korea on the nose and descended in a forty-five-degree dive. The airspeed accelerated through five hundred and fifty knots as he punched through the undercast layer.

"Music on," Kruger announced from the backseat, indicating that their DARPA jammer was now on and cloaking them from North Korean radar. As far as the North Koreans were concerned, that would be Spectre's last known location as if he'd crashed into the water.

He shallowed his dive as they punched through the clouds, breaking out at two-thousand feet. The airspeed climbed through six-hundred knots as he reached one hundred feet off the water and leveled off.

The Advanced Flanker screamed by a few fishing vessels as Spectre did his best to keep the Flanker straight and level. The thrust from the lone operating engine caused a severe yawing moment to the right, requiring a near full boot of left rudder.

"Feet dry," Kruger called out as they made landfall and he sequenced to the next waypoint.

Spectre continued low over the flat land as he nervously watched the distance to Osan Air Force Base click down. They were low enough to see people in cars and make out foliage on the trees. The airspeed was pegged at five hundred and fifty-two knots – more than Spectre expected a lone engine in afterburner could hold.

As they crossed over highways and a water way, they reached mountainous terrain. Spectre used it as best he could, hugging the terrain and rolling inverted on the other side of ridges to stay beneath the radar coverage. Although the cockpit was cool, he was sweating as he tried to maintain the nose track with the rudder pedal. He had never flown a low level with only one working engine before.

"How are we looking?" Spectre asked as he looked at his radar warning receiver. It was showing an SA-2 SPOON REST surface to air missile target tracking radar active in the area, but it didn't appear to be tracking them yet.

"You're doing great," Kruger said. "The pod is still working."

The distance clicked down below fifty miles. Spectre worked the Flanker as hard as he had ever flown an airplane before, using every bit of terrain he could find to keep the aircraft hidden. He just didn't trust the technology to keep him safe.

As they neared Kaesong in their last dash toward the South Korean border, Spectre suddenly yelled, "Shit!"

"What's wrong?" Kruger said, grunting as he tried to stay balanced and keep his helmet from bouncing off the canopy through the violent maneuvering.

"That was a KN-06 SAM site we just passed!"

"They're not tracking us," Kruger replied. "We're good, bub."

"Yeah, but we might've just stirred them up for Woody and Cowboy!"

"Nothing we can do about that now," Kruger said.

Spectre knew Kruger was right. They had to maintain radio silence to stay cloaked throughout their run to safety. Any transmissions might be intercepted and triangulated. They also had to maintain the appearance that their aircraft had gone down over the water, to keep up their cover story once Il-Sung's death was eventually discovered.

They passed Kaesong and over the DMZ, climbing up and cancelling the afterburner as he traded airspeed for altitude over South Korean territory. Kruger flipped off the EA pod and switched the squawk to the pre-assigned code they had been given for their crossing into South Korea.

"Freedom One-Two, radar contact, cleared direct Osan," the controller said in English as Spectre checked in.

Spectre dropped his mask and breathed a sigh of relief. It was short lived, as Spectre immediately remembered that Woody was still in the middle of bad guy land.

"I hope Woody makes it okay," he said softly.

CHAPTER THIRTY-FOUR

"Empire One-One is ready," Woody replied to the controller as he looked over his left wing at Spectre's aircraft and saw him struggling to maintain position. He had pulled the power back to help Spectre maintain position in the climb, but the aircraft just didn't have as much thrust as Woody's fully-operational jet. It also appeared to be yawing heavily to the right.

"Fly heading two-seven-zero," Woody heard the controller's translated voice say. They were speaking in Russian, still under the assumption that Woody and Spectre were Russian demo pilots.

"Two-seven-zero," Woody replied as the DARPA device translated it.

"Enemy aircraft two-seven zero, one hundred and fifty, ten thousand, hot," the controller reported. It was a "BRAA" call in which the controller gave their target's bearing, range, altitude, and aspect. The two MiG-29s were due west of their position at a hundred and fifty kilometers, and ten thousand meters above the ground, pointed right at them.

It was an awkward transition for Woody, having exclusively used imperial measurements his entire career, but after some quick math in his head, he gathered that they were roughly seventy-five nautical miles and thirty thousand feet.

"I've got'em, mate," Cowboy reported from the back seat. "Two contacts on your screen."

The Flanker's AESA radar was easily tracking them. Woody was sure the MiG-29s still had no radar contact at that range. They were older Fulcrums with very basic radar and weapons systems. It was unlikely that the pilots had any situational awareness at all. They were being driven around by the controllers using standard third-world tactics.

As they climbed through twenty-thousand feet, Woody looked over at Spectre and called, "Action."

Spectre's aircraft suddenly rolled inverted. "Good luck, brah," Woody added.

"C'ya!" Spectre replied as he pulled away from the formation.

Woody watched Spectre's aircraft hurtle toward the undercast layer. He watched the jet scream toward the cloud deck with its single afterburner lit until it punched through the clouds and was out of sight.

"MiGs are at fifty miles, mate," Cowboy announced.

"Empire One-Two has crashed!" Woody yelled over the fight frequency.

"Say again?" the controller replied.

"My wingman has crashed!" Woody replied frantically over the radio.

Woody started a left-hand turn and shallow descent. "I am descending to look for them," he said over the radio.

"I sure hope they buy this," Cowboy said.

FINI FLIGHT   215

"They will," Woody said. "Just be ready to turn the pod on when I tell you."

"My finger is on the switch. Just say when."

"Empire One-Two, say position," the controller said frantically.

"Empire One-Two has ejected," Woody said. "I am descending to look for them."

"Negative. Maintain heading and altitude," the controller replied.

"Is the translator not working or are they just this dense?" Cowboy asked over the intercom.

"It's probably a North Korean-ism," Woody replied. "Mission at all costs."

"I see the parachutes," Woody said over the radio. "I am going below the clouds to look for the survivors."

Woody tightened his spiral down toward the cloud layer with his throttles in idle. As he reached ten thousand feet, a new controller seemed to take over. "Empire One-One, you are instructed to turn to heading one-two-zero and standby for escort to Pyongyang."

"Empire One-One," Woody replied while ignoring the instruction.

All he needed to do was buy Spectre a little time to get a head start before the North Koreans realized what was going on. With the DARPA jammers working and radio silence, there would be no way of knowing Spectre's status until they were both safely in South Korea.

Woody punched in the waypoint for Osan Air Base and dove toward the cloud layer. As he punched through, he yelled, "Now!"

"Music on," Cowboy replied.

Woody lit the afterburners and accelerated to six hundred knots as he punched through the bottom of the cloud layer. He descended down to fifty feet over the water as he put Osan on the nose and started their mad dash to safety.

Their radar warning receiver lit up as they crossed the southern edge of Pyongyang's airspace. A flight of two MiG-21s had been scrambled to intercept them. The jammer was doing its job and they were unable to lock on to Woody's Flanker, but they were airborne and likely trying to intercept the spurious primary radar returns Woody's jet caused as he maneuvered and blanked the jammer's signal.

Woody cancelled the afterburner as they hit seven hundred knots indicated airspeed. Although it was more than fast enough to outrun the MiG-21s, Woody needed to slow down to maintain maneuverability as they approached the mountainous terrain in front of them.

Cowboy grunted in the back as Woody exploited the limits of the SU-30's performance. He flew below the ridge lines, popping up just high enough to cross terrain in front of him and then pulling five Gs at 120 degrees of bank to duck back down below and out of radar coverage.

The MiG-21 indications went away as they continued toward Osan. A few random surface to air missile sites had their radars in search, but none found Woody's aircraft. The jammer was working beautifully.

It was the most taxing and exhausting maneuvering he had ever done, but deep down Woody was loving every minute of it. It was exactly what he had spent his whole life training for. It wasn't until they reached the southern edge of Kaesong that Woody's bliss suddenly vanished.

His radar warning receiver was silent, but Woody visually picked up two smoke trails heading toward his aircraft in the distance. He banked hard right toward the border as he realized they were missiles. He hoped they would trail aft of on his canopy – an indication that they weren't guiding on his aircraft.

FINI FLIGHT

Instead, they moved slightly forward and mostly maintained position. They had been launched optically and were being guided by a continuous wave illuminator by the technician in the surface to air missile battery.

"Missiles inbound!" Woody said over the intercom.

He turned to put them on his right wing, hoping the jammer would do its thing and they would lose track. When they continued for his jet, Woody yelled, "Get ready!"

He tried a last ditch roll over the missiles, hoping to out maneuver them in the end game. The first missile lost track and continued flying toward the city, but the second fused as it flew under Woody's aircraft.

Master Caution and Fire Warning alarms suddenly went off in Woody's helmet as he recovered from the roll and tried to turn back south toward friendly territory. The aircraft was sluggish. He looked down and saw the left hydraulic gauge drop to zero and the exhaust gas temperatures on both engines spike.

"We're on fire!" Cowboy said. "We gotta get out, mate!"

"Bailout, bailout, bailout!" Woody said as he steadied his helmet against the headrest, assumed a good body position, and pulled the ejection handle.

CHAPTER THIRTY-FIVE

Spectre's Flanker was surrounded by blacked-out SUVs with flashing blue lights as he and Kruger taxied clear of the runway at Osan Air Base in South Korea. The four vehicles escorted him to a remote hangar on the southwest corner of the field.

Armed men exited the vehicles as Spectre parked in front of the hangar. He was marshalled into position and given the "cut" signal to shut down his only operating engine. As the engine spooled down, crews immediately hooked up a tow bar and tug to his aircraft and towed the jet into the hangar.

The large hangar door closed behind them and ladders were hung on the side of the jet. Spectre and Kruger exited the aircraft and were greeted by Sierra Carter.

"Where are Woody and Reginald?" Sierra asked, referring to her brother by his first name.

"You haven't heard from them?" Spectre asked nervously as he started to unzip his G-suit.

"We were down to one engine, so he stayed behind as a diversion," Kruger explained. "Have you heard anything from Natasha?"

Sierra frowned. "I was hoping you had news. We haven't heard anything since your update when you landed in country."

"Okay, well, we need to-"

Kruger was cut off by Coolio sprinting into the hangar. "Kruger, I found them!" he yelled frantically.

"Found who? Natasha?" Kruger asked as he tossed his G-suit to the side and moved toward Coolio.

Coolio stopped in his tracks. "No…umm…Woody and Cowboy…I found them!"

"Found them? Where?" Sierra asked.

"Well, not them, but I found a possible location," Coolio said.

"Spit it out, bub."

"Right, well, intel reports a KN-06 surface to air missile engagement near Kaesong. I've got a satellite feed of the wreckage but no visual on survivors yet. North Korean military is all over it. They're calling it a defection attempt by Russian pilots," Coolio said.

Kruger grabbed Coolio and spun him around, turning him toward the door. "Let's go find them. Spectre, a jet will take you home shortly. Thanks for your help."

"Wait, what about Woody?"

"We've got it covered," Kruger said without turning around.

Spectre jogged to catch up to them. "That's it? After all of that?"

Kruger abruptly turned around and faced Spectre, causing him to abruptly stop. "You did your part. You will be compensated for your services. Now, it's time for you to go home. I know how you are and I'm not risking you getting yourself into a situation that we would have to get you out of in North Korea."

"I can't just leave Woody like that!"

"You can and you will," Kruger growled. "Look, bub, I don't have time to argue with you. We appreciate what you did, but right now, we have to focus on getting our people out of North Korea. Go home. Spend time with Michelle and Cal Jr. The money will be sitting in your account by the time you land."

"It's not about the money. Woody is my friend."

"And we will do everything we can to get him home. Now, if you'll excuse me."

Kruger turned back with Coolio and Sierra without waiting for a reply. They walked through the hangar into a SCIF where Coolio had set up his computer network to monitor their operations in North Korea.

Coolio rushed to his desk and pulled up the satellite view of the wreckage. At least fifty North Korean soldiers appeared to have secured the wreckage while others seemed to be combing the area, looking for the downed pilots.

"What about their personal locator beacons?" Kruger asked.

"Nothing yet, although it's possible they turned them off to avoid detection," Coolio said.

"Find them," Kruger said before turning to Sierra. "Where are Tuna and the rest of the team?"

"Tuna and Ringo are in the base command post having a video teleconference with Director Chapman," Sierra replied. "And the others are pulling security around the hangar."

"Can you please find them and get them here? We're going to need to put together a quick reaction force to go get our boys."

"I'm on it," Sierra replied as she turned and walked out.

"Coolio, get me everything you can on the crash site – terrain, strength of forces, possible hole-up locations. We're going to need it ASAP and-"

"Uhh, boss," Coolio said, interrupting Kruger as an alert dinged on his computer.

"What?"

Coolio clicked on the icon and brought up a video feed. It was North Korean state television.

"I set up an alert for anytime facial recognition software picked up Choe Il-Sung on North Korean television," Coolio said as he expanded the window.

The video showed Kim Jong-Un walking with Choe Il-Sung as they inspected a North Korean military unit in Pyongyang.

"When was this taken?" Kruger asked.

"It's live," Coolio replied. "Shouldn't he be…dead?"

Kruger looked at his watch. It had only been six hours since his handshake with Il-Sung. It was still within the window of four to eight hours for the specially formulated ricin to take effect, but his presence at the meeting was definitely a bad sign. He appeared completely healthy and unaffected.

"Can you pull up the latest satellite images of Sunchon Airport?" Kruger asked.

"Sure, but, why?"

"Just do it," Kruger barked.

Coolio did as instructed. With a few mouse clicks, he had a satellite view of the airbase Kruger and Spectre had just barely escaped.

Kruger pointed to the ramp where the viewing stand had been set up. "Can you zoom in there?"

As Coolio zoomed in, Kruger's worst fears were confirmed. Natasha and company were supposed to fly out after Woody and Spectre. They would head back to Russia under the pretense that they had been recalled due to the crash. The fact that their jet was still sitting in the exact same place it had been when Kruger and company had taken off was a very bad sign.

Sierra walked in with Tuna and Ringo in tow as Kruger stayed glued to the satellite image.

"What's going on?" Tuna asked. "Glad to see you made it!"

"We've got problems," Kruger said as he pointed to the screen.

"What's up?" Tuna asked.

"Take your pick. The target is still alive, Woody and Cowboy were shot down in North Korea, and Natasha, Viktor, and Anatoly are still in Sunchon," Kruger said. "Total mission failure."

"Wait, what?" Sierra Carter asked as she pushed Kruger aside to look at the screen. "What do you mean Il-Sung is alive?"

Coolio switched windows to the live feed of Il-Sung with Jong-Il in Pyongyang.

"That's impossible," Sierra said. "When did you administer the toxin?"

"Six hours and twelve minutes ago," Kruger said, looking at his watch.

"And you're sure it was him? And not a body double?"

"It was him," Kruger said.

"What about Woody and Cowboy?" Tuna asked. "Have we made contact yet?"

"Radio silence so far," Coolio said. "The only thing I've been able to find is the wreckage."

"Jesus Christ," Tuna replied, running his hands through his hair. "Okay, so we need to get a QRF package together to go get them, and then figure out what to do about Il-Sung."

"I think they've got Natasha," Kruger said.

Tuna grabbed Kruger by the shoulders and looked him in the eye. "We'll get her back. This is a shit sandwich that we're going to have to handle one bite at a time, but I promise you, no one will get left behind."

CHAPTER THIRTY-SIX

Cowboy finished hiding his parachute just as he heard the North Korean troops approaching his position. He had landed a few hundred meters from the crash site on the side of a hill overlooking Kaesong. He counted at least a half dozen armed soldiers spread out and searching for him and Woody.

He had no idea where Woody had landed. His in-the-ear communicator/translator had failed during the ejection sequence. It was nothing but high-pitched squealing and static, so he tossed it and instead went to work assembling the CQB M4 rifle from his seat kit. It had a 10.5-inch barrel with integral suppressor and was chambered in .300BLK. He had four thirty-round magazines and a Sig P320RX chambered in 9MM with two extra 17-round magazines. It was unlikely that he would be able to fight his way out of the country against the North Korean Army, but he hoped it would at least buy him enough time to move to high ground and radio for help with the PRC-112G rescue radio from his seat survival kit.

Cowboy applied the green and black face paint from his seat kit and then started moving slowly. The soldiers were spread out in a V pattern, holding their AK-74 rifles up and ready. Cowboy had no intention of engaging them – he just wanted to find Woody and work on getting out of there.

He moved slowly through the brush. The thick canopy of trees overhead blocked the afternoon sun, helping to conceal his movement in the shade. He heard a radio squawk as the voices grew louder.

As Cowboy moved further up the hill, the radio chatter and voices moved farther away. He could hear them yelling, but it was becoming evident that they were moving away from his position. Cowboy worried that they were onto Woody's trail, so he turned to parallel the patrol and followed the sound of their radios and voices.

He moved slowly through the trees, careful not to make any noise as he kept his rifle low and ready. He could see the soldiers in their dark green camouflage as they moved toward a small clearing at the base of the hill. They appeared to be moving with a purpose – no longer searching for signs of survivors.

Cowboy stopped as he saw the group of soldiers crowd around the base of a tree at the edge of the clearing. He pulled a small pair of digital binoculars from his survival vest and zoomed in. His stomach turned as he saw the one of the soldiers hold up dark green fabric. *Woody's parachute!*

His suspicions were confirmed as one of the soldiers moved out of the way. They were standing over someone, and appeared to be removing gear as they handed it from one soldier to the next. It was definitely Woody.

FINI FLIGHT

They bound Woody's hands and feet and then four men helped carry him out. Woody appeared to be unconscious – at least, that's what Cowboy was hoping. There was no way to tell Woody's condition, even using the advanced digital binoculars. All Cowboy could see was that Woody didn't appear to be moving and his head flopped loosely as the men carried him out into the open area.

Cowboy considered his options. He counted eleven soldiers, but he was sure there were more at the crash site. He was confident he could take out the soldiers surrounding Woody, but he knew they would be able to radio for help before he could take them all out. And getting Woody to safety in this terrain with the North Korean Army bearing down on them would present a significant challenge.

He decided to move to higher ground to send a SITREP back to Coolio and Sierra. If Kruger and Spectre had made it out alive, they would be able to help extract them. If Kruger and Spectre were also down and in country, Coolio would help them link up and possibly figure out a way to rescue Woody. Either way, establishing communications was priority one.

Cowboy continued moving through the thick brush and headed back up the hill. He could see a small ridgeline in the distance and decided that would be the best place to establish communications. As he slowly crept up the hill, he heard a helicopter approaching his position and quickly found cover.

The helicopter zoomed overhead and then banked hard right before it disappeared from Cowboy's view. Cowboy continued to the ridgeline where he could see the smoldering wreckage of their crashed fighter jet. The transport helicopter landed and men in white coats exited. Cowboy guessed that they were technicians sent by the North Korean government to extract as much of the secret technology from the aircraft as they could.

Cowboy found a safe place to hide and then pulled out the PRC-112G survival radio. He powered it on and sent an initial data burst with his location information as soon as it acquired the satellites. That would ensure Coolio and the team would at least have a general idea of where to look in the event he was interrupted while trying to establish communications.

When he was sure the data burst went through, Cowboy went to the free text feature of the radio and began typing a message.

EMP12 DOWN. 12A STATUS UNK/CAP. 12B MOB. ADV RV.

The message was shorthand to save time, but Cowboy knew Coolio would understand it. Empire 12 was down. Woody's status as to whether he had died or had been injured was unknown but he had been captured. Cowboy was mobile and able to move to an extraction point and he ended the messaged asking Coolio to advise the plan for rendezvous.

Two minutes after Cowboy hit send, Coolio replied.

EMP11 SAFE. HAVE U ON SAT. NK SURROUNDING YOUR POS. SENDING COORD FOR YOU TO MOVE. GO NOW.

Cowboy pulled out the handheld GPS from his survival vest as he loaded the next message from Coolio containing the coordinates. He plugged the coordinates into the moving map GPS. It plotted to a point near the Ryesong River about ten kilometers from his position.

Cowboy acknowledged the message and then powered down the survival radio. He placed it in his vest and then picked up his rifle. He waited a moment as he listened for signs of nearby troops, and then started to move when he heard none.

He transitioned across the "military crest" of the hill, staying 2/3rds from the bottom as he moved west toward the river. Cowboy made slow and methodical movements, careful not to make too much noise as he kept an eye out for North Korean soldiers looking for him.

FINI FLIGHT

Moving down the hill, Cowboy suddenly froze. He saw three North Korean soldiers moving up the hill to his left. They didn't appear to be headed toward his location, but they were moving in the right general direction. Cowboy decided to offset to the north and go back up the hill until he could be sure he was clear of them.

Carefully moving up the loose rocks and gravel on the side of the hill, a flash of black suddenly caught Cowboy's attention to his right. As he turned, he saw a North Korean soldier moving up the hill toward him with his rifle raised.

Cowboy froze, hoping the soldier hadn't seen him. The soldier fired a volley of rounds, sending rocks and dirt flying high and to Cowboy's left. He returned fire, hitting the soldier twice in the chest and once in the throat with his suppressed rifle.

As Cowboy turned to move down the hill, another volley of rounds peppered the side of the hill. This time from the opposite side. The other soldiers he had avoided had apparently moved in and heard the shots fired.

Cowboy tried to move quickly down the hill to escape, but the loose terrain made it nearly impossible. Cowboy started sliding down the side of the hill just as he felt a round hit him below his survival vest.

He started to tumble as he lost his footing and slid down the hill. His GPS and radio flew out of his vest. His rifle stayed with him only because the single point sling somehow kept it secured. He was only along for the ride as he descended the remainder of the hill.

A tree broke his fall, knocking the wind out of him as he came to a sudden stop. Cowboy tried to right himself as he slowly rolled over to find his rifle. He was dazed and disoriented but determined to push through.

As he turned to his right, a half dozen North Korean soldiers came running toward him from all directions. They yelled at him in Korean as they kept his rifles trained on him. Within seconds they were on top of him, beating him as they relieved him of his weapons and gear.

CHAPTER THIRTY-SEVEN

"No!" Coolio yelled out as he watched the near real-time satellite feed video and saw Cowboy captured by the North Korean soldiers.

Sierra rushed over to Coolio's workstation. She was alone with him in their makeshift operations center while Kruger and the rest of the team planned the rescue mission. "What is it? Is it Reginald?"

"He was just captured by North Korean troops," Coolio said.

"Bloody hell!" Sierra yelped as she leaned over Coolio's shoulder and watched them carry off her brother. "Can you track them?"

"I can try," Coolio said nervously.

"Don't try!" Sierra yelled in a sudden flash of anger. "Do it!"

"Okay, I'm trying," Coolio replied sheepishly.

"I'm sorry," Sierra said. "I know you're under a lot of stress."

"It's okay," Coolio replied as he tracked the group of soldiers hauling Cowboy through a clearing.

Kruger, Tuna, and Ringo walked in as Coolio and Sierra watched the satellite feed.

"What's going on? We heard yelling," Tuna said, leading the trio into the small room.

"Cowboy made contact and I gave him the evasion plan you gave me to send in the event of contact," Coolio said.

"That's great!" Ringo said. "So, why all the yelling?"

"Cowboy's been captured by the North Koreans," Sierra said.

"Are you sure?" Ringo asked.

"We saw the whole thing unfold as it happened," Coolio said, pointing to the screen as the group with Cowboy reached a small path and convoy of vehicles at the base of the hill. "He made contact and I found his location through his survival radio's coordinate burst. Once I had eyes on, I saw a group of North Korean soldiers looking for him. So, I told him to get moving to the next point and sent him coordinates. I never saw the soldiers that got him. They must have just arrived from a nearby area. But I watched him fight and then fall down the hill before they grabbed him."

"Fall?" Sierra asked. "You didn't mention a fall. Is he okay?"

Coolio shrugged. "I couldn't tell. He rolled down the hill and it looked like a tree stopped him. The resolution isn't good enough to tell whether he stopped himself or just stopped. I wish I could tell you more."

"What about Woody?" Kruger asked. "Have you found him yet?"

"Nothing from his seat's locator beacon, his personal location device in his G-suit, or his SAR radio," Coolio replied. "I'm searching every grid I can, but I haven't found him yet."

"Keep looking, bub," Kruger said. "And find out where they're taking Cowboy."

"I'll do my best, boss," Coolio said. "But this satellite isn't easily repositioned. If they take him outside the coverage area, I'll be blind. We need drone support."

Kruger turned to Tuna. "Can you make that happen?"

"I'll make a call to Langley," Tuna replied.

Coolio's computer chimed as Tuna headed out with his encrypted satellite phone in hand. Kruger turned to see the young analyst reading a classified file.

"What is that?" Kruger asked. "If it's not mission essential, skip it for now, and let's focus on recovery of our people."

"I hacked into South Korean intelligence services and set up a keyword search for anything related to Choe Il-Sung. I'm reading it now, but it looks like they believe he's planning to visit a missile launch and test facility near Kosong tomorrow," Coolio said as he skimmed through the secret document.

"Do they believe a launch is imminent?" Ringo asked.

"It doesn't say that, but it does say that the last time he visited a site, they did perform a rocket test and it is feared that he may do so again due to stalled peace talks," Coolio replied.

Kruger turned to Sierra. "Can you verify this intel with MI 6? I'll have Tuna look into it with the agency once he gets off the phone."

"Are we sure the agent you administered hasn't taken effect yet? This may not even be necessary," Sierra replied.

Kruger turned back to Coolio. He was back to tracking the vehicle that had taken Cowboy. "Any updates on the live feed of Il-Sung?"

"Nothing, boss. Feed ended twenty minutes ago and he appeared to be in good health," Coolio answered.

"We can't risk it," Kruger said to Sierra. "If there's any chance he's still alive and thinking about launching that EMP, we have to take him down."

"What about Reginald?" Sierra asked.

"We will send a team in to get him when we have a better idea of where they're taking him," Kruger said. "But the priority is Il-Sung."

"I agree," Ringo added. "We have to stop that little bastard before he starts a nuclear war. At all costs."

"Those are your teammates out there!" Sierra yelled. "My brother. *Our brothers in arms*. We can't just leave them there."

"Look, bub, I don't like it any more than you do," Kruger said. "No one is leaving anyone behind. Once you confirm the intel, Ringo and I will insert and take Il-Sung out. The rest of the team can work on extracting Woody and Cowboy."

"That's not enough people," Sierra replied. "If you and Ringo go to Kosong, and they take Reggie somewhere else, we don't have enough people to launch a rescue mission. They'll all die."

"Look, I get it. He's your brother and you're worried. In case you forgot, the woman I love is probably being held by the North Koreans right now as well. But we all knew what we were getting into when we signed up for this mission – including Natasha. Including Woody. And including Cowboy," Kruger said.

Tuna walked back into the room, carrying a small phone. He started to speak, but froze as he saw the standoff between Sierra and Kruger. "What's going on? I've got new intel."

"Kruger here wants to leave two of our own hanging in the wind to fend for themselves," Sierra said. The anger in her voice left no question as to what she thought of Kruger's plan.

"Well, not to throw a wrench into this any further, but Director Chapman just told me Il-Sung is expected to visit one of their test sites tomorrow. They're moving AEGIS cruisers into position expecting a launch. He wants us to go to Plan B if possible."

"Coolio just found the same thing," Kruger said. "I asked Agent Carter to verify with MI-6 and that's how we got into this."

"Well, if it makes you feel better," Tuna said to Sierra, "Director Chapman was also adamant that we bring our boys home. Not just because it's the right thing to do, but because Americans caught flying a Russian fighter in North Korea to assassinate a high-ranking cabinet member is a PR nightmare no one wants."

"Well then, I will join you," Sierra said suddenly. "You don't have enough men to do both."

"Ringo and I will execute Plan B," Kruger said. "Tuna, you can take the rest and grab Woody and Cowboy when we get more intel."

Kruger turned to Sierra. His voice suddenly softened. "I'm sorry. I know this is not easy, but I need you to confirm this through your sources. And if you can get us intel on where they might be taking Cowboy, that would help too."

"Okay," Sierra said softly.

"Coolio!" Kruger barked.

"Yes, boss?"

"Find Woody! *Now!*"

CHAPTER THIRTY-EIGHT

Cowboy drifted in and out of consciousness as the North Korean soldiers loaded him into the back of the troop transport. The soldiers had done a poor job of bandaging the gunshot wound on his left side, but they had at least tried. Cowboy knew they were only doing their best to keep him alive so they could interrogate him later. It was no act of mercy.

Four soldiers accompanied Cowboy as he lay on the floor of the transport. Its diesel engine was deafening as they bounced along what Cowboy could only assume was a dirt path to the main highway to Kaesong.

Cowboy ignored the pain of his injuries and tried focusing on formulating an escape plan. His wrists were zip tied behind his back, but his feet were unbound. He was working on wearing down the plastic restraints by slowly sawing them against the specially designed blade on the heel of his boot, but it wasn't easy due to the pain he felt from his wounds. In addition to the gunshot wound, he was pretty sure he had broken at least one rib during the fall and subsequent beating.

His guards seemed satisfied that he would stay put, ignoring him as the transport bounced around the rough terrain. They were chatting with each other and laughing, apparently comfortable with the idea that Cowboy posed no threat. They were each holding their rifle by the barrel with the butt on the floor – within arm's reach if Cowboy could free himself from his restraints. It was a longshot of a plan, but a plan nonetheless. Anything was better than ending up brain dead after spending any length of time in a North Korean prison.

Cowboy continued slowly working his restraints against the blade. He didn't want to completely sever the restraints, in case the transport made an abrupt stop to transfer him to another vehicle or the soldiers had to move him for some reason. He just wanted to weaken them enough so that he could easily break them once he saw his opportunity to escape.

The transport suddenly jolted, causing Cowboy to levitate momentarily before crashing back onto the floor on his side. The pain was blinding. He couldn't breathe as he struggled to maintain consciousness. He heard the guards laughing as he groaned in pain.

As Cowboy recovered, the ride suddenly turned smooth. The drone of the diesel engine was accompanied by the sound of the studded tires against the asphalt. They had finally hit the highway. Cowboy guessed they'd be arriving at their destination soon.

He did his best to shake off the pain and instead focused on the rifle nearest his head. He calculated that he could grab it and take out its owner before turning it on the guard next to him. After that, things became a little dicey as he would have to turn around and take out the other two guards despite his injuries.

FINI FLIGHT

Before he could finish his calculations, the transport suddenly slammed on its brakes. They came to a screeching halt, causing Cowboy to slide on the floor into the front wall. He heard yelling in Korean outside, indicating the stop was anything but planned.

Had the team come to rescue him?

The guards stood and grabbed their rifles. There was more yelling outside, followed by a rapid succession of gunfire, and then what sounded like return fire. If it was a rescue operation by Odin or Project Archangel, it was severely botched. Cowboy knew they would never go in loud with guns blazing like that. Stealth was almost always preferred – especially when trying to rescue a hostage.

Two of the guards pulled back the canvas and lowered the gate. They hopped out and joined the firefight that had begun outside. The other two exchanged confused looks and said something in Korean. Cowboy wished he had his translator, but from their facial expressions and based on his experience in the field, he was pretty sure they were asking, "What do we do now?"

He played dead as one of them looked down at him. As they turned their attention back to the outside, Cowboy used the blade to forcibly break his restraints. There was no need for stealth anymore. It was time to save himself while he still could.

The second guard walked to the opening of the transport to see how the fight was progressing, leaving the guard closest to Cowboy with his back turned to him. Cowboy decided to seize the opportunity.

With a surge of adrenaline, he leapt to his feet, using the sling of the nearest guard's AK-74U to choke him out. When the other guard turned to see what was happening, Cowboy drew the choking guard's sidearm and fired three rounds, causing the far guard to fall out of the transport.

Cowboy finished choking the guard and then relieved him of his rifle and sidearm as the man's body fell limp. He stuffed the handgun into his flight suit pocket and shouldered the rifle. The pain was almost too much to bear, but Cowboy pushed through. Every ounce of training he had received in the British Special Air Service and with Odin kicked in. He was in survival mode and refused to give up.

Hearing the noise, the third guard walked back to look inside. Cowboy fired a three-round burst, hitting the soldier in the chest with all three rounds. The guard fell back and Cowboy exited the transport, grunting as the drop jarred him. The impact on the asphalt caused his vision to blur due to the jolt of pain the impact sent through his body.

As he recovered, the gunfire suddenly stopped. Cowboy slowly moved to the edge of the transport, using it for cover as best he could. He had no idea where the threat was or who the North Korean soldiers had even been fighting, but he didn't plan on sticking around to find out.

He looked out and saw that they were on a two-lane road in a valley, surrounded by trees on either side. Cowboy looked down the driver's side of the transport and saw two North Korean soldiers taking cover. In front of the transport, two trucks were blocking the road. He couldn't see any other fighters.

He turned back toward the other side of the transport. Stepping over the body of the guard he had just dropped, Cowboy peered around the corner of the transport. It was a clear shot to the tree line and into the woods. It wasn't a clean escape, but it would at least give him cover to plan his next move. As he looked down, Cowboy saw that blood from his gunshot wound had soaked through his bandage and flight suit. He touched it with his left hand and pulled back a hand full of blood. He was rapidly losing blood. If he didn't get help soon, he'd be out of the fight completely.

He found an opening in the trees and brush and decided that would be the best place to make a run for it. Cowboy did a quick check over his shoulder to make sure the North Korean soldiers weren't approaching his position, and then started toward his target.

As he sprinted toward the opening, Cowboy heard an exchange of gunfire behind him. The pain in his side was nearly overwhelming and his legs were beginning to feel weak. He tried to push through the pain and weakness to keep his legs moving, but he could feel them starting to buckle beneath him.

Cowboy reached a small ditch and tried to jump without breaking stride. When he landed on the other side, his legs buckled, causing him to fall head-first into the brush. He had lost more blood than he thought and his consciousness was fading.

He tried to push through and get up, but he was too weak. As he rolled over, the last thing Cowboy saw was a man dressed in black carrying an AK-47 standing over him.

CHAPTER THIRTY-NINE

Plan B sucked. There was no getting around it. As Ringo checked Kruger's wingsuit and equipment a final time, the C-17 taking them to the edge of friendly territory and humane civilization depressurized to allow the cargo ramp to lower. Deep down, Kruger wondered if they had made the right decision, or if they were about to dive head first into making a bad situation even worse.

They were just over thirty-thousand feet above South Korea, wearing specially designed stealth wingsuits which integrated with their advanced body armor and allowed them to carry their gear while maintaining a small radar cross section. Their helmet-mounted displays gave them the ability to glide forty miles into enemy territory undetected while precisely popping their chutes and landing at their intended overwatch position. It also had infrared and night vision capabilities, since they were jumping nearly three hours before sunrise.

It sounded good on paper, but the technology was largely untested and it did nothing for them to get them out of the country once they were done. They would have to hump it out on foot after taking the shot, a feat that both realized meant it was likely a one-way mission.

But that's what they had both signed up for. They knew it. They didn't like it. It was the cost of freedom. That was the price of saving hundreds of thousands of U.S. lives from the war that the man behind the North Korean curtain was trying to start. It wasn't an ideal plan, but it was the only one they had left. They had no time to worry about Woody or Cowboy or Natasha or the others. They just needed to finish the mission.

Ringo finished checking Kruger's gear and then tapped him on the shoulder. Kruger turned around and Ringo gave him a thumbs up.

"Comms check, Raven One," Kruger said, using the secure radio. They were both wearing oxygen masks attached to the advanced helmets that housed the head up display for their wingsuits.

"Raven Two," Ringo replied.

"You ready, bub?" Kruger asked.

"I'd bloody well better be. I didn't put all this on for nothing."

"I hate jumping out of perfectly good airplanes," Kruger replied.

Ringo laughed and pointed to Kruger's wingsuit. "Not jumping, mate. *Flying* out of a perfectly good airplane. There's a difference."

"Ugh," Kruger groaned without keying his radio.

Other than the crew chief, they were the only two in the empty cargo hold of the massive C-17. The crew chief gave them the "one minute" warning as she opened the rear cargo ramp.

Kruger and Ringo exchanged a fist bump as they waited for the jump light to turn green. When it did, Kruger led the way, running off the back of the ramp and jumping into the dark abyss on the other side of the DMZ. To help minimize their radar cross section, Ringo waited thirty seconds before following.

As he safely separated from the C-17, Kruger deployed his wingsuit. His head up display showed a diamond over the landing zone in North Korea thirty miles away. All he had to do was maintain his glide.

With Ringo out of the aircraft, the C-17 started a hard turn back south and closed its cargo door. They were on their own, and on their way once again to kill Choe Il-Sung. Anything that happened from this point forward would be denied by the U.S. government and they'd be left to fend for themselves. Even Project Archangel and the rest of the team would be helpless to rescue them.

Kruger watched the distance between Ringo and himself in the HUD. Ringo was exactly where he was expected to be as they glided through the clear, moonless sky. *So far, so good.*

As they glided deeper into North Korean airspace, Kruger's radar warning receiver suddenly beeped, indicating a P-18 SPOON REST D early warning radar had been detected. On Kruger's display, a line with the letters SR indicated that the surveillance radar was off to his left.

"Heads up, I'm getting SAM indications," Kruger said to Ringo over the secure radio.

"Roger, I see him," Ringo responded.

Kruger kept an eye on the indication as the beeping continued. With the early warning radar in acquisition mode, there was nothing he could do. Their suits were specially designed by DARPA and MIT to give them the radar cross section of a small bird. The radar warning receiver was only receiving the radar energy from the acquisition radar as it looked for threats within the airspace.

If the SPOON REST air surveillance radar found them and handed off to a nearby SA-2 surface to air missile tracking radar, that would be cause for alarm. It would mean that the site had locked on and was actively targeting them. The next indication after that would be a missile launch from the SA-2, and at that point, survival would depend on visually picking up the large telephone-pole-sized missile and defeating it with the suit's limited countermeasures and evasive maneuvers.

While it was survivable, it was not ideal. They were on an optimum glide profile to their designated area with only a small amount of wiggle-room. Any maneuvering to defeat the missile would likely put them miles off course, and possibly into populated areas.

"The bloody thing is targeting me!" Ringo said a few seconds later.

"Just stay on course, bub," Kruger said calmly. "We're halfway there."

"Easy for you to say!"

"Start worrying if you see a big telephone pole flying toward you," Kruger reassured him. "Until then, they can't see us and they're just fishing in the dark."

After a few tense seconds of beeping, the targeting indications went away. Ringo looked up and saw an aircraft's anti-collision light flashing above him.

"You're right, mate. It was another aircraft."

"The landing zone isn't far," Kruger said. "Looks good from here."

Kruger followed the flight computer's prompts and descended down to two hundred feet. The steep descent allowed him to carry speed as he zoomed along the treetops. When he reached the predesignated point, a drogue chute automatically deployed to slow him down, followed by his parachute.

The opening shock was still severe despite the help from the drogue chute, but Kruger managed to shake it off and steer his parachute canopy down into the small clearing. It was an opening in the woods near the base of a hill where they would be setting up for their shot.

As he reached the clearing, Kruger made a sharp turn to descend beneath the tree line and then flared as he touched down. He gathered up his chute and took off the wingsuit, hiding it as Ringo landed behind him.

Once on the ground, Ringo collected his gear and hid it before joining Kruger. They retrieved their suppressed H&K MP-7 personal defense weapons and started up the hill toward their overwatch position.

After an hour of slow hiking, they were in position. Kruger assembled his modified CheyTac M200 Intervention sniper rifle chambered in .408. It was the perfect tool for the long-range shot they were planning.

Ringo set up his spotting equipment and the two set up for their shot. Kruger checked his watch. In six hours, the target would be in place and they would finally stand down the looming threat for good.

And then he could work on getting Natasha out of there.

CHAPTER FORTY

The intel on Choe Il-Sung was solid. It had been confirmed through three independent sources, including the CIA, British MI-6, and even the South Korean National Intelligence Service. It was as good as they were going to get, given the time sensitive nature of their mission.

Choe Il-Sung was Kim Jong-Un's second in command and arguably the most powerful person in North Korea. His existence was unknown to the Western world except in the most highly classified intelligence communities. He was rarely seen in public and the few times he had been spotted next to Jong-Il and Jong-Un, he was labeled simply as a "policy adviser."

But several defectors and inside sources confirmed that Il-Sung was actually the man behind the curtain. He was the puppet master guiding the despotic North Korean regime with a thirst for vengeance after losing his father in the Korean War. He believed the West was the source of North Korea's problems, and that the only way to be taken seriously on the world stage was through a military show of force – specifically a crippling EMP attack on U.S. soil.

According to their sources, all three intelligence agencies believed that Il-Sung was to make a rare appearance at a garrison in southeast North Korea at 0900 hrs near Kosong. It was believed to be the location of one of the ICBM silos capable of launching the EMP attack. Kruger would have only a fleeting shot opportunity as Il-Sung inspected the workers and surface facility before going into the underground bunker, but it was the best chance they had.

They had a partial view of the silo and a clear line of sight to the hangars next to it. Even if Il-Sung drove straight into the hangar, there was just enough opportunity for Kruger to make the shot. That's why they had chosen the CheyTac M200. Although it was unsuppressed, its accuracy was unmatched out to 2500 yards. At just over two thousand yards, they had just enough wiggle room to take the shot and get the hell out of Dodge.

"Vehicle approaching," Ringo whispered. He was lying prone next to Kruger, monitoring the facility with his electro-optical/infrared binoculars. "Bearing one-one-five, eighteen hundred fifty-five yards."

"Contact," replied Kruger.

The military SUV came to a stop just outside the hangar. Two men exited and forcefully pulled out a third person wearing a hood. Kruger watched through his scope as the men pushed the prisoner out into the open and stopped.

As Kruger watched the prisoner through his scope, Ringo called out a new threat.

"Tracked vehicle, bearing one-two-five, twenty-five hundred yards, moving toward the objective," he said.

"What is it?" Kruger whispered.

"Looks like triple A," Ringo said.

The M1992 self-propelled anti-aircraft gun was the North Korean version of the Russian ZSU-23-4 Shika. It was fitted with two 30 MM anti-aircraft guns capable of firing 800 High Explosive Incendiary (HEI) rounds per minute per barrel. It also had its own tracking and surveillance radar on the roof capable of tracking multiple air to air targets at once.

But as the tracked vehicle lumbered toward the open area where the prisoner was standing next to the two men, Kruger realized that the M1992 wasn't to be used for its intended purpose. They were about to witness an execution in the most brutal fashion.

The M1992 stopped short of the prisoner and the vehicle commander emerged from the turret. Moments later, two more vehicles approached from the same direction as the first SUV and stopped. As they stopped next to the SUV, Kruger realized they were the armored limousines known to transport Il-Sung.

Several men with suits exited followed by a man wearing a tan general's uniform. Kruger immediately identified him as Il-Sung. He approached the soldiers standing by the prisoner. They rendered a sharp salute and then stood at parade rest.

"Positive contact on the Wizard," Ringo said, using the codename they had come up with for the man behind the North Korean curtain. "One thousand, nine hundred and four yards, wind left to right at two."

Kruger adjusted his scope as he zeroed in on Il-Sung who was still walking toward the prisoner. At this distance, he needed to wait until Il-Sung stopped to get a clean shot to ensure their escape.

Il-Sung stopped a few feet short of the prisoner and gestured to one of the soldiers. Ringo called out the new dope as the soldier next to the prisoner ripped off the hood.

Kruger felt like he had been punched in the stomach as he saw who it was. *Natasha!*

The reality came rushing to him as Il-Sung said a few words and then walked back to the front of the vehicles where his security detail was waiting. He was about to watch the woman he loved be executed by North Korean artillery. It took every bit of restraint he had not to start shooting to give her a chance to run, but he knew he had no choice. Il-Sung had to die today.

"Jesus, mate, isn't that-"

"Just call it out," Kruger said.

The two soldiers forced Natasha to her knees. Kruger exhaled slowly as he tried to steel himself.

"We can take out the guy in the turret and save her," Ringo said. "One thousand nine hundred and-"

"No," Kruger interrupted. "Stay on the Wizard."

"They'll kill her, mate," Ringo protested.

"They're going to kill her anyway," Kruger said grimly. "And a lot of other people will die with her if I don't make this shot."

"You can make both," Ringo argued.

"Stay on Wizard," Kruger said angrily.

Ringo called out the information. Kruger made final adjustments to the windage.

Ringo took a deep breath and then said, "Send it."

The M1992 fired just as Kruger squeezed the trigger. The sound of its 30MM cannon masked the shot. The round impacted Il-Sung in the chest, straight through his heart. He crumpled instantly.

Kruger fought the urge to yell out as he heard the M1992 fire. A feeling of dread and despair suddenly overcame him as he tried to control his building rage.

"I'm so sorry," Ringo said.

Ignoring Ringo's gesture, Kruger shook it off and quickly started disassembling the rifle and rolling up his shooter's mat. "Let's move."

Ringo followed suit. As they slowly crept out of the woods, the M1992 started blindly firing toward the hillside. The security detail had obviously figured out the shot had come from that direction.

Kruger ducked as tree branches fell around them and the two started running down the hillside toward their preplanned extraction route.

"Oracle, we're moving to EXFIL," Kruger said over the secure satellite radio.

"Copy that," Coolio replied. "You've stirred the hornet's nest. Lots of chatter right now."

"Raven copies," Kruger replied.

Their exfil plan required them to make it to the water in Kosong where SEAL Team Six would rendezvous and take them to USS Mississippi, a Virginia-class submarine that was waiting just off the coast. It was tenuous at best, but the only chance they had since the airspace was contested and they were too far in-country to make it through to the DMZ on foot.

They raced down the hill as the M1992 continued launching unguided volleys toward them. Kruger was sure the operator had no idea where they were, but the splintering wood seemed to tell a different story. The operator of the artillery piece was making damned good educated guesses.

Kruger nearly ran into Ringo as he reached the edge of the tree line at the bottom of the hill and froze. As he looked past Ringo, he saw a small platoon of North Korean soldiers heading toward them.

The soldiers saw them and opened fire just as they took cover behind a fallen tree.

CHAPTER FORTY-ONE

Cowboy woke up in a cold sweat. His heart was racing. The room he was in was completely dark and he had no idea where he was. The last thing he remembered was falling in the woods. Everything after that was a blur.

As his eyes adjusted, he realized he was in a bedroom of some sort. The walls were barren and there appeared to be no windows, but he could just barely make out a door to his right. As he felt around and his eyes adjusted further, he realized that the hard surface he was lying on was a single-bed mattress.

Shifting in the bed, Cowboy felt something pulling in his forearm and saw that he had an IV attached. As he tried to sit up, a sudden pain shot through his body. He moved his hand to the source of the pain in his abdomen and found that it was heavily bandaged.

He felt like he was in a fog, but as he tried to sit up despite the pain, everything started to come back to him. He remembered falling down the side of a hill after taking a round during a firefight. He vaguely remembered being captured and then trying to run when their convoy was ambushed. There had been a man dressed in black standing over him after he fell. He didn't know who the man was, but he remembered the man saying something to him in English.

After that, he had no idea what had happened. He had lost consciousness at some point while being disarmed and dragged out of the brush. He had no idea who had him, where he was, or how long he had been there, but it appeared that someone had at least tended to his wounds – this time with more care than the field medic that had done a half-assed job of bandaging his gunshot wound earlier.

Cowboy gingerly sat up and swung his feet over the edge of the bed. He had been stripped down to his boxers and an undershirt at some point during his capture. He slowly stood and pulled the IV out of his arm. His bare feet felt the cold and dusty concrete as he tried to orient himself in the darkness.

Finding the nearby wall, Cowboy shuffled along the concrete floor. He was hoping to find another door or window to at least give him an idea of how to plan his escape. As he reached the corner, he suddenly saw a light come on illuminating the bottom of the door to his right.

With the new light illuminating the tiny room, Cowboy searched for something that could be used as a weapon. He saw that he was two steps down from the door in a room that was barely big enough to fit the bed. The IV had been hung from a small pole above the bed.

As he heard the door unlock, he moved as quickly as he could back to the bed. The pain was overwhelming as he reached the bed and pulled the thin blanket back over him. The door opened and the silhouette of a small man appeared. He lingered in the doorway and then stepped down, apparently carrying a box as he approached Cowboy's bedside.

The man set the box down next to the bed and then walked around to Cowboy's IV. Cowboy prepared to strike as the man pulled the loose IV up from the ground.

"How are you feeling?" the man asked in heavily accented English.

Cowboy said nothing, still pretending to be asleep as the man turned to face him.

"It's okay," the man said. "I am not here to harm you."

"Who are you?" Cowboy asked cautiously.

"I thought I would ask you the same thing," the man replied. "But my name is Pak."

"They call me Cowboy."

"*Cowboy?*"

"Good enough for now, mate. Now, where am I?" Cowboy asked as he sat upright in the bed.

Pak tried to push Cowboy back down. "You should rest. Your injuries need to heal. I managed to remove the bullet but your body will need time to heal. You lost quite a bit of blood, and we could only give you a small transfusion with what we had available."

"What is this place?" Cowboy asked. He reluctantly complied and slid down in the bed and let his head fall onto the pillow. Pak held Cowboy's arm and reinserted the IV.

"It is my home. We are a few miles from Kaesong. It is a small village called Changp'ung," Pak replied as he gently lowered Cowboy's arm back to his side.

"How did I get here?"

"You were rescued by our group. You are very lucky they brought me to you when they did. Otherwise you would be dead. Or worse, in a North Korean prison."

"Why? Who are you? What group?" Cowboy pushed. "Why would you help me?"

"Your accent...Brit? Aussie?"

"British," Cowboy replied.

"Ah, yes, of course," Pak replied. "It's so hard to tell the western accents apart. That would make sense. MI-6?"

"No," Cowboy replied flatly.

"Well, I have worked with MI-6 and the CIA for many decades. I have housed many of them in this very basement."

Cowboy suddenly shot back up in the bed. "Do you have a way to contact them?"

Pak waved his hand and tried to push Cowboy back down by his shoulders. "You mustn't work yourself up."

"I need to get word back home. I think my associate may be in trouble," Cowboy said anxiously.

Pak seemed to consider it for a moment and then said, "Ah, yes, the American."

"The American? So, you've seen him?"

Pak shook his head. "I didn't see him, but I know that an American was found by soldiers not too far from here yesterday when you were found. Your plane crashed, yes?"

"Yesterday? Is that how long I've been out?"

"You were badly injured," Pak replied.

"Do you know where they've taken him?"

"No, but they will take him where they take all of the spies – Hoeryong Reeducation Camp," Pak replied. "It was closed in 2012 and now serves as an interrogation and torture site for political dissidents and those caught spying. It is the most secure prison in all of North Korea."

"I have to get word out to my friends back home," Cowboy said.

"I'm afraid there's nothing they can do," Pak replied. "It is the most heavily guarded prison. Even if you could break in, your friends would never make it out alive. I'm sorry, but your friend is as good as dead."

"Do you have a way to get in touch with your CIA or MI-6 contacts?" Cowboy asked.

"Yes, I have a satellite phone that I can use in emergencies."

"Alright, mate, well this is a bloody emergency. Let's go get it."

CHAPTER FORTY-TWO

Kruger was running step for step with Ringo as they fled the North Korean patrol. They had managed to escape the initial volley of gunfire with a decent head start due to the terrain and downed trees, but the North Korean patrol was still in hot pursuit.

They weaved through the trees as they ran through the woods. They were both seasoned operators, and years earlier it would've been much easier to outrun their pursuers, but now they were a little older and slower. Despite their worn-out knees and aching backs, they were still gaining ground as the soldiers struggled with the terrain between them. Even at 70%, they were still better than the young soldiers giving chase behind them.

As they neared a stream, Kruger flashed a hand signal to Ringo and the two split up. They each found cover as the two soldiers ran toward them. Kruger did his best to slow his breathing as the two soldiers ran past him into the clearing by the stream. He watched as they stopped to look for them. The soldiers split up as one of them radioed back to base.

"We lost them at the stream. Send air support," Kruger heard one of the soldiers say through his in-ear translator.

Kruger made eye contact with Ringo and gave a silent countdown with his hand. When his fist clenched, they both slung their MP-7s and unsheathed their knives. They made quick work of the two soldiers and then dragged the bodies into the brush.

"More are on the way," Ringo said.

Kruger pointed to the bridge fifty meters to the north. "Let's go find a ride to the ocean."

Ringo nodded and the two moved toward the wooden bridge. The each took a side, hiding just out of sight beneath the bridge as an old pickup truck with a loud exhaust clamored toward them. It appeared to be a farm truck with a tarp covering whatever the farmer was transporting to a nearby village.

"Oracle, what's the status of the rest of that patrol?" Kruger asked.

"They're still searching the woods, boss," Coolio replied over the encrypted tactical frequency.

"Copy," Kruger said.

As the truck approached, Kruger nodded and Ringo stepped out into the road with his MP-7 raised and pointed at the farmer. The farmer slammed on his brakes and skidded to a stop on the dusty road.

Ringo pulled him out of the truck and pushed him off into the grass before hopping in the driver's seat. Kruger cleared the area and then hopped in the passenger seat. Ringo floored it and the little gas engine roared as they crossed the bridge.

"That was easy," Ringo said.

FINI FLIGHT

"You know better than that, bub," Kruger warned, reminding Ringo that any time an operator said "that was easy," it was a direct invitation for something to go horribly wrong.

As if on cue, Coolio keyed up the radio. "Heads up, you've got multiple patrols in the next village. Recommend you detour south."

Kruger punched Ringo in the shoulder. "What did I tell you?"

"Copy that," he added over the radio.

When they were across the bridge, Ringo turned right down a dirt path to avoid the village. It took them through a valley and then started winding up the side of a hill.

"Is this the way we want to go?" Kruger asked Coolio over the frequency.

"It's ten clicks longer, but it's clear of patrols," Coolio replied.

"Is the drone still overhead?" Ringo asked.

"It has about three hours of battery left," Coolio answered. "I may have to switch to satellite if you get delayed."

"We'll try not to get delayed," Kruger said. "What's our ETA on this route?"

"Assuming no further detours, one hour," Coolio replied.

"And the team?"

"Standing by off the coast," Coolio answered, referring to the SEAL Team that was standing by to help them egress to the Virginia-Class submarine parked off the North Korean coast and waiting to take them home.

They continued up the terrain as they followed the dirt road Coolio had vectored them on. When they reached the shallow peak, they could see a train yard and the national highway in the distance. It was only a few miles from there to the coast and their egress point.

As they started down the hill, Coolio called out another threat. "Heads up. North Korean police are approaching the railyard from the north."

"Which way do we go, mate?" Ringo asked.

"Standby...At the fork in the road in two hundred feet, go north. Your left," Coolio replied.

"Copy, my left," Ringo replied.

As he hit the fork in the road, he veered left. The truck's engine surged and then there was a loud knock followed by steam coming from under the hood. The truck jolted and then coasted to a stop.

"Fuck me silly," Ringo said, slamming his hand against the wheel.

"No time to be pissed, bub," Kruger said as he readied his MP-7 and exited. "We're humping it the rest of the way."

"Oracle, the truck is tits up. We're on foot," Kruger said over the radio. "What's the best way on foot?"

"There's no terrain if you cross the railyard and follow the road east. Or, you could go due east through terrain. That's the shortest distance," Coolio replied.

"How far?" Kruger asked.

"Two clicks," Coolio replied.

Kruger looked at Ringo who nodded in agreement. "We're heading east, call out any threats."

"Copy that," Coolio replied.

As they started walking toward the railyard, Kruger asked, "Oracle, any news on the other survivors?"

"Still nothing on eleven alpha," Coolio said, referring to Woody.

"What about bravo?"

"Their convoy was ambushed during transport."

"Friendlies?"

"We're still working on that, boss," Coolio replied. "Tuna and Sierra are both talking to their agencies trying to find out if it was one of ours. Tuna thinks it might be someone else."

"Someone else? Who?"

"He thinks it might have been Chinese intelligence," Coolio said.

"That makes no sense," Kruger said as he exchanged a look with Ringo. "The Chinese are buddies with the North Koreans. They would just hand him over."

"I don't know, boss. That's just what Tuna said he was worried about. I guess that was Director Chapman's best guess when he learned they had been ambushed and they evaded our tracking."

"Copy, keep me updated," Kruger said.

Ringo looked over at Kruger as they walked across the railyard. "You going to tell him what we saw at the missile silo?"

"No," Kruger said gruffly.

"Why not? Shouldn't that be part of our SITREP?"

"I'll handle it when we get back, bub."

CHAPTER FORTY-THREE

A lone bulb hung from a wire in the center of the ceiling, barely illuminating the small bedroom as Cowboy finished the beef rib soup and bread that Pak had given him. He had promised to allow Cowboy to go upstairs and use the satellite phone, but only after he ate. It was an unusual compromise for Cowboy, but he didn't push the issue. He was starving and knew he would need to get his strength up for whatever escape plan that lay ahead.

After finishing the last of the bread and downing the glass of slightly-tinted water, Cowboy relieved himself in the bucket in the corner of the room and then headed up the steps. He slowly opened the door, revealing the rest of the basement that Pak apparently used for storage. It was filled with boxes and old furniture, barely illuminated by a small window at the far end of the room.

As Cowboy stumbled through the clutter, he heard a door open and creaking as Pak descended the rickety wooden stairs.

"I told you to stay in the bedroom," Pak said sternly as he spotted Cowboy.

"Sorry, mate," Cowboy replied.

"Come with me," Pak said, motioning for Cowboy to follow.

Cowboy gingerly followed him up the stairs. His abdomen was still sore and every step brought about a sharp pain. He had no idea what the quality of Pak's patch-up job had been. It seemed okay, but for all Cowboy knew there could still be bullet fragments lodged in his gut.

He followed Pak up the stairs and into what appeared to be a small closet. Pak opened the door and Cowboy saw that they were in the living area of a small house. He guessed that it was no bigger than a thousand square feet. Pictures of Kim Jong-Un and Kim Jong-Il littered the floral wallpaper covered walls.

"I thought you weren't a fan of this regime," Cowboy said cautiously.

"In this country, you must love Dear Leader. *Or else.*"

"Even in your own home?" Cowboy asked.

"If someone from the government enters your home for inspection, it is best to show allegiance through approved methods," Pak replied as he nodded toward the montage on his wall.

"Approved methods?"

"Come, let us get the phone," Pak said, ignoring the question.

Cowboy followed Pak into the modest kitchen. There wasn't much on the countertops and he had no refrigerator. He felt bad for the man who had taken him in.

"What kind of work do you do?" Cowboy asked.

"I am a doctor," Pak said before opening a drawer. He shuffled through it and found a satellite phone that appeared to be from the early nineties. He pressed the power button, verified that it had turned on, and then handed it to Cowboy.

"How old is this thing?" Cowboy asked as he examined the phone.

"It hasn't been used in quite some time," Pak said before pointing to the door behind Cowboy. "You will have to go outside to use it."

"I hope it works," Cowboy said.

Cowboy slowly walked outside into what passed for Pak's backyard. There was no fence and he was only a dozen or so feet from the next house. Cowboy walked to the edge of the wall where he hoped no one could see him and carefully squatted down, grimacing due to his wounds.

Cowboy dialed the number by memory and waited for the phone to connect. The reception wasn't good, but the connection was made and a female voice answered.

"I need to order a pizza," Cowboy said, using the pre-defined code.

"What kind, sir?" the woman asked.

"Everything except pineapple," Cowboy replied.

"One moment please."

Cowboy looked at the bulky phone as it sounded like the line went dead. A few seconds later, someone came on the line.

"Cowboy!" It was Coolio. He had never been so happy to hear the cyber analyst's voice.

"I don't have much time, mate. Woody was captured and may be on his way to the Hoeryong Reeducation Camp. I saw him before I was captured, but I couldn't tell if he was alive, dead, or badly injured. I'm in a village near Kaesong. Can you pull the coordinates off this phone?"

"I'm working on it," Coolio said. "We're aware of Woody. What's your condition?"

"Banged up, but I think I can make it through an extraction," Cowboy said as he pulled up his shirt. Blood had soaked through the white bandage.

"We are working on that," Coolio said. "Kruger and Ringo are on an OP. Tuna and Sierra are in a meeting on the other side of the base, otherwise I'd get you to talk to one of them. Are you in a safe place?"

"I'm staying with a man who calls himself Pak. Late fifties, early sixties. Village doctor. Says he's been a CIA and MI-6 asset for a few decades. He seems confident on the location of Woody."

"I'll look into it," Coolio replied. "Will you have access to this phone?"

"It only works outside. I will call you back in an hour."

"Okay. I will let Tuna know. I'm so glad you're okay, man. We were worried we had lost both of you."

"I can't vouch for Woody and I'm not out of this shithole yet, mate," Cowboy said. "I'll be in touch. Cowboy out."

Cowboy ended the call and then powered down the phone. He slowly stood, using the side of the house as support. He heard voices coming from the front of the house and slowly walked to the corner of the house.

Peering around the corner, he saw a North Korean Army UAZ-3151 light utility vehicle parked out front. It was unoccupied, but he could see at least one soldier standing near the corner of the building.

Cowboy's adrenaline surged as he ducked back behind the wall. He searched for an escape route as he contemplated his next move. He was sure they were a search team going house to house looking for him. There was no way they had given up looking for him already.

He heard loud voices coming from within the house. The soldiers were inside with Pak. It wouldn't be long before they realized he was outside. He decided his only choice was to evade and hope to get a head start.

Cowboy turned to his right. There were more houses, but in the distance, he saw what appeared to be a farm. He figured he could hole up there and make contact with Coolio again to get a better egress plan.

As the voices inside grew louder, Cowboy took off in the direction of the farmhouse. The pain in his abdomen was overwhelming. Whatever pain medicine Pak had given him was now completely worn off.

Reaching the next house, Cowboy stumbled and fell to his knees. He pushed through the pain and willed himself to stand. He was only two houses away from the farm. From there, it looked like he would have to clear a dirt road and then it was a straight shot to the barn.

Cowboy continued moving as quickly as he could toward the next house. He stopped as he reached the alley between them and looked both ways to ensure he was clear. The pain was now all he could think of. He was starting to feel lightheaded.

He stumbled across the alley clutching his stomach. As he reached the final house, he fell once more. This time, he couldn't catch himself and fell face first into the grass. With one hand still clutching his abdomen, he pushed himself back onto his knees.

As Cowboy sat up, he heard movement off to his right. He slowly turned, suddenly staring down the barrel of an AK-47.

CHAPTER FORTY-FOUR

If he never saw another moldy, damp, and dark basement, it would be too soon. Cowboy sat on the floor in the corner of the room, watching the light bulb flicker as he heard footsteps above him. He listened intently, wondering if his luck would run out and those footsteps would suddenly be muted by gunfire.

The footsteps grew louder, descending the stairs until he could just barely make out legs in the darkness. Unlike his previous accommodations, this basement had no separate room. The only door was at the top of the stairs.

The ghost like figure reached the base of the stairs and turned toward Cowboy. The woman that had introduced herself as Maeng Min when he was taken to his new accommodations emerged from the darkness. She was carrying a bowl of something as she casually approached Cowboy.

"Here, eat," she said as he stood to meet her.

"Any word on Pak?" Cowboy asked as he gratefully accepted the bowl.

Maeng frowned and shook her head. "T'ae is searching for him."

T'ae Yeon-Woo had been the man standing behind the rifle in the alley as Cowboy tried to escape the approaching North Korean soldiers. He claimed to be a friend of Pak's – part of an underground resistance with ties to the CIA – that had come to help Pak and Cowboy escape when they learned that North Korean soldiers had narrowed down Cowboy's location to Pak's neighborhood.

Unfortunately, they had been too late. Pak occupied the soldiers just long enough for T'ae and his men to grab Cowboy, but they were unable to save Pak. He had been taken for questioning and would likely be killed when they were done with him.

"If you let me call my friends, maybe they can help," Cowboy offered.

"No," Maeng said sternly. "They listen."

"It's an encrypted satellite phone," Cowboy argued.

Maeng shook her head. "They will listen and find you."

"Okay, so what do we do now?"

"We wait," Maeng said. "Patience."

"No offense, but we don't have time for patience," Cowboy replied. "My friend and your friend need our help. I'm no good to you in this basement."

"We will make contact with your government," Maeng reassured him. "Do not worry."

"How?"

"We have drop," Maeng said.

"A dead drop? That could take days."

"Patience," Maeng reiterated. "It is only way."

FINI FLIGHT

"It's not the only way," Cowboy argued. "Let me talk to my friends and we can extract Pak as well."

"No," Maeng replied flatly as she turned to walk out.

"Where are you going? Maybe we could talk this over?"

"No," came the reply as Maeng continued up the stairs.

Cowboy returned to his corner and finished the bowl of soup. A few minutes later, he heard more footsteps and watched T'ae descend the stairs.

"How are you feeling?" T'ae asked. His English was much better than Maeng's. Cowboy wondered if he had spent time in America at some point.

"Like I'm wasting time here," Cowboy replied.

"You will be back in South Korea very soon," T'ae said, reaching down to pick up the bowl on the floor. "Do not worry."

"How soon? And what about Pak?"

"Do not worry about Pak. We will get you back across the border very soon."

"Now wait a minute, mate. Pak helped me. Why wouldn't I help him?"

"There is nothing you can do for him," T'ae replied.

"Let me call my mates back home. We can extract him. Do you know where he is?"

T'ae nodded. "He's in a place where even your friends cannot get to him."

"You don't know who my friends are, mate."

"It will be dark soon. Get some rest. We will move you tonight."

"Move me where?"

"We have arranged for your departure through established methods."

"Established methods?"

"We have a network to get you to the other side of the Demilitarized Zone. It is safe."

"Nothing's safe in this country," Cowboy replied.

"Please get some rest. You will need your strength for the journey," T'ae said, ignoring Cowboy's quip.

"You really should let me call back home. I can help you rescue Pak."

"We have been doing this for many years. We all know the risks. Pak will either be let go because they believe him when he says he knows nothing, or they will kill him."

"And you're okay with that?"

T'ae shrugged. "It is a risk we all take. Rest now. I will return when it is time to move."

CHAPTER FORTY-FIVE

Spectre had been lying in the bunk bed, staring at the ceiling in the back of the plush Gulfstream when the intercom buzzed. He was exhausted and had tried to sleep, but he couldn't get over the overwhelming sense of guilt he was suffering from leaving Woody behind in North Korea. Despite Kruger's assurances that they'd bring him home, Spectre just couldn't stand sitting on the sidelines.

He sat up and hit the intercom button on the touchscreen in front of him. "What's up?"

"Hey, sorry to wake you," Jenny replied from the cockpit. "Your wife is up on the VTC when you're ready."

"Okay, thanks," Spectre said as he swung his feet onto the floor.

He put his shoes on and headed for the video teleconferencing suite. As he logged on, he saw the incoming conference request and clicked on it.

"Hey sweetie," he said as he saw his beautiful wife and son on the screen. "What time is it there?"

"Cal! How are you? You look tired. Are you okay? How did it go?" Michelle asked. "It's morning here."

"Kruger sent me home. We left Woody behind," Spectre said as he looked away.

"Left him behind? What do you mean? Where is he?"

"His jet ingested a rock when we landed and destroyed one of his engines. So, we swapped aircraft to get out and I guess when I flew by a SAM site near the border, they were alerted and shot Woody down," Spectre replied.

"Wait, you did *what?*" Michelle yelped. "You flew out on only one engine?!"

"It doesn't matter. Woody didn't make it out and now they're trying to find him."

"Did they eject?"

Spectre nodded. "But when I left, they hadn't made contact yet."

"I'm so sorry, sweetheart," Michelle said softly. "I'm sure Kruger has a plan."

Spectre shrugged. "Natasha is still in country. I could tell that's his first priority. Can't say I blame him."

"She was part of the mission?"

"She was a big part of the deal with the other Russians. They were brokering our deal. We were supposed to be demonstrating Russian jets to them, but that all fell apart when Woody's jet broke."

"Goddammit! I can't believe I just left him there," Spectre added. "They'll kill him if they get to him!"

"Is there anything you can do?" Michelle asked.

"What do you mean?"

"I know you, Cal. You won't be happy unless you're helping. So, is there anything you can do to help bring them home?"

"I don't even know where they are. Cowboy was with him. They could both be dead right now, for all I know."

"It's going to be okay," Michelle said. "Kruger and those guys are the best at what they do. They'll bring him home safely."

"How's Cal?" Spectre asked, changing the subject. "Hey buddy! He looks like he's grown a foot taller since I was home."

As Michelle held up Cal Jr. for Spectre to see and talk to, a chat window popped up on his screen. He saw that it was Coolio trying to get in touch with him.

Hey Spectre, do you have a second?

Spectre ignored it as he interacted with Cal Jr who was eagerly showing Spectre the bright yellow toy crop duster Bear had bought for him the day prior.

I found Woody.

Spectre's eyes widened as he stared at Coolio's message.

"Hey babe, can I call you guys back in a few minutes?" Spectre asked, his eyes still fixated on Coolio's revelation.

"Sure, what's going on?" Michelle asked.

"Coolio just sent me a message on the messenger on here. Says he found Woody."

"Go! I'll put Calvin down for his nap and wait for you to come back."

"Okay," Spectre said. "I love you."

"Love you too."

Spectre kissed his hand and touched the screen before ending the chat session. He dialed Coolio and waited for the video to connect. Seconds later, Coolio appeared on screen.

"Spectre! Sorry to bother you. I just thought you'd want to know we found Woody and are getting intel on him right now. We also made contact with Cowboy."

"Where is he? Is he okay? Are they together?" Spectre asked nervously.

"Cowboy is with a separatist group that are CIA assets. They're working to get him out now."

"And Woody?"

"He's in bad shape. They've got him in a hospital in Kaesong and will be transporting him to a secret prison soon."

"How bad?"

Coolio shrugged. "We only just recently confirmed his location. Still trying to get eyes on, but they say he's in ICU."

"Jesus! Okay. Where's Kruger? What's the plan?"

"He and Ringo are moving to the extraction point after taking down Il-Sung."

"Taking down Il-Sung? You mean what we did didn't work?"

"We don't know for sure. Either it was a body double or it failed, but we have confirmation that he went to inspect a launch site."

"Does he know about Woody?"

"Yeah. Tuna is working on a plan to get him out and they'll finalize the details when Kruger returns. But there's one more thing."

"What's that?"

"Natasha's plane just took off on a flight plan to Moscow."

"That's good news, right?"

"I haven't run the facial recognition yet to confirm, but I think she was assassinated in front of Kruger when he took the shot to kill Il-Sung."

"What?!"

"I watched it on the drone feed. Kruger didn't say anything about it though when we talked, so I may be wrong. It sure looked like her though."

"So, he's distracted, but man that seems like something he might've mentioned."

"A little distracted, yeah. But I don't want to say anything, you know? What would I even say?"

"Okay, Coolio, thanks for the update. I'll call you back in a few."

"Thanks, Spectre," Coolio replied.

Spectre ended the call and called Michelle back.

"By the look on your face, I can tell it's not good. What's going on?" she asked.

"They think Kruger's girlfriend was killed, Cowboy is being held by a separatist group, and Woody is in a military hospital soon to be transported to a top secret prison where they'll torture and kill him."

"My God…"

"I have to go back," Spectre said. "I don't know what I can do, but I have to be there. I can't go home like this. I can't leave my friends behind like that."

"I agree," Michelle said. "Kruger needs you now more than ever. So does Woody."

"So, you're okay with this?"

"If Kruger just lost Natasha, he's going to be distracted. He may not be thinking clearly. He's been there for us, and Woody needs your help. You should go back and help, even if it's just for moral support."

"I don't know what I can even do. The jet we have is broken with no way to fix it."

"Don't they have other jets on base you can fly?"

"Well, yeah, F-16s and A-10s, but it's been years. And do you really want me going back in country?"

"No, but I know you're going to do whatever it takes to get your friends back, so I just want you to be safe and think this through. Of course, I'd rather you not go at all, but I know you. You would never be able to live with yourself if you did nothing knowing what you now know."

"I love you so much," Spectre said.

"I love you too," Michelle replied. "But don't think I'm giving you a blank check, sir. Your son needs a father and your wife needs a husband. Promise me you won't do anything reckless."

"I won't."

"No," Michelle said, shaking her head. "Say it."

"I promise I won't do anything reckless."

"Thank you," Michelle said. "Now go get your friends back."

CHAPTER FORTY-SIX

"Boss, we've got a problem," Coolio said as Ringo and Kruger reached the peak of the terrain while making their way to the coastal extraction point.

Kruger stopped and took a knee with Ringo. "Go ahead, Oracle."

"After Cowboy made contact, I located his position using his satellite phone. It looks like the home he was in was raided by North Korean soldiers," Coolio said.

Coolio had reported the news of Cowboy's contact as soon as the call ended. Tuna and Sierra were working on verifying whether Cowboy was under the care of an agency asset or if Tuna's suspicions were correct and Cowboy had fallen into the hands of Chinese operatives.

"Do we know if they have him?" Kruger asked.

"The phone was powered off, so I couldn't track it," Coolio replied.

"What about Woody and the prison Cowboy told you about?"

"We've located it, but we think Woody was taken to a hospital in Kaesong first. Tuna is working on an extraction plan," Coolio answered.

"Copy, keep me updated."

"Will do, boss. Heads up, in the village ahead, there's a North Korean patrol, but they seem to be preoccupied. You should be able to skirt the northern edge without issue."

"Raven copies," Kruger replied as he stood.

Ringo followed Kruger as the two started down the terrain toward the ocean. They were less than half a mile from the coast and could see the village and water in the distance. They would easily make their rendezvous with the SEAL team and be headed back to Osan soon.

They made their way down the rugged hillside without incident. As they neared the village, they saw the North Korean patrol that had surrounded a house. Kruger stopped as he watched a soldier dragging a woman toward a vehicle followed by another soldier carrying a small child that was screaming.

"Bloody awful," Ringo commented.

They took cover in a group of trees just to the north of the village as they watched the final soldier drag an unconscious – or possibly dead – man from the house. Kruger unslung his sniper rifle and viewed the soldiers through the scope.

"What are you doing, mate? We've got no time for this," Ringo whispered.

"Observing the threat," Kruger replied.

"The soldiers seem to be busy. You're clear all the way to the coast," Coolio reported.

"I see them," Kruger replied.

He slowly attached the suppressor to his CheyTac rifle and put the man he assumed to be the officer in charge in his sights.

He watched as they tossed the man in the back of their jeep and then one of the men drew his handgun. He pointed it at the screaming little girl's head as the woman appeared to plead with the soldiers.

"Kruger, this isn't like you," Ringo pleaded in a hushed tone. "We have to keep going, mate. We can't get involved with the locals."

"They're pointing a gun at a kid, bub," Kruger growled.

"One of many," Ringo replied. "This isn't our fight."

"Whose fight is it?" Kruger asked, as he rested his rifle on his forearm and knee in a modified sitting shooting position.

"Listen, mate, I get it. What we saw back there with Natasha was horrific. But the only way to make things right is to get safely to the extraction point. We still have to get Cowboy and Woody out of this godforsaken country, and the team can't do it if we get rolled up and they're having to come get us too."

Deep down, Kruger knew Ringo was right. All of the rage and sadness and despair he felt as he watched the woman he loved executed in the most gruesome of ways had bubbled to the top. He felt helpless watching these North Korean soldiers threaten a mother and small child. He didn't know the backstory, but then again, he didn't need to. There was no valid reason for what he was witnessing.

Kruger kept his sights on the man holding the handgun. It was just over a three-hundred-yard shot. The soldiers were close enough that he could easily take out the first threat and move on to the second before any of them realized what was going on.

"I'll support whatever you do, mate, but just realize what kind of hornet's nest you're going to kick if we get into a firefight out here," Ringo added.

Kruger flexed his finger against the side of the rifle and then inserted it into the trigger guard, gently resting it against the trigger as he contemplated squeezing the trigger and sending the assholes harassing the family to hell.

"Raven this is Oracle, are you guys okay?" Coolio chimed in over the radio. "I don't see you moving."

Kruger said nothing, still focusing on the man aiming his weapon at the child.

"Raven?" Coolio asked again.

"We're good, mate. Standby," Ringo replied finally.

"Copy," Coolio replied. "The SEAL team is en route. ETA fifteen minutes. And I have news about the Russians."

Kruger froze.

"What news?" he asked.

"Their plane just took off from Sunchon," Coolio replied.

"Going where?"

"Flight plan says Moscow," Coolio answered.

"Has Sierra talked to them?" Kruger asked.

"No, I was waiting for you to-"

"Copy, we're moving," Kruger said as he slung his rifle and stood.

He started to move through the trees and Ringo followed. They crossed the road and heard screaming followed by a single gunshot as they made it across.

Kruger froze, resisting the urge to look back.

"You did the right thing, mate," Ringo said.

Kruger took off in a jog toward the last wooded area before the coast. Ringo followed, scanning for threats as they quickly made their way through the woods and emerged on the other side.

As they arrived on the beach, four U.S. Navy SEALs emerged from the water with extra breathing gear for them.

"Your chariot awaits, sir," the leader said as he handed Kruger a rebreather and flippers. "Hope you boys know how to swim."

CHAPTER FORTY-SEVEN

Coolio hovered over Tuna's shoulder as he set up the laptop for the secure video teleconference. Next to him, Sierra Carter was set up with her own laptop as they waited for CIA Director Chapman and U.K. Secretary of State for Defence Nigel Williams to connect.

As an unacknowledged, compartmentalized top secret joint U.S.-U.K. organization, Williams and Chapman were the only leaders of their respective governments with knowledge and oversight of Project Archangel. It provided their leaders plausible deniability, while making them solely responsible for the fallout if things went south.

"Okay, they should be dialing in shortly," Coolio said, returning to his screen so he could also participate.

"Okay, we're all here. Let's begin," Chapman said. "You all know my assistant Daniel Ellison. He will be briefing us on the information we have on our end so far."

Chapman's screen flipped to a tall, lanky assistant who stood and adjusted his tie. "We have confirmed with our assets on the ground that the operative *Cowboy* is under the care of an agency asset, codenamed *BLACK ICE*. Black Ice made contact with us and confirmed that Cowboy's condition was stable and improving."

"Director, we received a satellite phone call from Cowboy about an hour ago reporting the same," Tuna interjected. "He used an Odin number that patched to Coolio directly and confirmed that he was in good condition and ready for extraction."

Ellison looked confused as he leaned over to read his notes. "You said one hour ago?"

"That's correct, sir," Tuna replied.

"That can't be right," Ellison said as he flipped through the pages of his yellow legal pad.

"Why can't that be right, Daniel?" Chapman asked.

"Sir, I was just about to get to that, but we recently learned that North Korean soldiers raided Black Ice's home and took him to an interrogation facility approximately two hours ago. Are you sure it was only an hour?"

"I am sure," Tuna replied, turning to look at Coolio who nodded and gave a thumbs up in return.

"Well, then are you sure it was Cowboy?"

"He passed all authentications through the answering service and I recognized his voice," Coolio added. "That was him on the phone."

"Is it possible your asset turned?" Sierra asked.

"Black Ice has been with the agency for nearly three decades," Ellison replied. "I find that hard to believe."

"Coolio, can you trace the sat phone that Cowboy used?" Tuna asked, looking back to Coolio.

"I had a location while we were talking, but it has since been turned off. It will take some time to remotely power it on and pull a location," Coolio replied.

"Do it," Tuna ordered and then returned to his screen.

"Sir, I will have Black Ice's case officer attempt to reestablish communications as soon as we adjourn," Ellison said.

Secretary of State for Defence Williams cleared his throat. "Miss Carter will have every intelligence asset available to our government at her disposal to ensure Cowboy's safe return."

"Thank you, sir," Sierra said, as she looked away to hold back tears over the potential loss of her brother.

"Okay, what do we know about Woody?" Chapman asked.

Ellison cleared his throat and put down his notes. "We have confirmed his status as a prisoner being held by the North Korean state. He is currently in a hospital in Kaesong under heavy guard. Our local assets believe he is in critical condition, which is better than we could have hoped for, considering…"

"Do they know who he is?" Sierra asked.

"That is not clear at this time," Ellison replied. "Our assets only know of a 'Russian pilot that attempted to defect' with no further data."

Sierra steeled herself and turned to Tuna. "If he's in critical condition, he is in grave danger. The North Koreans will attempt highly experimental treatments to revive him and get him to talk. They will try to move him to their secret prisons regardless of his condition. We must intercept him."

"We need confirmation that he's there, first," Tuna said. "Daniel, can any of the CIA's assets in country get eyes on?"

"I will work on it, sir," Ellison answered as he scribbled notes on his tablet.

"Tuna, have you heard from Kruger?" Chapman asked.

"Yes, sir, he just linked up with the SEAL team and should be on his way to the *USS John Warner* where a helicopter will bring him back here," Tuna reported.

"And we're sure the mission was a success?" Chapman asked.

"One confirmed KIA," Coolio answered. "Facial recognition confirmed it was the target."

The stoic Secretary of State for Defence chimed broke his silence once more. "Do we know what happened in Sunchon? How did he survive?"

"It's unclear at this time, sir," Sierra answered. "The North Koreans may have created a vaccine to counter the effects of the toxin."

"How is that possible?" Chapman asked. "This was specially created."

"We don't know for sure at this point. It could have been a failure of the toxin itself," Sierra said. "The formula could have degraded due to the delivery method."

"The lab was confident," Chapman said. "I can't see how it failed."

"The other option is that Il-Sung used a body double, either at Sunchon or the Kosong facility. But the latter, is not very likely," Sierra said.

"Why is that?" Minister Williams asked.

"Because our FSB operative Natasha was brought there to meet him and summarily executed. We were able to confirm her death with the drone footage," Sierra answered. "We attempted to confirm using the same facial recognition software, but were only able to obtain a partial match due to her condition and the distance. She appeared to have been tortured prior to her execution by an artillery piece."

"Jesus Christ," Chapman said, hearing the news of Natasha's death for the first time. "Does Kruger know?"

"He watched it live, sir," Coolio said softly. "We all did."

Chapman shook his head and closed his eyes. "And what of the others? Anatoly and Viktor?"

"Their aircraft is currently en route to Moscow," Sierra said. "We do not know who is on board and will not be able to verify it until they land."

"So, she was possibly double-crossed," Chapman said. "And that means the entire mission may have been compromised."

"Compromised how, sir?" Tuna asked. "We got the son of a bitch."

"I still find it difficult to believe that the target was immune to our toxin. If only Natasha was executed and their aircraft flew to Moscow, it's very possible our team was double-crossed at some point and he was expecting it."

"Then why allow the mission to go as far as it did? Why were our people allowed to fly out?" Tuna asked.

Chapman seemed to consider the question for a moment and then said, "That is something we will have to find out once we have our boys back. Focus on rescuing Woody and Cowboy for now. We can sort out the rest later. Keep me updated."

CHAPTER FORTY-EIGHT

T'ae Yeon-Woo walked into the room Cowboy was staying in carrying a tattered jacket. Cowboy sat up on the cot, having given up on sleep an hour earlier when he realized it just wasn't going to happen.

"Here, put this on," T'ae said, tossing the jacket to Cowboy.

He caught it and then looked it over.

"For what?" Cowboy asked.

"It is time to go."

"Go where?"

"We have arranged for your safe passage," T'ae replied. "We must go now."

T'ae walked up to Cowboy and tried to grab Cowboy's arm. Cowboy immediately withdrew as he stood to face off against the much smaller man.

"Hold on a second, mate," Cowboy said as he stepped back. "What's the plan here?"

"We have a very small window to get you across. There is no time to waste."

"And you've made arrangements with my government?"

"Yes, of course," T'ae said, motioning impatiently for Cowboy to come on. "You must hurry."

Cowboy slowly stepped back until he was backed into the corner. He tossed the jacket on the cot. T'ae stayed where he was and continued to motion for Cowboy to go with him.

"How do you know what government to contact?" Cowboy asked.

"Pak told us when he asked for our help. Now, come, you mustn't waste any more time!"

Maeng came down the stairs and froze as she saw the standoff between Cowboy and T'ae. "What is going on? We must go now! Why are you both just standing there?"

Cowboy relaxed slightly as he saw Maeng. His guard was up and his gut told him something wasn't right, but they were both saying all the right things to make him believe that they were allies. His head was still in a fog and he was in a lot of pain. He wasn't sure if his paranoia was caused by his injuries or something more.

"If you stay here, we cannot protect you," T'ae warned. "The army will find you as they found Pak."

"You must hurry!" Maeng said.

"I think I should call my friends, first," Cowboy said.

"You can talk to them when you are across. We have coordinated this through your government," T'ae said.

"Which government?" Cowboy asked.

"What do you mean?" T'ae asked.

"You said you made contact with my government – which one?"

"I understand your suspicion, but we truly must leave now. As I have explained, we work with the CIA and they are helping to get you out. We cannot allow you to use that phone because the North Korean government may be listening," Maeng answered.

"There is no more time," T'ae said.

Cowboy reluctantly complied. T'ae grabbed the jacket off the cot and handed it to him once more. "You must wear this and keep the hood up to help conceal your identity."

"I stand out no matter what I wear, mate," Cowboy said as he accepted the jacket and put it on.

"Please do as we say," Maeng said. "We are trying to help you."

Cowboy put the jacket on and followed them up the stairs and out of the basement. They led him through the tiny kitchen and outside, where an old, four-door sedan was waiting in the darkness.

"Please put the hood on," T'ae said before getting in the driver's seat.

Cowboy put the hood on and got into the backseat as Maeng took shotgun. T'ae put the car in gear and the diesel engine roared.

They pulled onto the empty highway. Cowboy did his best to keep track of their progress, but he had no idea where he was or which way was home. The pitch black highway and lack of cultural lighting from the many homes without electricity weren't helping either.

They droned along the highway for twenty minutes and then pulled off the highway onto a narrow dirt road. T'ae put the car in park and killed the car's engine and headlights.

"What now?" Cowboy asked.

"We wait," T'ae said.

Moments later a pair of headlights flashed in the distance. T'ae and Maeng exited, and then T'ae opened the door for Cowboy. The hair on the back of his neck was standing up. Something about it just didn't feel right.

"What's this?" Cowboy asked.

"These are our associates," T'ae said. "They will take you the rest of the way."

"Who do they work for?" Cowboy asked suspiciously.

"Come," Maeng said. "We mustn't keep them waiting."

Cowboy tried to get a feel for his surroundings as he limped along behind T'ae and Maeng. It was nearly pitch black with a moonless night, but Cowboy could see that there were fields on either side. He could just make out the silhouette of a mountain to his left and an abyss of darkness to his right.

His escape options were limited, but as they approached four dark figures, he at least had a plan.

"Wait here," T'ae said.

Maeng stood by Cowboy as T'ae continued toward the figures. As Cowboy's eyes adjusted, he saw that they were four men dressed in dark clothing. They spoke to T'ae in Korean. One of the men pulled out a lighter and lit cigarette. The glow from the lighter was just enough for Cowboy to see that they were wearing camouflage.

"Are they military?" Cowboy asked.

Maeng said nothing as she stood next to Cowboy and watched T'ae.

"Answer me," Cowboy whispered.

T'ae stepped out of the way and the four men approached. As they grew closer, Cowboy could now clearly see that they were all military.

"What in the bloody hell is going on?" Cowboy asked.

"I'm sorry," Maeng said.

Cowboy pushed her out of the way and started running toward the field to his right. The pain from his injuries was overwhelming, but he pushed through as he stumbled through the field. He could hear the men running behind him as they gave chase. He ran as fast as he could, pushing through the pain as he heard them shouting.

Cowboy ran through a drainage ditch and tripped. He did a forward somersault and tried to get back up. Within seconds, the men were on top of him. They punched him in the gut and started kicking him. The hits knocked the wind out of him as the men flexcuffed his hands behind his back.

As they rolled him over, Cowboy saw Maeng hover over him with a needle.

"I am sorry. I had hoped this would go easier for you," she said as she stuck it in his neck.

"Who are you? Where are you taking me? Why did you do this?" Cowboy mumbled before drifting into unconsciousness.

CHAPTER FORTY-NINE

Spectre was sitting in the hangar next to his broken Flanker as Kruger and Ringo walked in carrying their gear.

"What the fuck are you still doing here?" Kruger barked.

"Good to see you too, *bub*," Spectre said as he stood to meet them.

"I'll go check on the others," Ringo said, not wanting to get in the middle of whatever shitstorm was about to be unleashed.

"I asked you a question," Kruger said. "You were wheels up before I left."

Spectre stood his ground as Kruger aggressively approached. "That is correct."

"Well, what the fuck happened?" Kruger asked. "Why are you here?"

"I heard about Woody and Cowboy's situations and I want to help."

"Help?" Kruger asked and then pointed to the Flanker behind Spectre. "With one engine? Or one kidney?"

"Whoa, whoa, that is not my fault," Spectre said. "There's no reason to make this personal. *You* talked me into this and I talked Woody into it. We both owe it to him to do everything we can to get him out. You need my help."

"It doesn't matter who talked who into what, bub. What exactly can you do to help without a jet to fly?"

"I don't know, but Woody is my friend and I'm not just going to fly home and forget about him. Put one of those DARPA pods on an A-10 and let me escort you in. Fix this jet and let's fight our way in. Hell, put me in the command center and I'll make copies and get coffee. But I'm not leaving my buddy behind."

"Go home, Spectre," Kruger said, sighing as he shook his head.

"Not without Woody," Spectre replied. "You know me better than that. You need all the help you can get"

Sierra Carter walked into the hangar from Coolio's work center, interrupting the standoff. "Ringo told me you were out here, Kruger."

She walked up to him and hugged him, holding him tightly as he did little to resist. "I'm so sorry about Natasha," she said.

"I know you're upset, man, and I'm sorry for your loss," Spectre said. "But please just let me help you."

"We don't have time for this," Kruger said as he squirmed free of Sierra's grip. "What have you learned?"

"We think we have a location on Reginald," Sierra said. "Coolio is working on it now."

Kruger turned to walk with Sierra. As Spectre followed, Kruger turned and went face to face with him. "Go home. I won't ask you again."

"Not until everyone comes home," Spectre said defiantly. "You know damned well I'm not going anywhere. You're just wasting time now."

Sierra grabbed Kruger's arm and turned him back toward the door for Coolio's workstation. "Come now, Kruger. We don't have time for this, and we may need all the help we can get."

"Thank you, Sierra," Spectre said as he followed them.

"Don't think you won, bub," Kruger warned.

The trio walked into Coolio's workstation. Coolio was busy clicking through satellite feeds while Ringo and Tuna watched.

"What do you have, Coolio?"

Hearing Kruger's voice, Coolio spun around in his chair and attempted to hug Kruger. Kruger blocked him and pushed him back. "What the hell do you think you're doing?"

"I'm so sorry, Kruger," Coolio said. "About Natasha."

"Would everyone please stop trying to hug me? You can throw the pity party later. Right now, we have two of our guys in enemy territory and we need to get them out. Coolio, what do you have?"

"I found the satellite phone Cowboy used to call in," Coolio said as he rushed back to his desk. "I was able to remotely power it back on long enough to track it."

Coolio zoomed in on a satellite image. "I narrowed it down to this farm house, just north of Kaesong. I don't have any real time imagery on it yet, but I'm working on it."

Kruger turned to Tuna. "Any words from Chapman on the asset that contacted them about Cowboy? *Black Ice*, I think it was?"

"Last, I heard, he was captured by the North Koreans," Tuna said.

"What about Woody?" Kruger asked.

"Our asset on the inside visually confirmed his presence in the hospital. He's on a ventilator, but they're planning to move him to their Hoeryong Reeducation Camp. We think it's by train," Sierra replied.

"*Train?*" Kruger asked.

"The North Korean Army has a highly secure train that they use to move political prisoners and high value cargo from south to north. It has a medical car that we think they'll use to keep Woody stable during the transport."

"Do we know when?"

"The train is on its way there, boss," Coolio replied. "I am tracking it now. My guess is it'll be there within the next few hours – longer if it makes any stops."

"So, we'll have to split up the rescue forces, then," Ringo said.

"That seems risky," Tuna said. "It's going to take all of us to take down a train."

Kruger considered the options as he stared at the satellite image of the farm house on Coolio's screen.

"It's the only option we've got, mate," Ringo said. "We can't leave either of them behind."

"Could you do both? Extract one and then the other?" Sierra asked.

"No," Ringo replied. "That's way too large of a tactical footprint. We'll lose the element of surprise if a firefight kicks off and we have to hightail it out of there."

Kruger finally broke his silence as the debate continued. "Tuna, are the 160th boys still on standby?"

They had asked the 160th Special Operations Aviation Regiment – the most elite helicopter flying unit in the U.S. Army – to be on standby in case they needed a ride. While they previously used their own in-house pilots, their rotary wing capabilities had been eliminated with the death of "Shorty" Roberts and his crew in Iraq two years earlier.

"They're on the other side of the base, standing by," Tuna said. "Why, what are you thinking?"

"Did they bring the stealth Blackhawks?" Kruger asked, referring to the specially modified and highly classified MH-X Blackhawk helicopters that had been used in Operation Neptune to kill Osama Bin Laden.

"They did."

"Both of them?"

"That's what I'm to understand," Tuna replied.

"Good, we'll need them. We'll send a team to grab Cowboy or recon the farmhouse and the rest will intercept that train."

"Kruger, we can't possibly stop that train on our own," Tuna said.

"We can if you let me help," Spectre interjected from the back of the room.

Everyone turned to look at Spectre. Before Kruger could snap at him, Sierra asked, "How?"

"Take the DARPA pod off the Flanker in the hangar and hang it on an A-10. Let me do what A-10 guys do."

"That's suicide," Tuna said.

"No," Kruger said as he mulled it over. "It just might work. But we've got a lot of planning to do and a short amount of time. Let's get Chapman on the phone."

CHAPTER FIFTY

It was just after 3 A.M. when Spectre walked out to preflight the jet. He was operating on just a few hours of sleep, adrenaline, and a Rip-It energy drink Coolio had given him. It reminded him of his first combat tour in the Air Force Reserve flying F-16s in Iraq.

He was amazed at the efficiency of the folks working with their top secret operation. Within an hour of coming up with their plan, DARPA technicians had an A-10C in the hangar and were making the necessary modifications to make the aircraft survivable for this mission.

While they worked, Spectre had taken a short nap and then joined the other pilots from the mission for the briefing. He could tell none of them – except the 160th Nightstalker pilots who appeared to be used to such last-minute operations – were thrilled to be flying such a critical mission into North Korea with a plan that might as well have been scribbled onto a bar napkin.

When they were finished, the two F-22 and two F-35 pilots returned to their side of the base. They would take off shortly after Spectre and the helicopters, and would provide both air superiority and Suppression of Enemy Air Defenses (SEAD) as necessary to ensure all players made it to the objective and back across the DMZ safely.

The crew chief saluted Spectre as he approached the aircraft. "Beautiful night to go flying, sir."

"How's the jet?" Spectre asked as he returned the salute.

"Best flying jet on the base, sir. And it looks like your friends have made it even better," he said, indicating the DARPA pod on the left wing.

"It'll be our little secret," Spectre said.

"Of course, sir. I've been read in and I'm not telling anyone. Unlike Hillary Clinton, my ass would end up in jail if I was careless with a secret like this."

"That's funny," Spectre said with a chuckle. "And you can stop calling me sir. Call me Spectre. What's your first name?"

"Joe," the crew chief replied.

"Where are you from, Joe?"

"Fort Smith, Arkansas, sir…uhh…I mean, *Spectre*."

"Well, Joe, thank you for giving me such an awesome jet tonight. We're going to need all the help we can get for this one," Spectre said as he shook Joe's hand.

"My pleasure, Spectre."

Spectre pulled his flashlight out of his helmet bag and placed the bag next to the ladder. He did a thorough walk around, paying close attention to the DARPA EA pods on the wings. The engineers at DARPA had managed to find a second pod for the mission. Having two that worked in unison would prevent the blanking issue that happened during a sharp turn.

The aircraft was loaded for just about anything, carrying a mix of laser guided bombs, Maverick missiles, cluster bomb unit munitions, and rockets. Somehow the engineers had also managed to retrofit two AIM-9X heat-seeking air to air missiles as well, a feat Spectre had been told was impossible with the A-10 due to hardware and software limitations. And yet the technicians at DARPA had done it in hours.

When he was finished with the preflight and satisfied that everything was in good working order, Spectre climbed up the ladder and settled into the cockpit. Joe followed him up the ladder and connected his G-suit and the parachute risers from his seat to his harness and then shook his hand.

"Good luck, sir," Joe said and then descended the ladder.

Spectre took a minute to reorient himself with the A-10. He hadn't flown it in nearly two years, and most recently, he had been eating, sleeping, and breathing the Flanker and its systems since their trip to Europe. For a moment, all the systems knowledge he had of the A-10 seemed to blur with the SU-35 and the F-16 that he had spent most of his career flying.

After doing a quick cockpit sweep and methodically touching every switch to make sure it was in the right position, Spectre felt comfortable that his mind was recaged and he was ready to fly. If he had been back at the squadron, they would've insisted that he do an emergency procedures simulator mission for practice prior to returning to the air, but in this case, there was no time and those rules didn't apply.

Spectre went through the startup procedures in a deliberate and methodical manner. They had plenty of time, and Spectre wanted to make sure he didn't miss anything by rushing through it. He needed every system to be online and ready once airborne. It was a short flight and there would be little time to troubleshoot failed systems once in the air.

Joe finished up his final checks, wished Spectre luck a final time, and then disconnected from the intercom. Spectre switched the ARC-210 secure radio to the operations frequency that Coolio was monitoring.

"Jabos One-One is ready," Spectre reported.

"Oracle copies," Coolio replied. "Your fighters are just starting up now and Chariot One and Two are being loaded."

"Jabos," Spectre replied.

He held just outside the hangar with the position and strobe lights off while waiting for Chariot One to report ready. As he sat there running through the mission plan in his mind, he checked the specially installed control panel for the DARPA pods. They were both powered on and their built-in tests reported that they were functioning correctly.

"Chariot One is ready," the Nightstalker pilot reported with a slight southern drawl.

"Jabos copies. Oracle, Jabos One-One, taxi, words."

"No other words – press," Coolio replied.

Spectre switched to the ground frequency and called for taxi as he flipped on his lights. As he taxied out, he could see the two, ultra-secret stealth Blackhawks with their rotors spinning next to the hangar near his. Ringo and his team were still loading their gear into the second one.

"Jabos One-One, cleared for takeoff, left turnout to the high pattern approved," the Osan Tower controller said as Spectre reported number one for the runway.

"Jabos One-One, cleared for takeoff," Spectre replied.

Spectre taxied onto the runway and held the brakes as he pushed the throttles forward. He wanted to do a static takeoff to ensure both engines were operating normally since his jet was heavily loaded. When the engines stabilized at military power, Spectre released the brakes.

FINI FLIGHT

His seat-of-the-pants feeling was all wrong as the jet started rolling down the runway. The Flanker had really messed with his internal clock. It felt like he was barely moving as the A-10 lumbered down the runway. He kept checking his engine instruments to ensure he hadn't lost an engine because it felt even slower than the single-engine takeoff he'd done in the Flanker less than twenty-four hours prior.

The A-10 finally reached rotation speed and Spectre gently eased back on the stick. As he got airborne, he raised the gear and flaps and the jet slowly climbed away. He climbed to two thousand feet and made a left turn, turning downwind as he pulled the panoramic night vision goggles out of its case and attached them to his helmet over the Scorpion HMIT helmet-mounted cueing system that covered his right eye.

He looked off his left wing and saw Chariot One take off from the ramp and start to climb away. Reaching the end of the runway he had just taken off from, Spectre made a left-hand turn to follow the helicopter.

Spectre shadowed the helicopter as it turned north toward Kaesong. In less than twenty minutes, they'd be crossing into North Korean airspace, and from there, another fifteen minutes to intercept the train.

As he flew his racetrack pattern over the much slower helicopter, Spectre saw the datalink symbol for the second helicopter appear on his screen and start moving away from Osan Air Base. Moments later, the four fighters charged with protecting Spectre from surface to air missiles and enemy fighters also took off from Osan Air Base.

Spectre took a deep breath and exhaled slowly as the exhale valve on his mask clicked. *So far, so good*, he thought. *At least everyone has made it airborne.*

The helicopter flew at five hundred feet as Spectre flew overhead at two-thousand. As they neared the border, it descended to a nap-of-the-earth profile just a few feet above the terrain. Despite being stealth, they weren't taking any chances with the North Korean SAMs. Ideally, he would've had two A-10s to daisy chain around the helicopter to protect it from ground fire, but since Spectre was the only A-10 out there, the plan was for him to stay high and fly slow and slightly ahead until they neared the train, and then push out in front at low level to clear for threats.

"Chariot One LEROY JENKINS," the Blackhawk pilot called out over the secure frequency, using their code word to indicate they had hit the run-in point that started at the DMZ.

They had just breached North Korean airspace. They were completely committed now.

CHAPTER FIFTY-ONE

Ringo had only eaten a banana before loading up into the helicopter. It was a trick an old RAF helo pilot had taught him during his time with the Special Air Service. "Because it tastes the same coming back up as it does going down," the pilot had mused.

Although he trusted the bloke up front and had done hundreds of flights like this, Ringo could never quite shake the nervousness he always got when first strapping into a helicopter. It was just too many moving parts flying together in close formation, and he had lost too many buddies in helicopter crashes in training and in combat.

But Ringo was a professional and he knew he had to focus on the mission at hand. Cowboy and Woody were in trouble and deep in bad guy territory. They had to bring their boys home.

He shook off his doubts and compartmentalized his fears as he always did as the advanced Blackhawk lifted off the ramp. He was leading a six-man team with Churchill and Sledge and three SEALs from Seal Team Six who went by Tommy, Paco, and Lars. They were in the second helicopter heading straight for the farmhouse where Coolio had tracked Cowboy's satellite phone in hopes of recovering Cowboy and bringing him home.

Ringo and his team were carrying their custom suppressed H&K 416s, and wearing their specially designed and fitted Dragonsilk body armor jackets and pants, while the SEALs had more traditional lightweight ceramic body armor plates. Tommy and Paco carried suppressed H&K MP7A1s, while Lars carried a Knights Armament SR-25 sniper rifle.

After twenty minutes of calm, as he collected his thoughts and mentally walked through the mission, Ringo heard "Hold on!"

The pilot descended to just a few feet above the terrain. Ringo kept his night vision equipment off, having decided that it was better to just see a black abyss outside than to know how truly close to death they were.

Ringo held on as the helicopter started banking, climbing, and diving as it navigated the terrain. Across from him, Ringo saw that Paco had his eyes closed and was clutching something in his hands. His lips were moving – Ringo guessed that he was equally nervous about the flight and praying for a safe arrival. *Not the worst idea, mate,* Ringo thought.

As the helicopter maneuvered through the valleys, Ringo checked his GPS wristwatch. They were just passing Koesong and would be on station in a few minutes. He said his own silent prayer as he felt the helicopter suddenly climb and decelerate.

"Thirty seconds," the pilot said calmly over the intercom.

Ringo unstrapped from his seat and removed his headset. The crew chief opened the side door and Ringo flipped down the night vision on his helmet. While the SEALs were using Panoramic Night Vision Goggles, Ringo and the other members of Project Archangel had specially designed lightweight night vision devices developed by ODIN with both color night vision and infrared/thermal capabilities.

Tommy led the team of SEALs to the right-side door as Ringo made his way to the left-side door. The crew chief hooked up the fast ropes and tossed them down as the helicopter slowed to a hover. He gave them a thumbs up and both teams descended their respective ropes.

Ringo hit the ground first followed by Sledge and then Churchill. They quickly started toward the farmhouse as the rope dropped behind them and the helicopter moved away. They had been dropped just outside the perimeter of the fence surrounding the small farmhouse and headed to their designated ingress point on the north side of the compound. Churchill broke the lock using a small pair of bolt cutters and they entered the front yard.

Tommy and his team moved to the south side and cut through the barbwire to enter. Tommy held the wire up for the others to duck under and then the three men moved to the rear door of the farmhouse. "Cujo Two is in position," Tommy announced over the radio.

Ringo and company had stacked up on the front door. So far, no one had stirred and no lights had come on. They had passed a car on their way to the door that matched the one Coolio had tracked from Cowboy's original location.

"Execute," Ringo ordered.

Churchill breached the door using a small charge. As the door swung open, Ringo entered first, followed by Sledge. Simultaneously, Tommy and his team breached their assigned door and entered.

Ringo and company cleared the kitchen and then moved to the small living area while Tommy and his team cleared the two bedrooms. "We've got two in here," Tommy reported. "Bedrooms are clear. No sign of Cowboy."

"Cujo One copies," Ringo replied.

They found the basement door. After a silent countdown, Churchill once again opened it and Ringo entered with rifle up. Sledge and Churchill followed close on his heels as he descended the stairs into the dark basement.

They found signs of life – an empty bowl and glass and a cot with a ruffled blanket – but no sign of Cowboy anywhere. They searched for hidden rooms or compartments where Cowboy might have been held, but found none.

"It's clear down here, boss," Sledge reported.

"Cujo One is clear, Chariot Two, we'll be ready for pickup in sixty seconds with two HVTs," Ringo said over the tactical frequency.

"Chariot Two copies, still clear out here," the pilot replied.

Ringo led the team back up the stairs and met Tommy's team. They had the two prisoners on their knees with hoods over their heads. Even in the darkness, it was easy to tell they were male and female.

Ringo took his helmet off and then walked to the male and ripped of his hood.

"Where is your prisoner?" Ringo asked angrily.

The man looked up at him but said nothing. Ringo could see that the man knew exactly what he was talking about.

"I know you speak English, mate," Ringo said as he slung his rifle and drew his Sig P320 handgun. "Answer me."

The man continued staring at Ringo defiantly.

"Thirty seconds," the helicopter pilot called over the radio.

Ringo turned and pointed the gun at the girl's head. "Answer or I put a bullet in her head, mate."

"He's gone!" the man yelled out.

"Gone? Gone where?" Ringo asked.

"I don't know!"

Ringo pressed the barrel of the gun against the hood on the girl's head. "Of course you do, mate. Now, start talking."

"The Chinese," the girl said softly as she trembled behind the hood. "He went with the Chinese."

Ringo holstered his weapon as he heard the helicopter arrive outside. "Grab them and let's go," he ordered as he put his helmet back on.

"Oracle, Cujo One," Ringo said over the tactical frequency as his team escorted the two prisoners out of the door.

"Go ahead, Cujo," Coolio replied.

"We've got a problem. We're bringing back two HVTs, but they're saying they gave the package to the Chinese."

"Say again, Cujo?"

"I said Cowboy's gone, mate," Ringo said. "These two HVTs say they handed him over to the Chinese."

"Oracle copies," Coolio replied. "Will pass to Punisher."

CHAPTER FIFTY-TWO

Spectre armed the A-10C's 30MM GAU-8 as they approached the intercept point ten miles northeast of Kaesong, just outside of Changp'ung, while the train skirted the edge of the mountain range to the west. He could see the armored train barreling down the tracks on his Multi-Function Display (MFD) using the infrared mode of his Litening Advanced Targeting Pod.

So far, Spectre's Radar Warning Receiver (RWR) had been quiet. They had flown up the Ryesong River to avoid Kaesong and then turned northeast toward Changp'ung as they cleared the outer edges of the city. He could just start to see the glow of the sunrise off the coast as he saw the diamond representing the train off in the distance through his helmet-mounted display. It was right on time and if all went well, they'd have it stopped and Woody extracted before official sunrise.

The DARPA pods were working as advertised – the North Korean Air Defense System was none-the-wiser to their presence. On his Tactical Awareness Display, Spectre could see that the F-35s and F-22s were airborne and orbiting in their respective Combat Air Patrols, ready to strike if the situation changed. It didn't necessarily make him feel safe, but it certainly helped ease his anxiety.

Fifteen miles from the Ingress Point (IP), Spectre pushed the throttles to their stops and descended down to one hundred feet, leaving the helicopter behind as the A-10 accelerated through three hundred knots. They had worked out the timing to the second, giving him exactly two minutes to reach the train, disable it and the anti-aircraft artillery (AAA) in the third car, and call "RAMBO" to let the helicopter pilots know the area had been sanitized and it was safe to proceed. The margins were razor thin.

Spectre hit the Ingress Point (IP) and called "SHAGGY DOG" and banked to the right as he hacked the clock. He saw the anti-aircraft gun clearly through the targeting pod and slewed the pod to the train's engine. It locked on and began tracking the moving target. His heart started racing as he looked out to his left for any signs that the AAA had come alive and was engaging him. He had logged hundreds of hours in combat, but had never been up-close and personal with the World War II style AAA.

When Spectre's A-10 reached the appropriate "pop" point, he pulled the stick back sharply and climbed. He looked out behind the left canopy bow and found the train barreling ahead, still unaware of his presence. He rolled the aircraft and aligned it perpendicular to the train's path of travel.

Using the A-10C's gun reticle, Spectre used the symbology to calculate the lead required based on the speed the targeting pod estimated the train was traveling. At just over a mile,

Spectre pulled the trigger, causing the A-10's GAU-8 to roar to life. *BRRRRRT.*

He tracked the train's engine until four thousand feet and then released the trigger. The combat mix of high explosive incendiary and armor-piercing rounds shredded the train's engine as Spectre pulled off into a right-hand turn.

Spectre checked the clock as he turned back east to gain separation. He still had a minute and fifteen seconds. He looked over his shoulder and saw the train's engine erupt in a fireball, but he couldn't see what the artillery was doing yet.

He flew east until the distance to target in the HUD read five miles and then turned back toward the train. Using the targeting pod, he slewed over to the AAA train car and began lasing as he switched from gun to the AGM-65 Maverick. He could see flashes as the artillery tried to shoot in his general direction, probably hearing him off in the distance.

The moving target indicator in his targeting pod showed that the train was slowing. At least the first part of his objective was a success, but without killing the AAA piece, it wouldn't matter. The helicopter would never be able to land in a hot LZ.

With the Maverick tracking the artillery, Spectre pressed the pickle button on the top of the stick. The Maverick's rocket motor fired and headed toward the target. Spectre made a hard turn to the left to remain outside of the effective range of the AAA as the Maverick sped toward its target.

The AAA picked up Spectre's jet and fired toward him as he turned back to the east. Spectre could see the flak exploding in the air in his mirrors as he remained well outside its effective range. The targeting pod masked momentarily in the turn and then Spectre watched the Maverick impact on the MFD, washing out the FLIR image. He looked up at the clock and saw that he had forty-five seconds left. Still plenty of time, but he would need to be sure the AAA was dead before clearing the helicopter into the target area.

Spectre turned back north as he made his battle damage assessment. His stomach turned as he saw the picture settle and the AAA start firing again. The Maverick had either hit short or failed to do anything against the armor and would require another attack run.

With just under forty seconds remaining, Spectre quickly considered his options. He could try another Maverick attack, but there was no guarantee that it would work. He had other options, but all he could think of was what one of his instructors had always told him, "When in doubt, go to the gun."

Spectre switched back to the gun and turned back toward the train. He could see the flak exploding in the air in front of him through his night vision goggles. The GAU-8 had a better standoff range, but it would be close. With less than thirty seconds remaining, it was his best and final option.

"Jabos, status," Oracle called over the tactical frequency. "Chariot One is approaching the IP."

"Standby," Spectre replied as he lined up the AAA in his HUD.

The flak grew more intense in front of him as Spectre lined up the gun cross. The muzzle flashes made it easier to single out the AAA car in the long train, but also meant he was getting close to its effective range.

Spectre opened fire as the flak started exploding around him. He was in a gun to gun standoff, praying that the A-10's prolific cannon would win. He squeezed the trigger, holding it on the AAA as he tried to ignore the hail of explosions going off around him.

He held the trigger down until, pressing well into the range of the AAA since he knew he only had one shot. He released the trigger at two thousand feet and then pulled up high and right, away from the now-stopped train.

As he looked over his left shoulder, he saw the artillery on fire and blowing up with secondary explosions.

"Jabos, status!" the helicopter pilot called out over the radio.

Spectre looked at the clock. *Ten seconds.*

"*RAMBO!*" Spectre replied as he maneuvered his jet back toward the IP to escort them to the train.

"Chariot One, IP inbound," the helicopter pilot replied coolly a few moments later.

CHAPTER FIFTY-THREE

"Boss, we've got a problem," Coolio said, transmitting over a direct, secure frequency to Kruger.

"What's going on?" Kruger asked as he held on while the helicopter maneuvered through a valley toward the train carrying Woody.

"Cowboy's not-"

"One minute!" the pilot called out, interrupting Coolio.

"Say again? Make it quick. We're approaching the LZ."

"Cowboy was not at the farmhouse. The team grabbed two prisoners for interrogation, but one of them said he was given to the Chinese."

"Copy. Focus on their exfil and our current mission and then you can work on finding him."

"I think I can work on both-"

"Thirty seconds!" the pilot called.

"There's nothing we can do about it anyway, Coolio. Just focus on this one. I've gotta go. We can talk more on the exfil."

"Understood, boss, it looks like the LZ is clear for you guys," Coolio replied. "I'm switching back to the main channel."

Kruger looked to his left at Tuna who gave him a questioning look while mouthing *Cowboy?* He shook his head in reply and then looked across at the three SEALs across from them – Bud, Cecil, and Bullet. They were part of the eight-man team to go get Woody, including Tuna, Dusty, and an Air Force Pararescue Jumper that went by Donnie.

"You squids ready?" Kruger asked as he felt the helicopter slow as it approached the train. Before Odin and Project Archangel, Kruger had been a member of the Army's SFOD-D "Delta." Despite having been out for over a decade, his sense of interservice rivalry with the SEALs was still alive and well.

"Try to keep up, old man," Bud shot back as he readied his rifle.

Kruger unstrapped and moved to the door as the helicopter stopped and did a pedal turn. The pilot gently set the main wheels down on the top of the car they had identified as the medical car. One by one all seven members exited and the helicopter took off again to provide overwatch with a fourth SEAL that went by "Rico" providing aerial sniper support.

Explosions rocked the front of the train as Spectre dropped CBU-87 cluster bombs over the troops that had dismounted and were in the open. The soldiers on board were scattering like ants, attempting unsuccessfully to fight back against the onslaught from the helicopter's mini-gun and the A-10.

Dusty and Tuna went to work with their specially designed advanced handheld plasma cutters on the roof of the medical car as the rest of the team set up a perimeter around them. Kruger picked off a few soldiers with his suppressed modified

H&K 416, but so far resistance was lighter than expected. The air support appeared to be occupying the North Korean soldiers' attention.

It took them less than two minutes to cut through the steel and create an opening large enough for them to get through and return with the litter carrying Woody. Bud and his team stayed above to maintain the perimeter while Kruger, Tuna, Dusty, and Donnie went down into the medical car to retrieve Woody.

Kruger went down the newly made rabbit hole first and picked off an armed North Korean guard. The medical technicians and doctors fled as they saw the armed men enter from the ceiling. The ones that didn't were flexcuffed by Dusty and Tuna as Kruger and Donnie proceeded to the makeshift intensive care unit at the back of the car.

As they reached the door of the sterile tent, a guard emerged holding his hands in the air. Kruger grabbed him and threw him to the ground, flexcuffing him before rejoining Donnie and entering Woody's ICU tent.

Kruger's heart sank as he entered behind Donnie and saw Woody hooked up to the ventilator. His face was bloodied and swollen and he had bruising all over his body. A nurse in a white uniform held her hands up as she stood next to his bed. Donnie grabbed her and forced her toward the door where Tuna and Dusty flexcuffed her and moved her out of the way.

"We've got three minutes," Kruger said, looking at his watch.

Donnie shook his head and grimaced as he examined Woody. "I may need more time. This is a rat's nest."

"You've got three minutes, bub," Kruger repeated.

"This is way worse than I expected," Donnie said as he took his backpack off and went to work on Woody. "I'm not sure we'll be able to move him."

"We don't have a choice," Tuna said as he guarded the entrance to the tent.

"I'm just saying," Donnie said. "I don't know how long I can keep him alive in this condition. He may not make the flight home."

"Just shut your manpleaser and get to work, bub," Kruger snapped. He could feel the rage building inside him – from losing Natasha, failing to kill Il-Sung the first time, and potentially losing both Cowboy and Woody. His ability to compartmentalize his feelings was being overwhelmed by the growing rage.

"Hand me that Ambu bag," Donnie said to Dusty as he started disconnecting tubes.

Dusty did as he was ordered and then Donnie stepped aside as he connected the Ambu bag where the ventilator had been connected. "Count to six, squeeze. Count to six, squeeze. Got it?"

Dusty nodded and squeezed the bag as Donnie continued prepping Woody for transport.

"Two-minute warning," Kruger announced.

Donnie moved quickly and efficiently around Woody. As he pulled back the sheets, Kruger saw that Woody's legs were broken and not splinted and there was dried blood all over the sheets. He knew Donnie had given his honest and professional assessment – Kruger just didn't like it.

"Alright, let's get the litter ready," Donnie said.

Tuna removed it from his back and Kruger helped unfold it next to the metal bed.

"Okay, I'll be at the head. Dusty, you keep bagging him. We'll use the sheet to transfer. Any questions?"

"Chariot One will be inbound in thirty seconds," the helicopter pilot announced over the tactical frequency.

"3...2...1...Lift!" Donnie said as they moved Woody to the litter.

"Nice and slow, let's move him," Donnie said as they started toward the opening thru which they had entered the medical car.

They reached the opening where Tuna and Dusty had assembled a collapsible ladder. The helicopter could be heard outside making its final approach to pick them up.

"Coming up!" Kruger yelled.

Bud dropped to his knees to grab the end of the litter. Down below, the team carefully lifted Woody up above their heads and walked him up the ladder. Bud helped pull him onto the remaining roof of the car just as the helicopter did its pedal turn and the crew chief exited to help carry Woody aboard.

The rest of the team climbed the ladder, leaving it behind as Dusty resumed his station at with the Ambu bag. They carried Woody onto the helicopter and then Dusty connected an IV and checked Woody's vitals as the team loaded up.

"He's not good, Kruger," Donnie said as he pulled the stethoscope from his ears and the helicopter lifted off.

"Please..." Kruger said, dropping his gruff demeanor for the first time. "Please...Just keep him alive until we can get him across the border."

CHAPTER FIFTY-FOUR

"Heads up, Jabos, threat, BRAA three-zero-zero, thirty, twenty thousand, hot, hostile, two ship," Spectre heard the flight lead of his F-22 escort call out as he finished his safe escape maneuver after shooting rockets at an approaching convoy of soldiers. "Status, Chariot?"

As Spectre turned back toward the train, he looked down and saw them load Woody into the helicopter. "Millertime," he replied, indicating they had completed the mission and were returning to base.

"Razor One-One copies, green southwest, Razors commit," the F-22 flight lead called, indicating that Spectre's path to the southwest was clear and that he and his wingman were turning to engage the potential threat of fighters thirty miles behind Spectre and the helicopter.

Spectre banked hard to his left and put the egress waypoint on his nose. The plan was for him to fly out in front of the helicopter, scanning for and engaging threats along the egress route to South Korea. It would have ordinarily been done with two A-10s, but Spectre had long since learned to work with what he had.

The sun had started to rise by the time the team had loaded Woody. Spectre had taken off his night vision goggles and was visually scanning for threats. Their egress was far more treacherous now since they no longer had the cover of darkness to help conceal their escape.

Spectre pushed the throttles to the military power stop and accelerated as he descended to one hundred feet above the ground. He was searching for any ground threats along the route as the helicopter trailed behind him. He still had around five hundred rounds of 30MM, one Maverick, and rockets to use if he found any troops, tanks, or other threats along the way.

As he flew just above the treetops, Spectre's Radar Warning Receiver (RWR) suddenly detected a MiG-21 coming from the direction of Kaesong. Neither the F-22s nor Coolio watching the AWACS and early warning radar feeds had mentioned it, but the RWR indicated the MiG-21 clearly heading right toward Spectre and the helo. He had no idea what the distance was, but given the direction and their distance from Kaesong, he assumed it was inside of fifteen miles.

Spectre looked down at the EA pod control panel, confirming both pods were working. There was no way the MiG was tracking him, but his RWR was still picking up its radar. The MiG was heading toward the site of the train attack and would soon become an imminent threat. The EA pods seemed to be working but would not stop the approaching fighter from picking them up visually.

"Jabos One-One spiked one-six-zero," Spectre called, informing the Raptors that he was receiving the radar signature of the MiG-21 from the southeast.

"Razor One-One clean," the Raptor lead replied, indicating that he had not picked up the threat on his sensors. "Recommend lean west."

With terrain to his southwest and his fighter escorts out of range, Spectre had no choice but to turn to engage the threat. "Chariot, lean west, Jabos One is engaged."

"Chariot copies."

Spectre switched to an air-to-air mode and selected the AIM-9X. It wasn't the F/A-18 that he had spent most of his career flying air to air in, but with a helmet-mounted cueing system and the high off-boresight capability of the 9X, Spectre liked his chances against the old Soviet fighter.

The sunrise made it hard for Spectre to see anything, and with no radar in the A-10C, visual was all he had. All he could do was put the RWR indication on his nose and hope the DARPA pods continued doing their thing to mask him while he looked for the threat.

As he accelerated through three hundred knots and started a shallow climb, Spectre saw a speck on the horizon. He used his helmet reticle to uncage the AIM-9X on it. A solid tone in his headset indicated that the AIM-9X was tracking and ready to unleash hell.

Spectre held the shot, wanting to get the visual ID as he had trained to do so many times in his career. As he started to turn to engage the single fighter, it suddenly made a hard turn away from Spectre. Its afterburner plume was clearly visible as it rolled out heading northeast away from the helicopter.

"The MiG has gone cold!" Spectre announced over the frequency.

"Should no longer be a factor," Coolio replied. "I was able to give their early warning radar system a false target twenty miles north of the train. Should be clear to the DMZ now."

"Nicely done!" Spectre replied as he banked hard to his left to intercept the helicopter and escort it the rest of the way home.

Spectre used the datalink to find the helicopter and rejoin ahead of it. The rest of their egress route was clear. Spectre watched it land on the roof of the hospital at Seoul and then he landed at Osan Air Base.

He went to the de-arm area where crews safed his remaining weapons and the gun. When they were done, he taxied to the isolated hangar they had been working out of and shut down. As he opened the canopy, Joe climbed the ladder to meet him. Spectre put his helmet on the canopy rail and exhaled as the stress finally caught up with him.

"Welcome back, sir! Looks like you cleaned off most of your ordnance over there. Mission accomplished?"

"I think I just started World War III actually," Spectre said as he started to unstrap. "No biggy."

"Holy shit, sir," Joe replied, descending the ladder to allow Spectre out.

"I'll be back later. Good jet, by the way!"

Spectre left his gear in the jet and headed straight for the hangar. He went straight in and headed for Coolio's workstation.

"Well?" Spectre asked impatiently. "How is he? Did he make it?"

Coolio spun around in his chair, his eyes were bloodshot. Spectre wasn't sure if it was from crying or just the lack of sleep in the last two days.

"I don't know," Coolio said softly.

"What do you mean, you don't know?"

"The Air Force PJ said he crashed twice on the flight to the hospital. They just rushed him into emergency surgery. Kruger is staying with him."

"Dammit! What about the North Koreans? Are we going to war now?"

Coolio shrugged. "Their artillery is quiet so far. I hacked their intelligence servers and blamed it on a separatist group. That might buy us a few hours or even a day or two until they sort it out."

"And then?"

"And then we hope having Il-Sung out of the picture is enough to keep the peace talks going."

CHAPTER FIFTY-FIVE

Cowboy awoke dazed and confused. He suddenly sat up, realizing he was in a king-sized bed with soft white sheets and a plush comforter. As he did, a pain shot through his side and he looked down to see that he was wearing dark blue silk pajamas.

Cowboy raised his shirt and felt the bandaging on his side. He felt like he was in a haze, but memories of being shot and captured were starting to come back. His whole body was sore and he had a massive headache.

The room was dark, but there was just enough light to see his surroundings. There was a flat screen TV and a dresser in front of him, and a chair by a large window off to his left. It looked like he was in a hotel room suite of some sort. *That can't be right*.

Cowboy slowly moved to the edge of the bed. As his feet hit the floor, he looked down and saw slippers that had been pre-positioned for him. He put them on and stood, grimacing as pain shot through his body.

He shuffled to the window over the hardwood floors, looking around the room for clues as to where he might be. He remembered bits and pieces from North Korea – Pak and calling home. Some of it seemed real, but most of it seemed like remembering a bad dream. The headache wasn't making it any easier to concentrate.

Cowboy pulled back the blackout curtains and looked out the window, revealing a busy metropolis at mid-morning. He was on a high floor in whatever building he was in, eye-level with the tops of a few of the buildings across from him. Down below, there were cars and people bustling through the streets as they went about their work day.

"Would you like breakfast?" a male voice asked from behind him.

Cowboy spun around and took a defensive posture. The man appeared to be Asian and was wearing a suit. His arms were at his side and made no advances as Cowboy stepped back.

"Who are you?" Cowboy demanded.

"It is okay, Mr. Carter," the man said with a thick accent. "I am not here to hurt you."

"I don't know who that is, mate, but you'd better tell me what's going on or else-"

"Please, Mr. Carter, there is no need for that. I know who you are. It is pointless to keep up such a charade."

"Alright, well, just who the bloody hell are you?"

"You may call me Khang. I am not here to hurt you."

"Where am I? Where did you take me?"

"Shanghai," Khang said, still maintaining his position across the room. Cowboy had moved back to the corner near the nightstand and had contemplated using the lamp as a weapon to aid his escape.

"Shanghai? What is your plan, mate?"

"Would you like breakfast?" Khang asked. "I have a chef that can make you anything you like using only the finest ingredients."

"I would like to go home, if you don't mind, thanks."

"I'm afraid that's not possible, Mr. Carter. But, in the meantime, my goal is to make your stay as comfortable and pleasant as possible."

"My stay? Just what the fuck is this?"

"I will return with a variety of options for your breakfast," Khang said as he turned and walked out of the room.

Cowboy followed him. The bedroom was only part of a much larger suite that looked more like an apartment than a hotel room. It had a small kitchen, two bathrooms, and a large living area. Khang walked through the kitchen and living area and out the door.

Cowboy attempted to follow, but the door locked behind Khang and Cowboy couldn't get it open. Despite Khang's pleasant demeanor, there was no doubt that he was a captive. To what end, Cowboy didn't know, but he suspected it was some sort of Chinese intelligence operation.

After unsuccessfully trying the door, Cowboy searched the room for weapons or a means of escape. He looked up and saw surveillance cameras with glowing red lights mounted on the ceiling at every corner. He ignored them as he went to what appeared to be a sliding glass door leading to a balcony. He tried to open it, but it too was locked and unable to be budged.

Straining to open the door caused more pain in his side. Cowboy stumbled to the nearby desk and sat down in the swivel chair. He caught his breath and then searched the drawers of the desk for anything that might help him, finding nothing as he grew increasingly frustrated.

As Cowboy sat contemplating his next move, the door to the penthouse opened. Khang entered with two servers trailing behind him carrying food trays. They headed straight for him and placed the trays on the desk as they removed the covers.

"I hope you will find this sufficient to your needs," Khang said as he poured orange juice into a glass for Cowboy. "If you have any special dietary requirements, please do tell me."

Cowboy studied the food as the servers left the room. Khang stood in front of Cowboy, waiting for his reply and acting more as a personal servant than the captor Cowboy believed him to be. He looked up at Khang as he unfolded the cloth napkin, revealing a set of silverware including a steak knife and fork.

"It would be unwise for you to use them for anything other than their intended purpose," Khang warned as he saw Cowboy eyeing the potential weapons. He showed no emotion or judgment, as if merely stating a fact.

"I don't know what you mean, mate."

"Of course you do," Khang replied. "You will be treated with dignity and respect in your time here, but any attempts to commit violence will be met with greater force. As the person charged with your safety and well-being, it is my duty to inform you of the consequences of such a miscalculation."

"Fine," Cowboy said as he picked up the fork and stabbed a piece of sausage. "Can I at least eat in peace?"

"Of course," Khang said. "My employer will be in to speak with you shortly."

"Your employer? You don't work for the government?"

"It is of no concern to you," Khang said dismissively. "Finish your meal. There will be plenty of time for discussion later."

"Great," Cowboy said.

Khang nodded and walked out. Cowboy watched him until the door closed and then stuffed his face as quickly as he could. He hid the knife in his sleeve and went back to examining the room for a means of escape.

He went to the sliding glass door and tried using the knife to jimmy the lock. As he futilely tried to open it, he suddenly heard the door open and a voice called out behind him.

"It is a waste of your effort."

Cowboy spun around upon hearing the voice. Khang walked in behind the speaker as Cowboy suddenly dropped the knife and his jaw.

"Oh, bloody hell."

CHAPTER FIFTY-SIX

Spectre was escorted by South Korean police with Sierra, Kruger and Tuna to the hospital that Woody had been taken to an hour earlier. He sat in the backseat with Kruger, and Sierra rode shotgun, while Tuna drove the blacked-out SUV in the convoy of police vehicles with their lights on and sirens blaring.

They arrived at the hospital just before noon and were escorted to Woody's room by a South Korean military liaison. He was in ICU with armed guards standing watch. Spectre led the way into the room, heading right to his friend's side as the others followed him in and stopped at the foot of Woody's bed.

"Jesus, buddy," Spectre said softly as he looked over Woody's wounds. Both legs were broken, his left arm was in a cast, his face was heavily bandaged, and he was on a ventilator.

Spectre turned back to Kruger. "There's no way all of this was caused by the ejection."

"The North Koreans had him, bub," Kruger said. "We're lucky he's alive."

Woody's doctor walked in carrying a chart. He was an older man with gray hair and thick glasses. He didn't bother to acknowledge any of them as he walked to Woody's bedside opposite Spectre.

"How is he, doc?" Spectre asked.

"He is recovering from surgery to relieve cranial swelling. We're keeping him in a medically induced coma for that reason. He also has a partially collapsed lung, several broken bones, and we had to fuse two vertebrae."

"Will he walk again?"

"Only time will tell. For now, our goal is to keep him stable and give him a chance to heal."

"How long will he be in ICU?" Spectre asked.

"If he remains stable and the swelling stays at bay, I hope to move him to a room when I go on call tomorrow. Tonight will be very telling."

"When will you bring him out of the coma?"

"If he makes it through the night, possibly tomorrow morning," the doctor replied.

"Thanks, Doc," Spectre said.

The doctor nodded and finished reviewing Woody's chart before excusing himself. When he was out of the room, Spectre joined Kruger and company.

"I'll stay with him until they discharge him," Spectre whispered. "We need to call his wife and fly her out here."

"I'll do it," Tuna said.

"No, I dragged him into this. I'll do it," Spectre replied. "Besides, she knows me. It'll mean more coming from me."

"I'll have Jenny send a jet to pick her up," Kruger said.

"Thank you," Spectre replied. He still couldn't get used to the idea of Kruger being a billionaire. It was just weird to hear him say things like that.

Kruger's phone vibrated in his pocket. "Excuse me," he said as he walked out of the room.

"What do you have, Coolio?" Kruger asked as the encrypted phone connected.

"Ringo just finished his first interrogation session with the people they picked up at the farmhouse. They're both former North Korean intelligence playing both sides of the resistance movement."

"Did they say who they gave Cowboy to?"

"A Chinese intelligence operative named Khang Zhou. They said he was taking Cowboy to China."

"Do we know where?"

"They said they were intentionally kept in the dark about that. Ringo believes them. I've run a search for all flights out of that area that went to China during that time frame."

"And?"

"I found three. One to Beijing and two to Shanghai. But there's something else."

"What?"

"The Russians didn't stay in Moscow."

Kruger froze after pacing around the ICU waiting area. He looked around to make sure no one was listening and then retreated to the corner of the room. "Where did they go?"

"The plane was on the ground for less than thirty minutes and then took off again with no flight plan."

"No flight plan? Can you track it?"

"It's going to take some time and processing power, but yeah, I think so."

Kruger exhaled slowly. He wanted nothing more than to track down Anatoly or Viktor and find out what the hell happened. More than anything, he wanted vengeance for Natasha's death. But despite his sadness and pure rage over what happened, he knew he had to keep his emotions in check and focus on the mission. One of their own was in hostile territory. Getting him home safely was priority one.

"Work on it only when you have time. Right now, I want every available asset devoted to finding Cowboy. We have to get him home safely."

"Hey boss, hold on a second, Ringo just walked back in," Coolio said abruptly. "He may have something."

Kruger waited impatiently as he tried to listen to their conversation. He overheard "Shanghai" and "Ministry of State Security." He heard Coolio typing as the phone sounded like it had been placed right next to the keyboard. After a few minutes of back and forth with Ringo, Coolio finally picked the phone back up.

"I think we found him!" Coolio said excitedly.

"Spit it out, bub," Kruger snapped.

"The girl – Maeng Min – said she overheard one of Khang's men mention Shanghai when they were carrying Cowboy off after they drugged him. I just confirmed that Khang is an operative with the Ministry of State Security and cross-referenced his name with our various databases. Turns out, he's been known to operate out of a hotel in Shanghai called the Starlight Tower. I'm running facial recognition against their security cameras to confirm, but I think we may have at least found Khang."

"Send a helo to come get us. We'll meet it on the roof. And tell Jenny to have the jet waiting for us to go to Shanghai when we arrive. We'll plan and brief the mission airborne."

"Copy that, boss. I'm on it."

Kruger ended the call and headed back to the room where the others were whispering with each other as they stood at the foot of Woody's bed.

"Let's go," Kruger barked as he stopped in the doorway. "We've got a lead on your brother."

"Where?" Sierra asked.

"Not here. It's not secure. Helo is on its way. I'll tell you when we get airborne."

"Is Reginald okay?"

"Unknown. Coolio thinks he found the guy who took him, so that's a start."

"Then we have no time to waste. Let's go."

"If you get time, ask Coolio to send up a go bag for me. I'll need clothes and a shaving kit while I'm here. And don't forget about Woody's wife," Specter interjected.

"Got it," Kruger said.

"Good luck, Kruger," Spectre said as the trio walked out and headed for the helipad on the hospital roof.

CHAPTER FIFTY-SEVEN

The Starlight Tower was one of the newest luxury hotels in Shanghai. It was modern, sleek, and one of the tallest buildings in the city. No expense had been spared in making it the premiere location for business travelers – from ultra-modern gigabit WiFi throughout the hotel to video teleconferencing equipment in every suite. It was the highest rated hotel in the city.

But what most business travelers staying there didn't know was that the hotel had been constructed under close supervision by the Chinese Ministry of State Security. And that meant that every room had video and audio surveillance and the WiFi was closely monitored. China's primary intelligence service used the hotel not only as an intelligence gathering source to steal from visiting businesses, but also as a means to keep tabs on its own businesses. It was one of many hotels they monitored throughout the country.

The Chinese had built a surveillance network within the hotel that had been largely impenetrable by most foreign intelligence services. Its multiple layers of encryption and firewalls shielded it from the average NSA hacker.

Luckily, "Coolio" Meeks was no average hacker, and the technology he had at his disposal between Odin and Project Archangel allowed him to make quick work of the various encryption protocols. Before the team had even landed at Shanghai, Coolio had managed to access the entire system and was pumping a real-time feed to Sierra's laptop.

After hacking into the software, Coolio had used facial and voice recognition software to search every floor except one. The sixty-second floor appeared to be a dead zone. There were no WiFi hotspots, no networked cameras, and no listening devices. The building schematics showed that it had four penthouse suites located at each corner, and the only access was through a service elevator on the south side of the building.

They deduced that this was where Chinese Intelligence agents conducted operations and likely relied on closed-circuit cameras and networks to prevent inadvertent access, despite the high level of security protocols on their surveillance network. If Khang had taken Cowboy to this hotel, the sixty-second floor was where they were keeping him.

Tactically, the lack of camera access posed its own challenges. By hacking the hotel's feeds, Coolio could easily get them to the service elevator, but they were mostly flying blind after that. The best they could do was use the thermal imaging from the micro-drone. It would give them an incomplete picture of the threat layout, but it was still better than nothing.

The infiltration team consisted of Kruger, Tuna, Ringo, and Sierra dressed as hotel maintenance workers. Churchill and Dusty manned the getaway van parked in the underground parking structure that connected to the service elevator. They each had suppressed Sig P320RX compact handguns chambered in 9MM in case things went sideways, with Churchill and Dusty standing by with heavier firepower if the OP really went south.

Coolio talked them to the service elevator, keeping them clear of roving security patrols in the garage as he looped the security feeds just long enough for them to get by. They entered the elevator pushing a small tool cart and selected the 62nd floor. A prompt appeared on the touchscreen, asking for an employee verification ID.

"Oracle, it's asking for an employee ID and access code," Kruger said over the tactical frequency.

"Standby," Coolio replied.

Kruger waited impatiently as Coolio did his magic. He was sitting in the MI-6 safe house a few blocks away that Sierra had arranged on the flight over.

"Give me something, Oracle," Kruger pressed.

"Try three-seven-eight-six and the passcode is four-four-seven-eight-two-one-one."

Kruger entered it in as instructed. He winced as the system processed the information, but to his surprise, the screen turned green and the elevator began to move.

"We're on the move," Kruger reported. "How?"

"Personnel database. There appears to be a small number of employees with unique access permissions and possible associations with the Ministry of State Security, so I took a wild guess based on their movements through the hotel."

"You're a bloody genius, mate," Ringo said.

"Focus, boys," Sierra said. "We don't know what's waiting for us up there."

"I'm showing six heat signatures, concentrated on the western corner of the building," Coolio said.

"What about the other rooms?" Kruger asked.

"They appear to be unoccupied," Coolio replied.

"Copy," Kruger said.

The elevator stopped and they drew their weapons as the doors opened. The corridor was empty.

"Left turn and the room should be on your right," Coolio said, monitoring them with the drone feed.

Kruger took point and headed straight for the room on the right. He pulled out an RFID cloner and went to work on the door lock. The LED on the small black box turned green simultaneously with the indicator on the door.

After a silent countdown, Kruger pushed the door open, button-hooking left as Tuna and Sierra followed close on his heels. Ringo covered the door, watching for anyone entering from the elevator they had just used.

As Kruger cleared left into the living area, he saw two men in suits standing next to four women dressed in maid uniforms. One of the men saw him and yelled something in Chinese as he saw Kruger's weapon.

The man tried to draw his own weapon, but Kruger dispatched him with two shots to the throat. Tuna had gone right, leaving Sierra behind him who hit the second guard in the left arm and shoulder as he attempted to draw his weapon.

Startled, the maids raised their hands high above their heads and dropped to their knees. As they reached the living area, Kruger and Sierra suddenly froze. Next to the buckets, scrubbing brushes, and bottles of bleach, a six-foot mass was wrapped in Visqueen.

"Are we clear in there?" Ringo yelled from the hallway.

"Jesus Christ," Kruger muttered.

"Oh no!" Sierra yelled as she holstered her weapon and dropped to her knees next to the body.

Tuna ignored the obvious and finished clearing the apartment as Sierra pulled out a knife to cut through the plastic. "Clear," he said as he walked back.

"Oh God!" Sierra cried as she pulled back the plastic and saw her brother's lifeless face. "Reginald!"

"Fuck!" Kruger yelled.

"What's going on over there?" Coolio asked. "I'm showing the elevator in motion. Might be headed to you."

"Cowboy is dead. We're moving to extract," Kruger replied.

CHAPTER FIFTY-EIGHT

Coolio watched the feed from the team's body cameras in stunned silence. When Kruger and Sierra peeled back the plastic on the body they found and said it was Cowboy, Coolio ran the image through his facial recognition software hoping they were mistaken.

The software only confirmed Coolio's fears – 99.87% match. That was Cowboy and those people had been caught trying to dispose of his body and clean up the aftermath. It made Coolio sick to his stomach.

"Oracle, we're going to clear the floor and look for intel and then move to the extraction point. What's the status on the elevator?" Kruger asked over the tactical frequency.

Coolio checked the drone feed and then the hotel's cameras that he could see. "They stopped on a different floor. You're clear for now."

"Copy."

The team cleared the room and then moved on to the other rooms. Methodically, Sierra and Kruger went through each penthouse, gathering as much intel as they could while Tuna and Ringo covered the hallways. Coolio couldn't imagine what Sierra was going through knowing that she had just lost her brother, but he was impressed with how she seemed to compartmentalize it and continue with the mission.

"We have a laptop," Sierra reported as the finished with the final room. "Moving to the elevator."

"Still clear," Coolio replied.

Coolio shadowed the team with the drone as they made their way into the elevator and back to the parking garage. They had loaded Cowboy's body on the maintenance cart and covered it with a sheet. They made it to the getaway vehicle without incident and were clear of the hotel in just a few minutes.

"Headed back to you, Oracle," Dusty reported as he drove the panel van out of the garage.

When the team was safe, Coolio went to work trying to find Khang. He opened the video chat window on his screen and dialed the first contact in his favorites.

"Hey Becca," Coolio said as MI-6 cyber analyst Rebecca Mallory appeared on screen.

"Julio, you look dreadful. Is everything alright?" she asked, brushing her red hair out of her face as she tried to get a closer look at the screen.

Coolio had become friends with Becca while working with Odin. She had worked for Sierra Carter and assisted Coolio during missions with the British intelligence service. And although they had only met a handful of times in person, the two were in constant communication in a close friendship that Coolio hoped would eventually turn into something more.

But for the time being, her beautiful green eyes did nothing to cheer him up. Seeing Cowboy's lifeless face was something he'd never get out of his head. It chilled him to his core and even Becca's bubbly personality and beautiful smile couldn't fix that.

"Cowboy's dead," Coolio mumbled.

"Oh my God!" Becca replied, covering her mouth with her hand as she started to cry. "Oh my God! Are you sure?"

"I'm sure," Coolio answered. "I ran facial recognition off their body cameras. It's him."

"My God. Does Sierra know yet?"

"She was on the team that found him."

"My heart aches for her," Becca said, wiping away tears. "Just awful."

Coolio steeled himself as he sat up in his chair. "That's not why I called. I need your help. I'm going to find the son of a bitch that did this to him."

"Of course. I'll do anything – anything at all."

"I'm sending you what I have now," Coolio said as he uploaded the files to the secure server. "His name is Khang and he's a Chinese intelligence operative. He managed to avoid all of the hotel cameras, and the room Cowboy was being held in had a closed-circuit system. I'm hoping MI-6 has something on him."

"I'm on it, love," Becca replied.

"Thanks, Becca, I-"

Before Coolio could finish, Becca had cut him off. He could hear keystrokes in the background and she worked furiously on her computer.

"I found that bastard!"

"Seriously?"

"I ran his information against our database. He has another alias called 'Ming' that has a safe house in Shanghai. I'm trying to get into their traffic cameras now, but I think this is it. Sending you the address."

"I'll help," Coolio said, momentarily forgetting about his sadness as Becca's enthusiasm and incredible talent lifted his spirits.

"Yup, this is it, I found his car."

"You're right," Coolio said as he simultaneously found a match via the traffic cameras. "That's him. He's there."

"That's not all," Becca said. "I'm trying to retrace his route. It looks like he went to the airport first."

"Can you send me the camera and timestamp you're looking at?"

"Already did," Becca said with a grin as she continued to work on their puzzle.

"Thanks," Coolio said as he went to work trying to beat Becca to the punch. "Who's that with him?"

"Don't know. Looks like he dropped someone off at the airport."

"Whoever it was didn't want to be seen. Hat, sunglasses, hoodie. I'm getting nothing."

"Same here," Becca said. "But I did find the aircraft he dropped his passenger off at on the military side of the airport. Looks like it's registered to the Russian FSB with a flight plan to Moscow."

"Shit, I know that plane!" Coolio said as he pulled up the data Becca sent him. "I tracked it to Moscow. It was involved in our operation."

"Whoever it is, didn't stay long."

"Oracle, status?" Kruger asked over the tactical frequency. "Did you find that fucker yet?"

"Yes, boss, I'm sending you the address now," Coolio replied.

"He sounds angrier than usual," Becca commented as she overheard the radio.

"Yeah, whoever did this is about to feel the wrath of Kruger. First Natasha, now Cowboy. It's going to get ugly when he finds Khang and whoever is on that airplane."

"Good," Becca said. "They bloody well deserve it."

"Oracle, we'll be at your location in two minutes. Be ready to give a full briefing," Tuna said over the radio.

"Oracle copies," Coolio replied before looking at the screen and smiling sheepishly. "I've got to go. Thanks for everything. It really means a lot."

"That's what I'm here for, love. Go get'em. Let me know what happens."

"You'll be the first person I call. Thanks again."

CHAPTER FIFTY-NINE

The last thing Khang remembered was dropping off the Russian and heading back to his apartment. Everything after that was a blur. He could parse bits and pieces together, but none of it made sense. One minute he was sleeping peacefully in his bed, and the next he was wherever *this* was.

He drifted in and out of consciousness. The floor seemed to sway beneath him as he groaned groggily. His hands and feet were bound to a metal chair and there was a hood over his head. It smelled like sweat and vomit, quite possibly his own.

Khang heard the power drill before he felt it. At first his brain couldn't process the sensation, but as the drill plunged deep into his kneecap, the pain center in his brain was suddenly wide awake and every neuron was firing.

As he started to scream, the hood was violently ripped from his head and he was blinded by bright lights.

"Wake up, bub," his tormenter growled as the drill suddenly stopped and the bit was ripped from his knee.

A gurgled scream was all he could muster. He had been through resistance and torture training before with the Chinese Ministry of State Security, but nothing could have prepared him for this. The pain was unlike anything he had ever felt. He was disoriented, scared, and in excruciating pain all at the same time.

"Let's talk," the voice said. "My name is Kruger. What's yours?"

"Khang," he managed as he grunted through the pain.

"Full name, bub," Kruger ordered.

"Khang Zhou. I know who you are, Mr. Kruger."

"Then you know what I'm capable of," Kruger said menacingly as he leaned in close. "Now, tell me who you work for."

"The Ministry of State Security. When they find out what you've done, they will come for me. Your country will be starting a war."

"You said you know who I am, bub," Kruger replied.

"Yes."

"Then you know that none of that matters."

Kruger held up the drill and squeezed the trigger. The blood that had been dripping from the bit sprayed onto Khang's face.

"Please…I'm cooperating with you!"

"Tell me about the man you took from North Korea," Kruger said as he pulled open a folding chair and sat next to Khang with the drill in his lap.

"The Brit?"

Kruger nodded.

"We learned that he was being held by North Korean resistance fighters. They contacted us to make a trade."

"Trade for what?"

"Weapons. Money. Medicine."

"How did they get him?"

"They said they rescued him from an old man during a North Korean Army raid. I don't know how he got him. All I know is that he was British SAS."

"How did you know this?"

"I had his file."

"Why did you bring him to Shanghai?"

"It was our closest interrogation facility. I was charged with keeping him safe and secure. When we landed, I was told the Russians would be taking over."

"The Russians?"

"I am told we had another operation with them in North Korea, but I do not have clearance for that, I swear."

"Who were the Russians? What were their names?"

"I only knew codenames. The one that came to Shanghai was called *Scorpion*. They were only supposed to ask a few questions before we began our interrogation, but when I came back in the room, the Brit had been shot and I was ordered to bring *Scorpion* back to the airport."

"*Scorpion*?" Kruger asked as his mind started to race. *No fucking way.* "Try again, bub."

Khang nodded. "I don't know! That's the only name I was given. I have no reason to lie to you. Please!"

"Where did Scorpion go?" Kruger asked as he stood.

"Moscow. That's all I know. I am telling you the truth."

Kruger walked to the corner and picked up his suppressed Sig P320. He dispatched Khang with a headshot and then removed the suppressor and holstered it on his hip. "I believe you," he said.

He opened the door of the shipping container and walked out into the misty air. The cargo ship had entered a dense fog as it steamed across the South Pacific. Kruger walked straight to the operations center where the team was waiting.

"Well?" Sierra asked. "What did he tell you?"

"The North Korean resistance fighters gave him up to the Chinese. Khang was there to interrogate Cowboy for Chinese intelligence."

"Why did they kill him?" Sierra pressed.

"He wouldn't tell them anything," Kruger lied.

"They barely had him twenty-four hours. That doesn't make sense!"

"Did he tell you who he brought to the airport, boss? Maybe we could find out that way," Coolio interjected.

"No," Kruger snapped. "It's over."

"What the bloody hell do you mean *it's over*? My brother was killed and you're just walking away now?" Sierra asked angrily.

"Khang is dead. I put a bullet in his head. *That's* who's responsible for Cowboy's death. The rest doesn't matter."

"*Doesn't matter?* Did you hit your head in there? Lost your bloody mind? Of course it matters!"

"Kruger, what's going on here, man?" Tuna asked calmly. "This isn't like you."

Kruger ignored Tuna and turned to Coolio. "Get me a helicopter and have Jenny standing by. The rest of you are going home. The mission is over. You'll be compensated as promised."

"The weather is kind of sketchy for that, boss, I-"

"Then find a pilot that will land in it or turn this fucking ship around and find good weather!" Kruger barked.

"Got it, boss. Will do."

Kruger stormed out as the rest of the team was left standing in shock. Tuna gave chase as Kruger headed toward the bow of the ship.

"Kruger!" Tuna yelled as he jogged to catch up. "Kruger, wait."

"What?" Kruger asked angrily as Tuna grabbed his shoulder and spun him around.

"Dude, what's going on with you? I get that you're upset about Cowboy, but this isn't like you. What the hell happened in there?"

"I already told you."

"I've known you longer than that," Tuna said. "We've fought and bled together. Don't give me that bullshit. I'm asking as your friend."

Kruger clenched his jaw and then finally answered. "Scorpion."

"What about Scorpion?"

"That's who the Russian was. That's who betrayed us."

"You're fucking shitting me!"

"Khang wasn't lying."

"Scorpion is dead though."

"I know. That's why I have to do this alone."

"Do what alone? Kruger, you're not thinking clearly here."

"I'm going to handle it. By myself."

"Bullshit! You have a team – two of them, actually. Remember? Odin? Archangel?"

"If Scorpion betrayed us, then both Odin and Project Archangel are dead, bub. You know that as well as I do. That means the Russians know everything."

"It doesn't matter what you call us, you still need a team. You can't go into Russia alone."

"This is not your fight, bub."

"Bullshit! Cowboy was one of ours! *You* are one of us! No one does this shit alone."

"Cowboy is dead because of *me*!" Kruger yelled angrily. "I brought this on us. And I'm going to fucking finish it. Now get the fuck out of my way, bub!"

CHAPTER SIXTY

Kruger had plenty of time to think about what he was going to say. He had spent the last two days doing surveillance to confirm Khang's statements. His worst fears had been confirmed.

He sat quietly in the living room chair of the one-bedroom apartment. He had turned it to face the door as he waited for its tenant to arrive. No one knew where he was, and as far as he was concerned, no one ever would. The go bag next to him had enough money, fake passports, and IDs to keep him off the grid for years. He had no plans of ever going back.

Kruger adjusted his grip on the suppressed Glock 21 SF in his lap as he heard footsteps outside the door. He didn't need to look at his watch to know that his target was right on time as he heard the key enter the door lock.

The door opened and a tall, slender silhouette appeared in the doorway. Kruger said nothing as the light came on and the door closed.

"I was wondering how long it would take you to stop following me and come to say hello."

"Hello, Natasha," Kruger replied. "Or are you going by *Scorpion* again?"

Natasha ignored him as she walked into the small kitchen. She opened the cabinet, pulling out two glasses and a bottle of vodka before she approached Kruger.

"You won't need that," Natasha said, nodding to the gun in Kruger's lap.

She sat down on the sofa next to Kruger and placed the glasses on the coffee table. She poured vodka into each glass and then took the one nearest to her.

"To us," she said, as she held up her glass. "And what might have been."

Kruger remained still as he stared at her, trying to figure out how the woman he thought he knew so well could have betrayed him so deeply.

"I understand most of what you did, but why did you kill Cowboy?" Kruger asked.

Natasha downed the vodka and then slammed the glass on the coffee table. "I didn't."

"Khang said you did."

"Khang is a low-level imbecile. He needed to believe that I killed Cowboy. But the truth is Cowboy killed Cowboy."

"You gave him a choice?"

Natasha nodded. "The friendly tactics the Chinese were planning never would have worked on Cowboy. They would have had to resort to their more brutal ways. I knew that. Cowboy knew that. Khang was the only one who didn't know it. So, I gave Cowboy a choice. One bullet to use as he saw fit."

"We could have saved him!" Kruger shouted angrily. "His body was still warm when we found him!"

Natasha laughed as she poured herself another drink. "We both know they would have moved him as soon as you landed. Why do you think I had Khang drive me to the airport? I had to protect you, sweetheart."

"Protect me from what?"

"Yourself. I know you, Freddie."

"I thought I knew you, and yet here we are."

"Yes, here we are," she said.

"Was it ever real? Or were you just doing your job?"

"Both," Natasha said as she leaned forward and gently put her hand on Kruger's knee. "I cared very deeply for you and I looked forward to our child together. That's why I intervened when I found out about your friend. I didn't want him to suffer."

"But you wanted me to believe you died?"

"I wanted to prevent this very meeting, my love," Natasha said before taking a sip of vodka. "I did not know the Chinese would capture your friend. That was never part of the plan."

"What was your plan?"

"It's complicated."

"I trusted you!"

"I'm a spy, love. You knew that."

"I watched you die."

"You watched a North Korean political dissident in a wig and very convincing mask die."

"What about Viktor and Anatoly? You kill them too?"

"*Da*," Natasha replied coldly. "It had to be done."

"It had to be done? How? How did any of this have to be done?"

"The Chinese wanted Choe Il-Sung removed. War is a threat to the Chinese economy."

"So why didn't they do it themselves?"

"Do you remember Colonel Deng Jinping?"

"Yes," Kruger replied flatly. Jinping had been behind the kidnapping and attempted assassination of then-President Madeline Clifton on Midway Island. Capturing, interrogating, and killing him had been one of Kruger's first missions with Odin.

"The confession you coerced from him caused great embarrassment within the Politburo."

"I didn't coerce anything."

"Well, true, not directly. But Rage is dead. And you're the new head of Odin. It matters not to the Chinese. Jinping was very well-connected within the Politburo and the Chinese government. They wanted retribution for the embarrassment."

"The embarrassment was their shoddy operation."

"In either case, killing a Bratva boss had the same effect. When you killed Suvarova, the Bratva that still had connections in the FSB wanted revenge. They tasked me to infiltrate your operation. But I fell in love with you, so things became complicated."

"Did you really love me?"

"Da."

"What do the Chinese have to do with that?"

"Suvarova intended to sell the computer that he stole – Helios – to the Chinese. When you destroyed it and killed him, the Politburo and the Bratva wanted to know everything they could about your operation. 'Odin' was merely something whispered in passing. A ghost. No one believed it to be real."

"So, your whole goal was to gain intel?"

"When you and your team killed Kuznetsov in New York, the Bratva only grew stronger. They paid off more people. More attention was brought to Odin. That was when they told me to arrange the operation. We needed to see how the operation worked first hand. That is why the mission to kill Il-

Sung happened. We found out that one of the American assets within the North Korean nuclear program was defecting and intercepted the thumb drive he had before the CIA could retrieve it. We replaced it with information about Il-Sung. I knew the mission was too risky for normal channels. It was a convenient way to kill two birds with one stone, as you say."

"But it failed."

"It failed because the Chinese warned the North Koreans of an assassination plot so he sent a body double instead. They wanted to see what you would do if the mission failed. They wanted to know how you would follow through."

"How did they know we would?"

"I told them you would. I know you, Freddie. I knew that if we let it leak that Il-Sung was visiting the site, you would personally see to it that he died. You wouldn't be able to help yourself. And it would also be a perfect opportunity for you to see me die. Because I knew you would take revenge. You are too predictable."

"You killed your own agents for that?"

"The North Koreans needed blood and I gave it to them. Viktor and Anatoly have been trying to rid the FSB of Bratva influence for many years now. It wasn't my call."

"I can't believe how much of a heartless bitch you are," Kruger said, shifting his hand over the Glock in his lap. "I should have known better."

"Yes, you should," Natasha replied. "But that is the problem with love. It is such a weak emotion. It clouds our judgement. Makes us crazy. I nearly turned against them after we lost the baby. I could almost see us living a real life together. Almost."

"It's not too late," Kruger said, slightly shocked by his own words.

"It was always too late, love," Natasha said. "I grew up on the streets of Moscow. This is how I survive. It is the only way for a woman like me. You shouldn't have been so naïve."

Kruger picked up the weapon and pointed it at Natasha. "I thought this was going to be a hard decision."

"Harder than you know," Natasha said with a nod.

Before Kruger could squeeze the trigger, he heard a crack and the sound of glass breaking. He felt the round hit him in the chest, causing him to drop the gun as he pulled the trigger, missing Natasha and hitting the wall behind her.

Natasha stood and picked the handgun off the ground as Kruger doubled over onto the floor.

"I'm sorry my love," she said as she nodded in the direction of the sniper and then looked down at him. "I wish we could have had that life together."

CHAPTER SIXTY-ONE

One Month Later

The Gulfstream G650 landed at the Louis Armstrong International Airport just after 1 A.M. Spectre, Michelle, and Woody's wife helped Woody down the stairs where Louisiana State Troopers were waiting to escort them home.

"You know we could've used a lift instead, right?" Spectre asked as he held onto Woody's arm to keep him from falling.

"Not my style, brah," Woody replied. "My legs work and I'm gonna use them."

Michelle shot Spectre a look and shook her head before he could make a sarcastic comment in reply. They helped Woody down the stairs and stopped at the base.

"Emma, my pimp cane please," he said to his wife as he stood and stretched, gently swaying as his legs struggled to keep him upright.

Emma rolled her eyes and accepted the cane from the flight attendant that had followed them down. Woody took it and used it to help prop himself up as he turned to Spectre.

"Well, sir, thanks for the magic beans," Woody said with a grin.

"I'm sorry," Spectre said. "About everything."

"Sorry? Well, besides being gimpy, I'm fifteen million dollars richer and still alive. I don't know why you'd be sorry," Woody replied. "Not your fault, brah."

Spectre and Michelle agreed that giving Woody half of their ten-million-dollar share was the right thing to do, given all that had happened. Woody was permanently disabled and would likely never be able to fly again at all. His military flying career was definitely over.

"I talked you into this mess," Spectre said.

"You did," Woody said. "But we're still friends. And look at all the stuff you can write about in your books now! Woody better get a starring role! My face better be on the cover of *at least* three books."

Spectre laughed as he shook Woody's hand. "You got it, buddy."

"Hey, did you ever hear what happened to Kruger?" Woody asked.

Spectre shook his head. "Tuna said he went to Moscow on his own. That's the last anyone has ever seen or heard from him."

Woody frowned. "Do you think they killed him?"

"I'd like to think he's just off the grid somewhere laying low while he deals with losing Natasha, but it's definitely not a good sign."

"What's going to happen to the teams then?"

"Odin wasn't much of anything anymore anyway, but with no one to run it, I think it'll be done. And Tuna's team is officially disbanded. Cowboy being interrogated by the Chinese put everyone in cover-your-ass mode. Everything related to either group has been burned. They never existed."

"Poor Cowboy," Woody said. "I feel like it's my fault."

Spectre shook his head. "It was a risk we all knew and accepted when we went into that shithole country. It sucks, but you can't blame yourself for what happened."

"Have you heard from Sierra since they all said goodbye?" Woody asked. A week after Kruger's disappearance, Sierra, Tuna, and the rest of Odin and Project Archangel had all stopped by Woody's room to check on him and bid farewell. The only connection that remained was the promise that when Woody healed enough to go home, the CIA director would send his personal jet.

"She was reassigned at MI-6. Tuna said she probably went to a desk job."

"Damn, brah, that sucks. She lost her brother and her job."

"I think it was voluntary. When the team was disbanded, they gave her a choice and she decided that seeing her brother like that was the last straw. I can't say I blame her."

"Alright man, well, mission accomplished, I guess. Don't be a stranger," Woody said as Emma and one of the State Troopers assigned to his security detail helped him into the unmarked white SUV with flashing blue lights.

"Get well soon, man. Tell Sparky hello for me when you see him."

"Will do. He emailed me the other day. He bought a Canadian F-5!"

"I'm glad he's feeling better," Spectre said.

They watched Woody and Emma drive off in their motorcade, leaving the second motorcade assigned for them.

Spectre turned and hugged Michelle. "I'm ready to go home," Spectre said before kissing her.

"No more saving the world?"

"Not unless I'm writing about it in my books. I'm done. I got lucky this time, but one of these days the luck is going to run out. I want to watch our son grow up while I still can."

"What about Kruger?"

"I would do anything for that man, but if Tuna and Sierra believe he's dead…well, there's nothing I can do. They would know better than anyone. And if he's not dead, then he doesn't want to be found. Who am I to intervene if that's the case?"

"I guess," Michelle said as she got into the back of the unmarked SUV taking them home. "What a shame."

Spectre got in behind her and put his arm around her, pulling her close.

"When I first met Kruger, one of his favorite quotes was from Patton. 'It is foolish and wrong to mourn the men who died. Rather we should thank God that such men lived.'"

EPILOGUE

Special Agent Maddie Tanner owed much of her success within the FBI to a chauffeur assignment called in as a favor just two years earlier. It was during that detail to escort Cal "Spectre" Martin that she uncovered Odin, helped them take down a group of rogue billionaires bent on destroying the U.S., and was subsequently hand-picked to be the FBI's liaison to a newly formed CIA-MI-6 covert operation known as Project Archangel.

She was the youngest agent in the Bureau to be picked for such a prestigious assignment, and her time with Project Archangel led to even more success. She had helped them take down terrorists, human traffickers, and a Russian Bratva boss. Through her grit, determination, and toughness in the field, Special Agent Tanner had made a name for herself and anyone watching knew she would be able to write her own ticket.

So, when Project Archangel was disbanded, it made sense that Tanner would transition to the Counterterrorism Division and continue her career progression. It was exactly where she wanted to be.

And it was exactly why she didn't expect to find herself walking through the rubble of what once was the Freddie "Kruger" Mack estate that had been left to him after the death of Jeff Lyons.

The arson investigator with the Virginia State Police Special Services Division had requested an FBI team due to a cryptic message found in what once was a panic room within the heart of the mansion. That request had been flagged by the CIA and a special request was put in for Tanner to take the case as the liaison from the Counterterrorism Division.

Upon seeing the symbol and message written on the wall and visible only under UV light, Tanner had immediately requested that the case be classified Top Secret / Sensitive Compartmented Information and called former Project Archangel front man Ty "Tuna" Turner out to see it.

It was just after 9 P.M. when he arrived in his pickup truck at the burned down estate. She barely recognized him without his scraggly hair and operator beard. He had taken a job in the civilian sector in the wake of the team folding.

"I told you over the phone, I'm not interested in helping," Tuna said as she met him at his truck. "With Kruger gone, it's time to put it all behind us. I'm finally getting some semblance of a normal life and finishing up his estate."

"Well, you're here at least. By the way, how's the estate going?"

"Kruger will help more people in death than he could have ever imagined. I'm starting the most well-funded veterans' assistance group in the history of our country. It's incredible."

"Well, you're going to want to see this," Tanner replied as she led him toward the rubble.

"What the hell happened?"

"Local sheriff's office received reports of multiple explosions visible from the highway. The mansion and every building on the property were burned to the ground. The armory was cleared out."

"Robbery?" Tuna asked as he followed Tanner to the only structure still standing in the center of what once was the mansion.

"That's what they thought at first, but during the investigation, they found a message on the interior walls of the panic room."

"Walls? Plural?"

"Yes, it was on all of them."

"Same one?"

"See for yourself," Tanner said as they reached the panic room. She pulled a black light wand from her back pocket and handed it to Tuna as she turned off her flashlight.

Tuna held it up against the wall.

"Jesus Christ," Tuna mumbled as he saw a skull and valknut painted on the wall. Under it, were two phrases written in Latin.

"The investigators didn't know what to make of it. Thought it might be a new terrorist group due to the weapons. I recognize the first one – *Stamus Contra Mallum.* It means *We Stand Against Evil*, right? Wasn't that the Odin motto and symbol?"

"Yeah," Tuna said as he leaned in close to look at it.

"But what does this one mean? *Quidquid Victor Ero. Come what may, I shall be victorious*? It's also Latin, but what is that from? What do they mean together?"

Tuna stared at the wall and then suddenly spun around, shining the light on the other walls. "Fuck me."

"What? What does it mean? Is it a warning?"

"This isn't a warning," Tuna said as he turned to face her. "It's a declaration of intent from a very dangerous person."

"What? Who?"

Tuna handed the UV light back to her and took the flashlight out of her hand, shining the light on their path out. "Let's go. We've got work to do."

If you enjoyed this book, please leave a review!

VISIT WWW.CWLEMOINE.COM FOR MORE INFORMATION ON NEW BOOK RELEASE DATES, BOOK SIGNINGS, AND EXCLUSIVE SPECIAL OFFERS.

ACKNOWLEDGMENTS

To all my readers, thank you for continuing on this journey with me. I appreciate the comments, feedback, and reviews. It has been an honor.

To **Mrs. Beverly Foster**, thank you for everything you do. You're an awesome editor, even when I am hard-headed. I appreciate your hard work and dedication even with the loss of dear Jäger.

To **Dr. Doug Narby**, as always, thank you for your help in content-editing. I appreciate having your wisdom and feedback. Your notes are always on point and help me to be a better writer.

Marc "Deuce" Dufresne, thanks for the feedback and input on some of the flying stuff. You're a great friend and supporter. Thank you for keeping me on track and making the flying stuff as realistic as possible.

Trevor "Gonky" Hartsock, thanks for the Flanker gouge. I know you're sad that Gonky didn't get another cameo, but there are much greater things ahead!

Jonathan "Frenchy" French, thanks for being such a great fan, man. I hope you enjoyed the book!

Michael Hayes, you rock, man! I can't tell you how great it is to have you as a beta reader. It is awesome to get instant feedback and to have someone pushing me along to write more. Thank you!

Pat Byrnes, you've been there since the beginning. Thank you for being my first fan and beta reader. I appreciate your comments and reviews.

Thanks again to everyone that has supported me. Hopefully it is just only just beginning. I can't wait to see what the future will hold.

Thanks for reading!

C.W. Lemoine is the author of *SPECTRE RISING*, *AVOID. NEGOTIATE. KILL.*, *ARCHANGEL FALLEN*, *EXECUTIVE REACTION*, *BRICK BY BRICK*, *STAND AGAINST EVIL*, *ABSOLUTE VENGEANCE*, and *THE HELIOS CONSPIRACY*, *I AM THE SHEEPDOG*, and *FINI FLIGHT*. He graduated from the A.B. Freeman School of Business at Tulane University in 2005 and Air Force Officer Training School in 2006.

He is a military pilot that has flown the F-16 and F/A-18. He currently flies for a Legacy U.S. Airline and flies the T-38A as an Adversary Pilot in the Air Force Reserve. He is also a certified Survival Krav Maga Instructor and sheriff's deputy. He also hosts a popular YouTube channel called *Mondays with Mover.*

www.cwlemoine.com

Facebook
http://www.facebook.com/cwlemoine/

Twitter:
@CWLemoine

Instagram:
@CWLemoine

YouTube:
https://www.youtube.com/cwlemoine/

Made in the USA
Monee, IL
07 June 2021